Praise for *Double Dare* by Jeanne St. James

"Sensuality and passion combine to create a sizzling erotic romance with a flair for the intense."

– *Sensual Reads*

"St James has constructed a fantastic world filled with hot lust and wonderful emotion."

– Danica, *A History of Romance*

"Jeanne St. James' *Double Dare* is one of the steamiest, sexiest stories I have read."

– Lila, *Two Lips Review*

"Ms. St. James has created a marvelously sensual story that is a winner from start to finish. Double Dare is a richly decadent and emotionally-charged novel that tantalizes as it intrigues the reader…"

– Shannon, *The Romance Studio*

"Jeanne St. James writes a compelling story, keeping the reader entertained from start to finish."

– Gabrielle, *You Gotta Read Reviews*

LooseId®

ISBN 13: 978-1-60737-293-6
DOUBLE DARE

Originally released in e-book format in January 2010

Cover Art by Anne Cain
Cover Layout and Design by April Martinez

Printed in the U.S.A. by
Lightning Source, Inc.
1246 Heil Quaker Blvd
La Vergne TN 37086
www.lightningsource.com

DOUBLE DARE

Chapter One

Logan Reed jammed a finger into the neck of his white oxford and pulled. He needed some fucking air.

What the hell was he doing here anyway?

As he surveyed the church, a bead of sweat popped out on his forehead. His breathing had become shallow and quick. He was going to hyperventilate right there and pass out, making a fool of himself in front of everyone.

He realized one of the ushers was speaking to him.

"What?"

"Bride or groom?"

Bride or groom? Did he look like a bride?

All he wanted to do was strip off his stiff shirt, strangling tie, smothering jacket; throw on a soft, worn pair of jeans and one of his comfortable shirts; sink into his couch; toss his feet on his coffee table; and chug a nice, frosty beer.

Ah, now that was a fantasy!

But here he was, standing in a monkey suit in a church, about to be struck down by lightning at any second. He blew out a long breath to settle his thumping heart.

Logan stared at the confused usher. Unfortunately he understood the feeling.

"Neither."

"Are you okay?"

Logan had vowed to himself to never do this again. Never be in a church again.

He reminded himself he was only there to observe. He didn't have to participate. But it didn't help. Anyone with as many sins as Logan should have been barred from religious houses. That should have been a law. But it wasn't.

For chrissakes, he had to get a grip. This was a wedding, not a crucifixion.

He had promised his sister he would be here. And even though Logan was a sinner, he never broke a promise. Never.

The usher cleared his throat.

"Dude—"

Logan pinned the suddenly flushed, sweating kid, whose suit looked two sizes too big, with a glare. "Dude?"

He watched the teen's Adam's apple bob up and down a couple of times before he felt a whoosh of air against him, and someone grabbed his elbow. Hard.

"Logan! How nice of you to get here on time." The female voice was singsong and syrupy sweet. And it held a lot more meaning in the tone than in the words.

Logan turned to face his sister. He had to look down because she was nearly a foot shorter than him. "Hey, Shorty. Good timing."

The petite brunette gave him a tight smile. "I see that." She turned to the usher. "We're with the bride," she said sweetly. "We'll just seat ourselves. Thank you."

The usher looked relieved, and Logan almost felt bad. Almost.

The grip on his elbow tightened, and without warning, his sister dragged him down the aisle and over into one of the pews on the left.

"*Sit down*," Paige said through gritted teeth, even though her face held the biggest smile.

He sat.

She smoothed her dress and tucked it ladylike as she settled into the pew beside him.

"Jesus Christ, Shorty. What the hell is your problem?"

Logan watched her plastered smile falter.

"Logan, you are in a church, for God's sake. It's not the best place to take the Lord's name in vain. And if you keep doing that, I might have to move to another pew so when lightning strikes you dead, I'm in a safe spot." She smoothed her done-up do and gave a pacifying smile across the aisle to the older couple staring at them, mouths agape.

"Hey, I didn't want to be here in the first place."

"I ask you for one favor—"

"One? Hmm. You must have a short memory."

"Okay, okay. Knock it off. Believe me, I appreciate your coming."

"And the thanks I get is a bruised elbow?"

"Sorry, I thought you were going to make that guy piss his pants."

"Well, shit, he called me *dude*."

"Oh yeah, that's so much worse than you calling me *Shorty*."

"I thought you liked it—" Paige elbowed him in the gut before he could say anything besides "ooof."

The wedding march started, and the double doors opened to reveal the bride.

His sister owed him big-time.

* * *

Quinn Preston almost choked on her Alabama slammer when her friend elbowed her in the ribs. "Ooof."

She saved her drink before it could spill all over her ugly bridesmaid dress. Yeah, that would have been a shame: to ruin such a nice, frumpy, pukey pink taffeta dress. One the bride had said she would be able to wear in the future. Like to a cocktail party. Or maybe her own funeral. *Yeah, right. No one in their right mind would want to get caught dead in this thing.*

Ruining the dress wouldn't have been a loss, but losing her drink would have. She was drinking slammers for a reason—to get good and drunk.

Lana nudged her again. "You see that?" She nodded her head toward the back of the room.

"What?" Quinn really didn't care what Lana was excited about. She just wanted to get this day over with. She was tired of watching the happy couple. She was tired of pasting on a plastic smile for the photographer. And she was really tired of listening to the sappy congratulations. All things she might never have—the wedding, the husband, the bridal bliss. And something her parents never failed to remind her.

Especially now that she was in her early thirties. And single. Again.

"Not what. Who."

"Huh?" She sucked on the dainty little straw the bartender had put in her drink. Hardly anything would come out of it. Maybe it was designed just for stirring. She pulled it out and threw it onto the bar. She really needed one of those big giant straws that came in those fancy frozen drinks.

"Him. Over there." Lana grabbed Quinn by the shoulders and turned her around to face whatever had caught her friend's attention.

"Oh, him." She took a deep draw of the punchlike drink, only there wasn't a bit of punch in it. Not the fruit kind anyway.

"Yeah, him." Lana dragged out *him* like she was sucking on a maraschino cherry and enjoying the sweetness on her tongue.

Quinn didn't even take a good look. Men were on her shit list at the moment. She didn't care how hot they were. The potent drink in her hands was all the company she needed. She smiled into her glass; it was the best date she'd had in a while.

Another pink taffeta blur whizzed up to them, out of breath.

"Jeez Louise. Did you see that hunk of man meat?" Paula, another victim of the wedding fashion nightmare, was flushed and had a bead of sweat running down her chipmunk-like cheeks. "Do you think he's single?"

Quinn raised one shoulder in a half shrug and turned back to the bar. It was bad enough when the three of them had to stand next to each other at the altar, then throughout the grueling pictures, followed by having to sit beside each other at the head table. All in that awful pink froth. But now that it was all over, and they had done their duty for their friend Gina, there was no reason they all had to stand there looking like someone threw up Pepto-Bismol.

She leaned into the bar and asked the semicute bartender the time. When he answered that it was six, she gritted her teeth. They had only been at the reception for an hour. It was way too early to bail.

Damn.

With a sigh, she turned back to her friends. They were still ogling the male eye candy across the room.

Paula's sigh drifted over her. “I wonder if he likes women with a little meat on their bones.”

A little meat? She opened her mouth to correct Paula, but shut it quickly. Her friend didn't need to be on the receiving end of her miserable mood.

“Quinn, I bet he'd make you forget Peanut.”

Quinn winced and took another long draw from her drink. She loved the flavor and the tanginess on her tongue. And she was trying to forget Peanut. She hated the nickname her friends had called her ex-boyfriend, Peter. Once they had actually called him Peanut in front of his face—by accident, of course. *Right.* It had taken her a while to brush that one under the rug. He had never liked her friends after that.

On the other hand, her friends had never liked Peter from the beginning. Unlike her parents, who loved the bastard. Probably more than they loved her.

"Yeah, Quinn, he could probably fuck your brains out, and you'd never remember that douche again."

Quinn frowned at Paula. She noticed her friend's string of pearls hiding in the skin around her neck. Quinn's hands automatically went to her neck to finger a similar necklace—a part of the stupid wedding costume. *Ugh.* She hated pearls!

She hated taffeta. She hated pink. She hated frilly dresses.

She took a long swig from her glass.

And she hated Peter. The asshole.

His gift to her last Valentine's Day wasn't an engagement ring. Oh no, after five long, wasted years of dating the shit, he couldn't have gotten her a ring. Nope. Instead he sent her a text message.

That was it.

A stupid little text message. One line.

We've grown apart and I've found someone new.

She deserved more than that. Something better. After all those years of loyalty, standing by his side, being the "good, proper" girlfriend. As Peter had expected. As her parents had expected. The girlfriend any decent man would want on his arm. Right?

Not even a sorry. Not even an explanation. Nothing.

And the next day, FedEx had delivered a box with all the things she had left over at his apartment during the last half decade.

Quinn emptied her glass and turned back to the bar, blocking out her friends' chattering over that man.

She needed another man like she needed a hole in the head.

She slid her glass over the bar top, and before she could ask for another, a deep voice washed over her.

"Put her next drink on me."

Dumb ass. The drinks are on the house. She turned to ream whoever it was, and stopped. Her mouth opened, but nothing escaped.

"You look like a fish out of water with your mouth hanging open like that." When he smiled, the lines around his eyes crinkled. He was tan, an outdoorsy tan, not a manmade one. And he had beautiful green eyes. Shit. She had never seen such beautiful eyes on a man. His nose was a little crooked, like it had been broken, and it made him even more beautiful. No. Not beautiful. He was… He was…

Quinn closed her mouth and swallowed hard. He was so *unperfect*, he was perfect. His hair was a dark brown with natural highlights, more proof he liked being outdoors. It was long and pulled back into a neat ponytail.

She hated long hair on men. But it was right on him.

He had a beard that wasn't a beard. It was like a longer five-o'clock shadow.

She hated facial hair.

He had a strong, corded neck that disappeared into a stiff dress shirt. The collar had been already released and one more button undone below that. The knot of his tie was loose and hung crookedly from around his neck.

The sleeves of his crispy white shirt were rolled up to his elbows, and his forearms were tan covered in dark hair. His hands…

Oh. Damn.

His hands were large. They were working hands. They weren't soft and pampered. But calloused and thick and strong.

Capable. Capable of doing all kinds of things.

Quinn's nipples hardened under the scratchy taffeta.

His hands could do all kinds of dirty, nasty things.

Things Peter had never wanted to do…

Quinn ripped her gaze from him and spun back around to the bar, bracing herself against it for a second to catch her breath. She grabbed her fresh drink and took a gulp.

"Whoa. Slow down there."

She pressed the cold drink against her forehead in an attempt to cool herself off.

She needed to go change her panties, she was so freaking wet.

She could feel his heat next to her; his body was like a furnace. She wanted to plant her hands on his chest and feel how hot he really was. Her fingers convulsed around her glass.

"Are you okay?" The deep timbre of his voice sent a shot of lightning down her body, landing right in her pussy.

Quinn could only nod her answer.

He palmed her bare shoulder and turned her to him. He stared down into her eyes, his lips widening into a smile.

His lips. Oh man. Those lips probably could do all sorts of things to her, with her. Lips that were made for more than kissing…

"*Yes.*" Oh my God, she thought. That was the kind of yes she blurted when she was in the midst of an orgasm. At least from what she could remember. It had been so long since she'd come…with a partner, anyway.

She felt the heat crawl up her neck, and she stepped back, breaking the contact.

"I…I'm fine." She cleared her throat. "Thank you for the drink." She took another sip before raising the glass to him in thanks.

"It was nothing." When he laughed, her knees almost buckled. "Enjoy it."

He stepped away and then paused. But it looked as though he thought better of whatever he was contemplating, and he continued on his way.

Quinn leaned back against the bar and let out a shaky breath.

She was suddenly flanked on either side by her friends. She had been so distracted, she hadn't even realized that they disappeared.

"Quinn—"

"Quinn!"

"Oh. My. God!"

"I told you he was hot!"

"Oh! I wish I weren't married already."

"I wish he liked chubby chicks."

Quinn couldn't take any more. She raised her palms in surrender. "Stop. Enough."

"But, Quinn—"

"But nothing," Quinn answered Paula.

"You're just going to let him walk away?"

"Paula, he isn't going anywhere. Unfortunately I'm not going anywhere. We have to be here for two more hours, at least."

Lana said, "Are you going to let Peter ruin the rest of your life? All men aren't assholes like him."

Quinn harrumphed and took another sip of her slammer.

"Why don't you at least dance with him?"

"No."

"Why not?" Lana asked.

Why not? Because if she did, she might come right on the dance floor? Because she might end up in a puddle of her own juices? The picture in her head shocked her: it was of her lying in a heap in the middle of the dance floor in the throes of an orgasm. Surrounded by all the wedding guests…

This drink was stronger than she thought.

"Because no one is dancing yet."

"Sure they are. Look."

Quinn glanced over at the area cleared for dancing, and sure enough, a crowd of people were out there shaking their groove thing. Quinn had been too busy trying to get her drink on to notice.

From the looks of the participants on the dance floor, a few of them had been partaking in the open bar also. Even the bride and her new husband were bouncing and shimmying in the crowd.

At least *they* were a happy couple.

Quinn took another drink.

Lana frowned at her. “Are you just going to drink tonight, or are you going to do something about your situation?”

“Situation? What situation?”

“Getting laid.”

Quinn checked over her shoulder to see if the bartender was listening. He was. He had a big grin plastered on his face. *Great.*

The father of the bride came up and asked for a gin and tonic. While he was waiting, he turned to them. “Hi, girls. Enjoying yourselves? You look great in those dresses. My wife picked them out.”

Oh joy. Quinn would have to remember to smack—she meant thank—her. She couldn't wait to rip the scratchy, ugly piece of shit off.

All three women gave him a smile but bit their tongues. Eventually he wandered away, and Lana and Paula jumped right back to harassing her. Good thing they were her friends.

“C'mon. It's not going to hurt to have a one-night stand. Look at him.”

“I already saw him.” Holy moley, she knew they meant well, but they were getting on her last nerve.

“Yeah, and we saw how you were drooling too.”

She had not drooled. Her hand automatically went up to her mouth.

Paula said, "He probably isn't interested in you anyway."

"Yeah, you couldn't get someone like that. You attract losers like Peter," Lana said.

If they thought their reverse psychology was going to work, well, it wasn't.

"Looks like he's with Paige Reed, anyway."

Quinn's gaze shot over to the corner of the ballroom where the tall man stood next to the petite, dark-haired beauty. Paige Reed. *Figures.*

"I thought Paige was dating Connor Morgan," Quinn mumbled.

She must have mumbled loud enough, because Lana answered her. "She is. Connor had to fly to Australia for something to do with his job."

"So why is she with him?" Quinn asked. Why was she so curious all of a sudden? Why did she care?

She didn't. She nursed her drink. After one and a half Alabama slammers, she was starting to feel pretty tipsy. She wasn't used to drinking. And when she did drink, she usually had wine, not hard liquor, and especially not such a hard-hitting mix of liquors.

Paula leaned into the both of them and said in an exaggerated whisper, "Maybe he's an escort," like it was a scandal, and then laughed.

Maybe he *was* an escort.

He was probably worth every penny too.

His back was to them now, but that just gave Quinn the opportunity to study how broad those shoulders were in his dress shirt. When he moved, the fabric bunched and pulled with his muscles.

Lana gasped, jerking Quinn out of her thoughts. "He's not an escort! That's Logan Reed, Paige's brother. I haven't seen him since we were kids. Holy shit, did he grow up."

"I'll say." Paula agreed. "Quinn, I dare you to go ask him to dance."

"Not interested."

Lana joined in. "Yeah, I dare you too. Don't be a wuss."

If she were a wuss, she wouldn't have come out in public in this pink atrocity. And the matching shoes were killing her feet. The last thing she needed was to be dancing. She'd be crippled.

"That's a double dare, you know, with the two of us daring you."

Oh, boy, a double dare. She would definitely do it now—not. "You're crazy."

"No, you are, if you pass up this opportunity."

"How do you know he's available?" Quinn asked them.

"You don't know until you ask him," Lana said. "But if I remember correctly, his wife left him a while ago. There had been some rumors…"

There had been some rumors about her and Peter too, but rumors were just that: rumors. She didn't take any stock in them.

Paula suddenly shouted, "Truth or dare?" making Quinn jump. It was like they were teenagers all over again.

Lana quickly said, “Truth.” And bounced on her toes like she was fifteen.

Jesus, would someone please put a bullet in my head? Quinn needed to be put out of her misery.

Paula asked Lana, “Do you shave or wax?”

“Shave. Okay, Quinn, your turn. Truth or dare?”

Quinn was not playing this juvenile game. It was stupid; she was not going to fall into what was clearly a trap.

“Truth.”

“How bad was Peter in bed?” Lana asked.

Damn. She wasn't going to answer that one. Even as drunk as she was. She didn't want to relive their vanilla, boring lovemaking. And she definitely didn't want to admit it or talk about it.

There was only one thing left for her to do.

Chapter Two

Logan ran a finger around his collar one more time. Why did it feel like a freakin' noose?

His sister was out on the dance floor with someone's husband, having a good time. With the man's wife's blessing, of course. The eight-months-pregnant woman had her feet propped up on a chair on the other side of the room, and she was smiling and encouraging her husband to have fun while she rested.

Logan sighed and glanced at his watch. It was only seven. He looked down at the plate of food in front of him. He'd hardly touched it. He didn't want any tilapia or whatever the hell it was. He wanted a thick, juicy steak slathered in spicy BBQ sauce. With a big, fat baked potato dripping in butter and sour cream. Yeah, now that was a meal. Not some twigs of asparagus and a dried-up fish filet. He got that crap at home as it was.

The only highlight of the night so far was the chick at the bar. The way she'd looked at him had made him instantly hard. He had to finally turn around and walk away before he threw her on the bar and tossed her freaking ugly-ass dress over her head.

That would have gone over well with his sister, banging one of her friends on the bar. In public.

He unwrapped one of the little Hershey Kisses decorating the table and popped it into his mouth. He chased it with a sip of Jack and Coke—the whole reason he had approached the bar in the first place.

He could probably slip out of the party, and no one would even notice. But his sister would never forgive him, and he'd been on the receiving end of her anger in the past. Many times. It wasn't pleasant.

Basically it was suffer now or suffer later. Hell, he was already here anyway.

He looked at his watch again: 7:02. He groaned.

When he glanced up again, he saw a pink vision stalking toward him, and he sat up straighter. Shit, the cause of his earlier hard-on was coming his way.

She looked determined, and she still had a grip around her glass like it was a lifeline.

She stopped directly in front of him and put one hand on her hip.

"Are you Logan Reed?"

Oh shit. "Yes?"

"You don't know for sure?"

"Oh, I'm sure."

"Are you fucking anybody right now?"

"Right this minute?" He glanced around to see if anyone else was hearing this surreal conversation. Luckily no one was paying attention.

"No. Do you have anyone who is going to get mad if I ask you to dance?"

"Uh. No." Well, hell, that was a unique way of asking someone to dance.

She placed her drink on the table, and he asked, "Is that still your second one?"

"No, third."

"I was afraid of that."

She grabbed his hand and pulled, but he was too heavy for her to lift, so he unfolded himself from the chair to accommodate her.

"Are you asking me to dance?"

"You have a problem with that?"

"Not at all." He interlaced his fingers with hers and led her to a corner of the dance floor. Luckily for him, the DJ had turned the lights down and was playing a series of slow tunes. Ones he could dance to. There was no way he was doing the chicken dance or line dancing. He had his limits.

As the slow, wailing tune blared through the large speakers, Logan slid his palms around her waist, his splayed fingers coming to rest at the small of her back. The fabric of her dress felt terrible, and he didn't know why women wore shit like that and suffered. The dress certainly wasn't flattering.

But it wasn't the outer package that mattered to Logan; it was the prize he found inside when it was unwrapped.

He stepped in a little closer and pulled her hips against his. He swore he heard a little gasp. He smiled into her overstyled, dark blonde hair and nuzzled it. Underneath all the hairspray, he caught a scent of wildflowers. It smelled nice.

"What's your name?" he murmured into her hair.

"What?" She turned her head a bit, and she ended up nuzzling his neck. Her lips, the shape of which reminded him of an archer's bow, were warm and soft, and he could detect the fruity scent of the slammers on her breath.

She was average height for a woman, which made her a bit shorter than him, so he had to lean down a bit to place his lips against her ear.

"What's your name?"

He felt the shiver of her body against him, so he traced the delicate shell of her ear with the tip of his tongue. The touch was light enough, but she unmistakably felt it. In response, she arched her back slightly, pressing her hips harder into his.

"Quinn," she finally answered him, her voice breathless.

"Quinn," he repeated while moving one hand up her back to the bare skin rising out of her dress. He drew the pad of his thumb along the smooth expanse of flesh, along her exposed spine, moving up to her neck to cradle it in his palm. His thumb continued to stroke her skin along the vein in her neck.

He pulled away a little and looked down into her face. Her eyes were heavy, and her lips were parted. Her breaths were short and quick.

He struggled to keep from thrusting against her. If she looked this good in that god-awful dress, he wondered what she looked like in normal clothes. Or no clothes at all.

Or just a pair of handcuffs.

His balls tightened, and he released a long breath out of his nose to steady his pulse.

"Quinn, do you like sex?" He placed his cheek against hers, and they swayed to the music, their hips, their thighs brushing against each other.

Her eyelids fluttered a bit before she answered, "Sometimes."

"Why only sometimes?" he whispered against her ear.

She shrugged slightly, and one of her off-the-shoulder sleeves slid down a bit, exposing more creamy flesh.

Logan brushed his lips along her collarbone. It was delicate and covered with smooth skin. When he got to her shoulder, he worked his way back, and in the hollow of her neck, he placed a kiss.

There was a groan. He didn't know whom it came from. Her? Him? He didn't care. His hand at the small of her back slipped lower, to just where the rise of her ass was. The fabric of the dress kept him from feeling details, but his imagination took over.

One song transitioned into another, and they weren't even aware of the other couples dancing nearby.

His hips kept a steady side-to-side rhythm, while his hand on her back kept her close and in perfect time with him.

He was hard. There was no doubt she could feel it. Even with the yards of fabric around her midsection, her belly brushed against his length, teasing his cock.

"What kind of sex do you like?" His voice sounded low and gruff to his own ears.

"The kind when I get to come."

Logan chuckled against her temple and slipped the hand he had around her neck to her shoulder. His fingers brushed her skin lightly. He couldn't help but notice goose bumps suddenly appearing everywhere he touched her. Which meant her nipples were probably hard and aching for his fingers and mouth.

Her dress had slipped down a bit, and the neckline rode low on her chest. The fabric rested just on the crest of her breasts; he could see she wasn't wearing a bra. In fact, he thought he could see the crescent edge of one nipple, even in the dim light.

He wanted to dip his tongue between her breasts.

"Quinn?"

"Hmm?"

"Why did you ask me to dance?"

"Because my friends…" Her soft voice faded off.

"Your friends?" He prodded.

"My friends dared me to. They think I am such a loser when it comes to men."

"Ah."

"I always pick Mr. Wrong."

"Am I supposed to be Mr. Right?" He brushed the backs of his knuckles over the rise of her breasts.

"No. Just Mr. Right Now."

She was direct. He wondered if it was just the alcohol talking. “So you just want to use me.”

“Basically.”

Her boldness wavered, disappointing him a bit.

He raised his eyebrows. “Huh. And you don't think I'd care?” He leaned back a bit and looked down at her, her skin a canvas for the colorful light bouncing off the mirrored disco ball above the dance floor.

She wouldn't meet his gaze. “Do you?”

Logan stilled, bringing their dancing to a sudden halt. “Do you normally drink this much?”

“No.”

“Maybe you need to sober up.” He stepped away from her, and his fingers curled into fists. He could be direct too. “I don't fuck drunk chicks.”

“Oh.”

And he left her standing on the floor, swaying. Only it wasn't to the music.

* * *

The world was coming to an end.

Okay, it wasn't. It just felt like it. Quinn hadn't drunk this much since college.

Outside the banquet-hall, she sat on the hood of her Infiniti. She had ripped the shoes off her feet and had winged them out somewhere into the dark parking lot. Good riddance.

She was just rolling her pantyhose down her thighs when she heard the clearing of a throat. She tried to catch her balance, but it was too late. She fell back, cracking her head on the windshield of her car.

"Ouch. Son-son of a bitch." She rubbed her head and started to pull out the bobby pins that were digging into her scalp, throwing them onto the ground. Another torturous ritual for women—unrealistic hairdos that needed metal pins to keep them in place. She flung a bobby pin with all her might, and it just plopped to the pavement with an unsatisfying *ping.*

"Need help?"

She looked up surprised to see—what was his name?—*Logan* watching her.

"No, I don't—I'm juss fine... Don't want help from you."

"Yeah, I can see that."

Her pantyhose were still midway around her thighs, her dress was pushed up to her waist, and half her hair was now falling around her face. She wouldn't be in this predicament if her friend hadn't gotten married. It was all Gina's fault.

"I hate weddings," she grumbled.

"Me too."

"It's juss a stupid ritch...ritual to make people suffer."

His lips twisted into a smile. "I agree."

"I need to go home."

She pushed herself to her feet and swayed a bit. She dug into a matching pink clutch and pulled out her car keys.

He was suddenly next to her, grabbing her hand, snagging the car keys from her fumbling fingers. "Oh no. You're not driving in this condition."

"Who says?"

"Me."

She frowned at him, and she tried to plant a hand on her hip, but she missed. "An' who dooo you think you are, huh?"

"I'm the one your friends dared you to have sex with." He cast a glance behind him, searching, his ponytail draping over his shoulder. "Where are your friends, anyhow? Shouldn't they be out here driving you home?"

She had the urge to wrap his ponytail around her hand and tug. Instead Quinn leaned against the front grille of her car, trying to keep her balance. "They leff a while 'go. I told 'em I was goin' home with you."

"You are?"

"No, I juss told 'em that so they didn't think I was a loser."

"Why would they think you are a loser?"

"Because I can't get anyone good."

"And you think I'm good?" He arched an eyebrow, waiting for her answer.

"No. Thass the point. I think you're bad. Very bad."

"You've got that right."

She planted her hands against the front of her car to push herself to her feet. "See? You're sooo bad, you're perfect."

That was the last thing she remembered.

Logan caught Quinn before she fell face-first onto the pavement. He grimaced. He hated drunk chicks.

But for some reason, he didn't think this was a normal event for her.

Even so, something had to be done with her.

He leaned Quinn's limp body back onto the front of her car and held her in place with his knee. Grabbing her clutch—purse, bag, whatever the fuck they called them—he dug through it for her wallet to find an address.

Nothing. There was nothing in the bag but a tube of lipstick! What the fuck? What was the point of carrying the stupid thing, then?

Women!

He threw her car keys into the bag and, with a grunt, hefted her over his shoulder. She was facedown, and her dress was draped over her head, covering her upside-down torso completely. Which, from what he could see, left most of her bottom bare.

He shook his head when he noticed her pantyhose halfway down her thighs. And she had no shoes on. Not his problem.

As long as law enforcement didn't spot him in this predicament, he was golden.

He strode quickly across the parking lot to his Dodge Dually and opened the back passenger-side door of the crew cab. He tossed her in the back and slammed the door shut.

He contemplated dropping her off on someone's doorstep. Maybe even his sister's. That would be good payback for dragging him to this nightmare. But he thought better of it.

No. He would deal with little Quinn.

It would be his pleasure.

And possibly hers too.

Chapter Three

Quinn groaned at the splitting pain in her head. The high-pitched whine didn't help. Where was that coming from?

She didn't want to open her eyes, because her bed still felt like it was moving. But she had no choice. She had to get the wretched noise to stop.

She shuffled around in the warm sheets and rubbed her face with a hand, before reaching down to scratch her…

Quinn's eyes popped open in horror. She was naked. She never slept naked. Her hand traveled lower until she touched the springy curls of her pussy. She was definitely naked.

And, holy shit, that wasn't her ceiling either. She sat up suddenly and gasped.

This was not her bedroom. This wasn't a bedroom of anyone she knew.

She looked around. The walls and the ceiling were made of logs. Smooth, stained, glossy logs. The floors were wood planked, and there was a window over the bed. She squinted at the sunlight glaring through the glass.

In the corner was a pile of pink taffeta…

Oh shit.

Now she remembered.

The dare.

She had gone through with it.

No. Wait. He had turned her down flat. She at least remembered that part.

Crap. Maybe they had dared her to screw some other guy, and that guy hadn't turned down a free piece of ass.

Oh no. It could have been anyone! She closed her eyes and started to do inventory of all the possibly single guys at the reception. There hadn't been that many. Had there?

Crap, she better not have gone home with a married man. She was going to kill Lana and Paula. Why didn't they stop her? They knew she didn't do these types of things!

She looked around for something to wear, but all she could see was that dress. And she'd rather be naked than put that thing back on. She spied a dresser and, with the sheet wrapped around her, went over to pull open a drawer. T-shirts. Mostly in black. She grabbed one and shook it out, looking at the size. It was large enough to cover her and then some.

Now, where was her underwear? Nowhere to be found.

There was no way she was going without underwear. She could be in a psycho's house, and she might have to make a quick escape. She was not going to be running out into the wild butt naked. She wanted something covering her goodies.

She dug in the next drawer down, pulled out a pair of men's boxer-briefs, and put them on. They were way too big, but they at least covered her like shorts. Sort of. If she didn't count the big, gaping slit in the front.

She couldn't believe she was in this situation. This was so unlike her.

Dumb. Dumb. Dumb!

She went to the door of the large bedroom—it had to be the master bedroom, especially with such a massive bed—and quietly opened the door to peek out. The coast was clear; the long hallway was empty, and she could see light at the end of it. It might be her chance to escape.

She tiptoed down the hallway and passed a bathroom with regret. She really needed to relieve herself. But it would have to wait. Priorities, she reminded herself. She crept farther down the hallway, and she realized the high-pitched sound had ceased.

The scent of fresh ground coffee wafted over her.

A pan clattered. Someone was making breakfast. It sounded like the kitchen was the next entryway down the hallway. She would have to try to sneak past it without getting caught.

But the curiosity was killing her. Who did she end up going home with last night? What had they done together?

Okay, did she really want to know?

She pinned herself against the wall, chewing on her thumbnail worriedly, and peered around the doorway into a huge kitchen.

She sucked in a breath.

Logan Reed stood at the stove, the hard lines of his back shifting as he messed with something in front of him. She was mesmerized by the powerful ripple and flow of his muscles under smooth, sun-bronzed skin.

His deep voice snapped her out of her trance. “What are you doing? Get in here and help.”

The breath rushed out of her. He hadn't even bothered to turn to face her. He just knew she was there.

She straightened up and stepped into the doorway. The man was barefoot and bare chested, with only a pair of soft, worn blue jeans encasing his lower body.

Her pussy pulsed, and her breathing became shallow.

“Well, c'mon. Don't just stand there.”

She took a tentative step farther into the kitchen.

“Coffee's brewing. Grab yourself a mug.”

He turned, and Quinn bit her bottom lip until she tasted blood. His hair was loose this morning, framing his face. It was long enough to brush past his shoulders.

Had she said she hated long hair? Oh, she'd have to rethink that one, for sure.

His chest was dark and lightly covered with hair from his well-sculpted pecs down his abs—oh God, he actually had abs—and disappeared into the front of his jeans. Visible veins popped out from his biceps, since the muscles were so distinct. And the tattoos…

He had a tribal band circling his left bicep, and the one on his right looked like a white stalking tiger. Yes, it was a white tiger, and it might have had green eyes. She wouldn't know for sure until she got closer. *If* she got closer.

Oh, did she *so* want to get closer.

No! No, she didn't.

His right nipple was pierced, which caught her off guard. She had never seen a man with pierced nipples.

Until now.

"Nice outfit. The mugs are in the cabinet over by the fridge."

Quinn made herself move, albeit stiffly, to grab two mugs from the cabinet, and she reluctantly moved closer to the man she wanted to throw on the kitchen table and eat for breakfast.

He had turned her down flat last night. What had changed his mind?

"There's aspirin on the table for your hangover."

She cleared her throat before answering, "Thanks, but I'm okay."

He had a carton of eggs on the counter next to the stove, and he turned back to crack four of them into a cast-iron skillet. Another first for her: real cast iron. She had never seen anyone cook in one of those before. She had only seen them used for decoration.

"How do you like your eggs?"

"Anything but runny."

"Easy enough," he said.

Her stomach felt slightly queasy, but the fried eggs smelled wonderful. She watched his muscles bunch when he flipped the eggs in the pan.

"There's juice in the fridge if you want."

Quinn shook her head. "Just coffee."

"It's ready. Help yourself."

She did and then sat at the large butcher-block table, curling her legs underneath her and pulling the oversize T-shirt over her knees.

He placed two plates of food on the table and sank into the chair across from her, his green eyes pinning her in place.

"Go ahead and eat."

She ripped her gaze from his and followed the line of his shoulders. "I'm not really hungry."

"You should try to get some solid food into your stomach."

She didn't answer but just stared at the gold ring protruding from his dark small nipple.

She was tempted to crawl over the table on her hands and knees and tickle the hoop with her tongue. She had the craziest urge to suck it into her mouth and tug… Where the hell had *that* come from? Why would she think that? She never initiated sex. Ever. None of her former lovers—all two of them—had ever made her even *want* to initiate sex. Especially not Peter.

She broke her gaze away and picked up a fork and took a small bite of egg. Her stomach rolled, and she quickly grabbed her mug to take a long swallow of black coffee. It made her feel a little better.

"It was a rough night."

Quinn jerked her head up, and their eyes locked. He wore a small, crooked smile. She quickly looked away and blushed. "What…what happened?"

"You don't remember?"

She opened her mouth and looked up again, only to realize he was teasing her. A flash of relief went through her. "Nothing happened?"

"I told you I don't fuck drunk chicks."

"You have a conscience, huh?"

"Maybe. Actually, if I'm going to fuck someone, I want it to be enjoyable for both of us. Or all of us."

"All?"

"Depending how many are involved."

Quinn cleared her throat. "Oh."

His smile widened, showing off his straight white teeth. He finished off his meal before sliding his chair back across the plank floor. After placing his plate in the sink, he turned to lean back against the counter and crossed his arms over his chest.

Shit, even his forearms were sexy.

"Are you done?"

She nodded, unable to answer.

He crossed the room to snag her plate. "Good, because you're not drunk anymore."He tossed her plate onto the counter and then came to stand behind her chair. Quinn's heart skipped a beat before it resumed thumping furiously. Her breathing shallowed, and her lips parted slightly.

"Your hair looks much better down." His warm, deep voice sent a shiver down her spine. She refused to turn to face him. She enjoyed not knowing what he was doing, what he was looking at, how close he was, what he was going to do next. Her nipples pebbled, and her breath caught. She never realized that the fear of the unknown could be so exciting. She barely got out, "So does yours."

His fingers curled over her shoulders, worked their way up into her hair, and massaged against her scalp.

His hands flexed into fists, pulling her hair tight, and he yanked her head back, forcing her to look up at him. Her neck was stretched over the back of the chair, and she looked up into his serious eyes and was afraid.

No. She wasn't afraid. She should have been, but she wasn't. She was titillated.

One corner of his mouth lifted, and he let out a low growl. "Who said you could go into my drawers and borrow my stuff?"

Quinn opened her mouth to answer. But she couldn't form any words. She didn't know what to do.

"Did you have permission?" He gave her hair a slight yank, and she groaned.

It hurt. But boy, did it hurt good. How could that be?

Her breathing quickened, and she whispered, "No."

Quinn wrapped her hands around his wrists but didn't try to pull him away. It would have been pointless anyway. He had to be three times as strong as her. At least.

"How dare you touch something that isn't yours?"

"I don't know—" Her answer was strained, her neck was getting sore in that position, and the blood was rushing to her head.

"That's right, you like dares."

"No."

"Yes, you do."

Her chest rose and fell rapidly beneath the tautly pulled T-shirt, her nipples hard beneath the cotton.

"Do you dare me to make you pay?"

"Pay?"

"Yes, punish you like this…" He buried his head into her neck, scraping his teeth along her strained throat, brushing his lips and tongue where his teeth had gone. His beard was too short to be soft; it was like sandpaper against her skin.

When his fingers loosened on her hair, she grabbed his biceps, meaning to push him away but pulling him toward her instead. Logan grabbed a handful of the T-shirt and pulled it up and over her head, covering her face, exposing her breasts.

Never having been blindfolded before, she sucked in a breath, and the cotton filled her mouth. She pushed it back out with her tongue and made herself calm down enough to breathe through her nose. His scent was infused into the fabric, and she imagined his cock nestled in the same spot of his boxer-briefs as her pussy was now.

Her nipples were tight and painful, and her pussy pulsated. Yet he did nothing. She sat in his kitchen, with a T-shirt covering her head, which was bent back over the chair, and she did nothing.

Only waited.

Her breathing was fast and furious. She tried to quiet it enough to hear something, anything. She couldn't. Her heart pounding in her ears didn't help either.

She should move, leave, not just wait like the mouse being ready to be pounced on by the cat…

But she didn't. She didn't want to miss what he was going to do next.

Her breathing finally caught when something brushed her nipples. The pads of his fingers circled the hard points. The touch was light. Feathery.

She moaned and arched her back, needing him to do…

More.

It was a rush, not seeing but just feeling. Not knowing what to expect.

He rolled both of her nipples between his thumbs and forefingers gently. Quinn twitched in the chair, and she dug her fingers into his arms. He rolled harder and harder, until he was twisting the hard nubs and tugging on them.

Quinn cursed him. She cursed herself—for reacting like this. For enjoying something that—in the back of her mind—she thought she shouldn't. For reacting so strongly. Wanting him so much…

She gritted her teeth and ground her pussy into the hard seat of the chair. She wanted relief, but she also wanted it to last as long as it could.

She wanted more of this, more of him.

"*More.*" She didn't even recognize her own voice.

One hand released her breast and slid along her belly to dip down into the loose boxer-briefs. Logan's fingers played along her damp pubic hair, close, but not touching where she needed him.

Still blinded, she felt along his arms to his chest and brushed her palms over his nipples. His were just as hard as hers. She smiled into the darkness of the shirt.

Punishment, her ass.

She tweaked both of his nipples and tentatively flicked the nipple ring with a finger. She felt him shift. She'd had no idea that such a small piece of gold jewelry would make his nipple so sensitive. The ring was more than decoration; it was a source of pleasure. Or possibly pain?

His finger found her hot button, and she forgot everything she had been doing.

He circled her hard, supersensitive clit with his thumb, while parting her pussy lips with his index and middle fingers. Her hips surged forward. She wanted him in her. She didn't care what part of him, anything—fingers, tongue, cock. The emptiness inside her desperately needed to be filled. *Now.*

His fingers played along her labia and continued to tease her clit, keeping a rhythm that made her rock her hips in time.

"Fuck!" exploded from between her clenched teeth.

His slick fingers found the small stretch of skin between her pussy and her anus, and he stroked it. He stroked back and forth, back and forth, occasionally touching her anus, making it clench, then back again to the edge of her pussy. Her pussy opened for him, wanting him, needing him.

"I'm going to fuck you," Logan murmured.

She tried to clear her mind. Bring herself back to her senses. But she couldn't…

"Okay."

"Not when you want. When I want."

"Okay."

His thumb dipped into her pussy slightly; her hips jerked forward to meet it.

"Patience," he murmured. She was shocked to find the heat of his breath right above her mouth. His lips brushed hers through the fabric. She'd never felt a kiss like this before. It was like kissing through a veil. The shirt prevented her from touching her tongue to his, from tasting him. His lips moved over hers, the cotton dampening from the contact.

He pulled away, and Quinn felt a sudden sense of loss. She wanted to taste him without the barrier; she wanted to explore his lips, his tongue.

He had other ideas for his mouth. He leaned over to cup her left breast; he raised it until she felt the suction of his hot mouth on her nipple. His tongue flicked against the hard tip, making her cry out.

She arched her back more, raising her chest to him. He sucked and pinched and nipped her breast.

Words were coming out of Quinn's mouth, but she had no idea what she was saying. She didn't even care. All she cared about was that he not stop.

Logan slipped two fingers inside her at the same moment he bit down on her nipple. Quinn cried out and blindly reached out to him, making contact with his rib cage. She dug her nails into his skin as he plunged a third finger into her and pressed them as far as they would go. Her nails raked against him, and she felt him shudder.

Her hips lifted off the chair, thrusting against his fingers; she was so wet and slick, they met no resistance.

Then, unexpectedly, he was gone.

He had stepped back out of her reach, and Quinn whimpered.

Before she could protest, he lifted her out of the chair and pushed it out of the way. Once Logan set her on her feet, he nudged her forward until her hips jammed against the heavy wood table. With a hand on her back, he pushed her over. With one yank, his borrowed boxer-briefs pooled around her ankles, and cool air tickled her heated skin. He grabbed the back of the T-shirt and slipped it over her head so it was now around the front of her neck like a collar, her arms still snared in the sleeves. Her head was free now, but because he was pinning her down with one hand, her sight was still limited. And she wanted to see him…

She wanted to see all of him.

As he was seeing all of her.

The rasp of his zipper mixed with the sounds of their accelerated breathing. The *swoosh* of denim against his skin as he stripped out of his jeans made her start to shake.

Hard thighs, wiry hair, pressed against the back of her thighs. She tried to push back against him, but he pushed down on her harder.

“Don't move.”

His palm skimmed down her spine and over one ass cheek, then the other.

"Don't move from that position," he warned. "Not even an inch."

Or what? she wanted to know. What would he do? What could he possibly do to her that would be more exhilarating than what he was already doing? The thought tempted her to move, but she wouldn't risk it. Not yet. She didn't know him. She didn't know his limits, what he was capable of.

And that made her cunt clench tight.

"Do you know what happens to bad little girls who borrow without asking?"

Oh, wait. That's right. She was still being punished. Somehow she had forgotten.

"They get punished," Quinn answered, not bothering to disguise the pleasure in her voice.

Then he smacked her ass cheek with his open hand, making her jerk forward in surprise. "That's right."

"Ow!" She was not expecting to be spanked. And it stung, to boot.

Logan smoothed his palm over the stinging cheek to soothe it.

"Not only did you borrow my stuff without permission, my shit's going to need to be washed. You got the crotch all wet."

He smacked the other cheek, and again, she jerked forward from the shock of it.

"Jesus Christ!" She wanted him to stop. No! No, she didn't. Oh God, what was wrong with her?

"No complaining, or it'll just extend your punishment."

Quinn felt the sweep of his long hair against her rear before his tongue smoothed along one of her smarting cheeks. He licked her again and again, long, slow strokes, until both cheeks were damp.

Then he smacked her once more, and it stung worse because her skin was wet, but made the pleasure more intense to Quinn. Never in her wildest dreams would she have thought she'd be spanked by an adult as an adult. But she realized now what she had been missing. It was naughty and exciting, and every time his palm made contact with her ass, a shot of lightning went right through her, making her nipples harder and making her inner muscles contract.

"Your ass is so red. It's so pretty like that. So fuckable."

"Then fuck me...*please*."

She waited to be berated for speaking out. But he said nothing. Instead he slid his cock over her burning cheeks and between them.

She tensed as a moment of panic shot through her. *Jesus.* He was large. Not as large as some of the men in the pornos she had seen in college. But larger than her ex.

She couldn't see him, because she was still pinned on her stomach, her arms bound in the T-shirt behind her back, but he felt as hard as steel, thick, and long. He would never fit.

His balls hung heavily, rubbing against her slit. He squeezed her ass cheeks together and slid his cock between them, thrusting against her.

Quinn raised her hips and pushed her ass toward him, encouraging him to take the next step.

Logan leaned over her, grinding his hips into her ass harder while he licked along her lower spine, avoiding her bound arms. He nipped a shoulder blade. Her hands were free enough that, when she stretched her fingers out, she made contact with the head of his cock. It was slick and smooth and very, very hot.

She tried to wrap her fingers around him, but Logan pulled away.

"Don't move," he warned her again.

She didn't. She didn't want to miss this for anything.

At least she thought so until she heard the slide of a drawer. What was he getting? Oh God, what was he going to do with a kitchen utensil?

Quinn relaxed when she heard the ripping of a foil packet, and the fleeting question of why he would have condoms in his kitchen left her when the tip of his cock pressed against her entrance.

He rubbed the bulbous head back and forth, over her clit, up to her anus, making her wetter, slicker, more desperate for him to be inside her.

She was ready to scream in frustration when she felt him push her thighs wider with his own, nudge his cock between her lips, grasp her ass cheeks with his large hands, and spread her wide.

"Are you ready for me?"

Quinn had her forehead pressed against the tabletop, and she rocked it back and forth in a nod.

His fingers dug deeper into her ass cheeks. "I can't hear you."

She let out a shuddered breath. “Yes.”

“Yes?” The crown of his cock bumped against her pussy, not quite entering her. But so close…

“Yes, I'm ready.”

“Dare me to fuck you.”

She didn't respond. She couldn't. She'd never demanded anything during sex before. Ever.

He slid his cock in only an inch. His head was wide, and it stretched her. He was barely in her, and she felt her orgasm already starting to build.

She tried to grind back against him, to drive him home deep within her, but he restrained her hips in his grasp.

A shiver ran down her spine when he barked, “Do it!”

She clenched her fingers into fists and let out a long groan. Why did he have to push her? Why did he have to hear how much she wanted him at this moment?

She whispered, “I dare you to fuck me.”

“Louder.”

She let out a long, low wail before screaming, “I dare you to fuck me!”

Quinn gasped as he drove his cock deep with a sharp tilt of his hips, deep enough to bump against her cervix. Her inner muscles clenched around him, not wanting to let him go when he pulled out. But before he pulled out completely, he plunged into her again. Her back arched, her body bowing to meet him. The pain and pleasure all mixed together.

"Shit, you're too tight. Relax." His voice sounded strained, but she couldn't answer him.

She *was* tight, to the point of being uncomfortable, but he stretched her out more with every thrust of his hips. He released deep, soft grunts with each thrust.

"Your pussy is so hot."

He smacked her ass cheek again, making Quinn cry out in surprise and jerk back against him harder. She wanted, she needed, to grab on to something, but she couldn't, her arms were still bound in the T-shirt, helpless. Her fingers wiggled, trying for something, anything to take ahold of.

"You're so tight."

Logan released her hips and leaned forward, pinning her fingers under his lower belly, and he changed the angle of his hips, thrusting down. His cock brushed against her magic spot, making her knees buckle. She no longer held her own weight on the balls of her feet. He held her in place, held her where *he* wanted her. Took her at *his* own rhythm.

Her pinned fingers felt each bunch of his stomach muscles as he conquered her. Took her for his own.

She had never felt so completely under someone else's control in her life. Never. And she loved it.

Quinn realized she had been moaning the same two words over and over in rhythm with each surge of his cock deep within her.

Fuck me.

Fuck me.

Fuck...me.

He leaned his chest into her back, putting more of his weight on her, pinning her arms between them even more. He freed up one of his hands and slipped it between her and the table, pressing his fingers against her clit, making rapid movements in contrast to his hips.

His other hand grasped her loose hair, and he sank his teeth into her shoulder as he ground against her, making small, quick thrusts, staying as deep as he could.

"Come with me."

She did.

Quinn screamed as the spasms overtook her, rocking her whole body from the inside out. Her muscles gripped and released his cock in the hardest orgasm she had ever had. She hadn't even known it was possible for it to be that intense.

Logan cursed, and she could feel his cock pulsating inside her, his hips moving uncontrollably as he came as hard as she did.

He stilled while she had some aftertremors. She felt weak and boneless. Her muscles were loose, and she didn't know if she could even stand by herself.

But that could wait. She was still full of Logan; he was deep inside her yet, and she wanted to take pleasure in the moment.

She had just had the best sex in her life, and it was all because of a stupid dare.

A laugh bubbled out of her as Logan slipped out of her and stepped back. He untangled the shirt from her arms gently and pulled her to her feet. The blood rushed to her freed limbs, and she groaned with the relief and the little bit of pain.

Logan turned her to face him with a look of concern on his face. “Are you all right?”

Rubbing her arms to bring back the circulation, Quinn smiled up at him. Couldn't he tell that she'd just had the best sex of her life? “Never better.”

He returned the smile and, with his index finger, tipped her chin up toward him. “Good.”

He leaned down and kissed her, giving her what she had wanted earlier but had been unable to get. His mouth slanted across her lips, and his tongue brushed against hers softly. She was disappointed when he ended the kiss, but he made up for it when he enfolded her in his arms and pressed her naked body against his. His cock was still large, but softer than what it had been, pressing against her hip; her nipples brushed against the light fur on his chest.

She usually felt self-conscious naked. But not now. With this man, it just felt right.

He laid a whiskered cheek on the top of her head and after a few moments said, “We need to stretch you out.”

It took a moment for Quinn to process what he had said. But she didn't get it. Yes, she had been tight, but he had fit just fine. Perfectly fine.

“For what?”

An unfamiliar deep voice came from behind her. “I guess I missed breakfast.”

“For him,” Logan answered her, tilting his head toward the kitchen entranceway.

Quinn tensed in Logan's arms and tried to pull away, embarrassed to be caught naked in front of another man. He wouldn't release her but turned the both of them until she could see the owner of the silky voice.

He was dark, his skin the color of baking chocolate. Dark enough that from the distance between them, it was hard to differentiate his facial features, but she could tell he had dark eyes and a very white smile.

Those dark eyes surveyed the two of them, and the smile got even bigger.

"Wow. I didn't expect you to bring home a wedding gift."

As he stepped closer, Quinn clung to Logan like he was a blanket, trying to keep the important stuff covered. But it was useless. Logan peeled her off and stepped away, his nakedness in front of the other man not seeming to bother him a bit. He held on to her hand, forcing her to face the new arrival.

"Ty, this is Quinn..." He looked at Quinn with a disconcerted expression. "I'm sorry. I don't know your last name."

"Preston." This was bizarre—being introduced to another man when she was totally naked. She glanced around for the T-shirt.

"Preston," Logan repeated. "Quinn, this is Tyson White. My...roommate."

The way he said *roommate* made her lift her eyes from her search.

Ty took another step closer and gave Quinn the once-over. "She's spectacular."

Since he had moved closer, Quinn could see Ty's eyes were definitely a dark brown, almost black. His scalp was shaved smooth, showing off a beautifully shaped head. He had a small gold hoop earring in each ear, which were nice complements to the rich shade of his skin. His nose was broad and his lips full. His shoulders looked even broader in the tight black T-shirt than Logan's did. And he was taller too. By an inch or so.

He was a very big man. And Quinn realized that was the least of her worries. She needed to cover up.

She spied the discarded T-shirt thrown over one of the chairs pushed away from the table. She started for it when Ty reached out and grabbed her elbow.

"Hold on. Let me see you."

His grasp was light, but when Quinn tried to pull away, he tightened his fingers.

Logan came behind her and wrapped his arms around her waist, putting his lips to her ear. "Shhh. It's okay. He's not going to hurt you."

Quinn's heart was pounding, and she was getting into a fight-or-flight mode when Ty ran a thumb over her jawline. He ran one of his long fingers over her parted lips, her rapid breath fluttering against the backs of his knuckles.

He gave her a soothing smile and said, "Beautiful."

His fingers continued a path down her neck, along her shoulders, and lightly traced along the undersides of her breasts. Quinn's nipples peaked again between the pressure of Logan's soft but still-heavy cock against her backside and Ty's fingers brushing over her rib cage. Ty lingered a bit before trailing them down her belly to her damp curls and the evidence of the sex between Logan and her just minutes before.

She sucked in a breath and held very still. She felt like a deer caught in headlights, knowing she should run but too stunned to do so.

"She's very tight," Logan said matter-of-factly, his voice sounding normal—like he was talking about the weather.

Quinn was thinking there was nothing normal about this situation, when Ty dropped to his knees in front of her and smoothed his palms over her hips and down her legs, running his hands over the slickness still on her inner thighs. His hands were not as rough as Logan's, but they caused shivers up her spine just the same.

He rubbed his thumb and forefinger together, testing the wetness between them. "She must be very responsive. Turn her around."

Logan turned her within his arms, and Quinn looked up into his eyes, questioning him without words. He placed a featherlight kiss on her forehead in answer.

If he thought that was going to be enough to pacify her, he was sorely mistaken. She did not like being inspected like a piece of horseflesh at an auction. But no protest made it past her lips. Maybe it was her natural curiosity to see where this would lead.

Or maybe he had just fucked her brains out. Literally.

Ty's hands skimmed over her buttocks. Then he stood, stepping close enough to press his jean-clad groin against the small of her back.

"Still pink," he murmured, referring to her spanked ass.

Logan and Ty shifted closer and met over Quinn's shoulder. Quinn was helplessly sandwiched between the two men as their lips met and they kissed.

It wasn't a brotherly kiss either.

"Holy shit," Quinn blurted out before she could stop herself.

The men broke the kiss, gave each other a look Quinn couldn't read, before they both stepped back, freeing her.

With her newfound freedom, she dashed to the chair and yanked the T-shirt over her nakedness. With hands on her hips, she turned to both of the men. Logan had slipped back into his jeans and was in the process of closing the top button.

"What the hell is going on here?"

"Quinn—"

"I mean, one minute you're having sex with me, and the next...the next you're kissing him. I mean, it's not like I'm jealous or anything. I'm not. It's just I'm..." She shook her head. "I'm confused."

Confused was a mild way of putting it. She sank into one of the heavy wooden kitchen chairs and stared at the men across from her. Logan leaned back into Ty's chest, and the darker man's hands languidly stroked Logan's arms.

For some reason, Quinn could not wrap her brain around what she was seeing.

"You're gay?" Her question was directed toward Logan, though she didn't care which one of them answered her.

"No, I'm not gay. I love women."

Quinn pressed fingers to her temples to try to relieve the dull throb taking up residence in her head. "But you like men."

"I don't see color or gender, for the most part. I see people."

She asked Ty, "Are you gay?"

He shook his head. "I enjoy women too. But I love Logan."

Quinn gave up the massaging and dropped her hands in her lap helplessly.

Logan squeezed Ty's forearm before pulling away and coming over to Quinn, then squatting in front of her. His fingers were warm and strong as they gripped hers.

"Quinn, when I went to the wedding yesterday, I didn't plan on meeting anyone. I was only going to do my sister a favor. And I definitely wasn't planning on bringing home a drunk girl"—at her frown, he corrected himself—"woman. Sorry."

His thumbs traced over the delicate skin of her wrists.

"But—"

"But I was attracted to you, and I was intrigued by your friends' dare. But…" His words faded off.

"But?"

"But when you got that drunk, I changed my mind."

"But I ended up here anyway."

"Yeah."

"Did anything happen last night?"

Logan didn't answer. Just his expression was enough.

"I still don't know how I ended up here."

Logan explained it to her while Ty moved around the kitchen, getting himself a mug of coffee and clearly keeping an ear open during the interesting tale of events.

Quinn was disappointed to learn her friends had deserted her while she was so incapacitated. She was going to have to have a little discussion with them. It was one thing for them to want her to get laid. Or to get over Peter. It was another to leave her drunk and expect her to go home with a stranger. Okay, maybe he wasn't a total stranger, but still...

Ty placed a fresh mug of coffee in front of her. Logan moved away and settled into a chair across the table, giving her some space. Ty leaned against the counter a couple of feet from her and crossed his ankles, just observing her. Both seemed to be waiting for some sort of reaction from her.

"So...you're a couple?" she asked them, keeping her eyes focused on her mug of steaming java.

"Four years," Ty finally answered.

Logan had cheated on his partner with her. She was the *other woman*. She would never knowingly cause a rift in a relationship. The guilt turned her gut.

"I'm sorry," she said.

"For what?" Ty asked her.

"You caught us... We... I didn't mean to..." Why was she apologizing? Feeling guilty? She hadn't known Logan was taken. She turned to look at him. He was leaning back in his chair, a concerned look on his face.

“There's nothing to be sorry about,” Logan stated firmly.

She faced Ty. “You don't mind sharing him?”

“Oh, I don't mind sharing him, as long as I'm involved.”

Quinn pinned her brows together, considering for a moment what he had just said. “Do you share him much?”

Ty laughed and took a sip of his coffee, effectively avoiding the question.

“Look, I know this looks kind of…odd. But Ty and I have a great relationship. It's secure. We both know what we want out of it and each other. We had been discussing bringing in a third person for a while.”

Quinn sputtered, “Whoa, whoa, whoa—”

“We wanted a woman to complete us. We weren't actively looking, but—”

“Apparently fate brought you to us,” Ty finished for Logan.

“Fate?” Quinn shook her head. “It was a stupid dare.”

Logan leaned forward over the butcher-block table and splayed his fingers flat against its surface. Quinn's eyes were automatically drawn to his large hands. The memory of what they had done to her made her wiggle in her seat.

“Quinn, I dare you to stay a few days with us.”

She forced herself to look up at him. He wasn't laughing…nor even smiling. He was dead serious! He wanted her to just drop everything and stay a few days with not one but two men!

Uh, yeah, right. "Logan, I have a job."

Not that she liked her job as a financial analyst, but it paid well, and she was not going to blow vacation days just to bang two guys... Shit! Not just two guys, but two guys at once.

As if she *would* do that...

One of those two guys—Ty—moved behind her and placed his hands on her shoulders, his fingers shifting until they stroked the hollow at the base of her neck. She cursed herself silently when her nipples peaked against the T-shirt.

What they were proposing—it was so wicked...so forbidden.

As if she *could* do that...

Ty's palms slipped down, and he cupped the outsides of her breasts while Logan kept talking.

"Okay, so stay with us next weekend. Go home for now, go to your job, live your life normally for the week. Then Friday after work, I'll pick you up and bring you out here for the weekend. Or drive out yourself, so you have your own way to escape if you decide it's too much. It'll be an experience you'll never forget."

Ty leaned over her and murmured in her ear, "We'll treat you to a weekend you'll never forget. Do you want a preview?" His thumbs caressed her pebbled nipples, and she involuntarily arched into his touch.

Quinn hissed out a breath, trying to gather her wits. She twisted away from Ty's touch and left her seat, creating some distance.

"I can't think when you're doing that."

The men gave each other a meaningful grin. They thought they had won her over. Just because she was like putty in their hands…

She let out a long, slow breath. The fact was, she *was* putty in their hands. And she liked it. Logan seemed to be a skilled lover, and Ty, well, she could just imagine.

Stepping over to the sink, she gazed out of the window at a distant row of trees.

Her dilemma was, one part of her wanted to say yes. She wanted to experience what it was like to be a bad girl, not caring what people thought of her. Throw caution to the wind.

The other part of her was scared to say yes, because…because…

Fuck it.

When was she ever going to have a chance like this again? No one but the three of them had to know. Right?

It was only a weekend. She could leave if it became overwhelming.

She was going to do it. No. No, she wasn't. She couldn't.

“Okay,” she told them without turning around. She had to get this out before she changed her mind. “Here's the deal. Next weekend, I'll drive myself out, just in case. And we have to be safe. And if there is something I don't want to do…”

She heard nothing behind her, so she turned to face them. Both of them looked sort of shell-shocked. They hadn't thought she'd agree! Oh boy, what had she gotten herself into?

"Now, do you have anything decent I can wear? I need to get back to my car and go home. I have dinner plans with my parents."

"We'll find you something. What do you want to do with your dress?"

"Burn it."

Logan laughed loudly.

This had to be the most bizarre day of her life.

Chapter Four

Friday couldn't come soon enough for Quinn. After leaving Logan's farm last Sunday, it was all she could think about.

Her concentration at work was lacking. She would stop in the middle of the hallway and have to close her eyes. The sensation of her stinging ass when Logan had been plunging his cock deep into her came back to her like it was all happening right then and there.

Sometimes she was so weak after reliving those moments, she had to grasp a nearby wall to catch her breath for a few seconds. Her nipples had been constantly hard peaks, visible through her blouse every day, catching the eyes of some coworkers.

In fact, it was no wonder she had had two guys ask her out so far this week. After the second invitation she had gone into the bathroom and taken a good look at herself. Her flushed face, heavy eyelids, and hard nipples made her look like she had just been well fucked or wanted a good fuck. And it was bad enough that the anticipation for Friday night was keeping her wet constantly. Some of the guys were probably picking up on the musky scent as she walked through the insurance company's offices.

She was like a bitch in heat. She had never thought about sex so much before in her life. It was constant. Almost an addiction. The memories of the pleasure she had discovered with the boys continually interrupted her workday.

On Monday night, she relieved the tension brewing in her with her vibrator.

On Tuesday, she didn't even bother with her toy; she just took care of herself with her fingers. In the bathroom at work, in her car, and at home on her couch.

By Wednesday, she couldn't stop reliving Sunday in her head. She sat in her office with the phone off the hook, picturing her ride back to the banquet hall in Logan's truck.

Not remembering the ride out to his place the night before, she was surprised to see how far out of town he actually lived. The driveway itself was about a mile long, surrounded by well-maintained grass fields. Logan had explained it was sod. He ran a sod farm that provided turf to all different types of businesses. That explained why he had his truck all lettered up with the name LGR SOD, INC.: *WHERE THE GRASS IS ALWAYS GREENER...*

Their parting by her car in the parking lot had ended with a kiss and a promise: if she dared to show up, she would have the best sex of her life. Quinn didn't think it would be hard to beat. After she had been almost bored to death with Peter's performance in the bedroom, anything was better.

Quinn imagined Peter over her in missionary style—like always—no foreplay, just pumping into her a few times before saying, "Ooo, ooo, baby," before grunting and shooting his load. It was all over before she was even wet.

In contrast, what could be better than spending a weekend with not one, but two gorgeous, experienced, not-uptight men?

Two, all for her. All for her pleasure.

At that thought she had to squeeze her thighs together to keep her pussy from quivering. But when she did, she came anyway. She gasped and slammed her hand over her mouth as her eyes rolled back from the pleasure skirting up her body. She was so glad she had closed her office door.

On Thursday she had second thoughts. When she got home from work, there was a message on her machine. It was from Peter. The prick started off with, “Quinn, I've been thinking…”

Quinn jabbed the Delete button before she could hear another word. That decided it; she was going to do it and enjoy every second.

After digging out an overnight bag from the bottom of her closet, she threw some essentials into it: panties (probably unnecessary), makeup and hair products, and… She needed something sexy. As she dug through her drawers, she realized she had nothing besides a glittery thong Lana had given her as a joke on one of her birthdays. She didn't think a thong stating *Come In, We're Open* would be very enticing, and decided to stop at Victoria's Secret on her lunch break the next day.

She had never shopped at the well-known lingerie shop before, preferring to buy her underthings at a local department store instead. But maybe it was time for her to shake things up a bit.

As she zipped up the bag, her doorbell rang. It had better not be Peter coming to beg for her forgiveness. It wasn't. When she opened the door, Lana and Paula pushed past her, chatting the whole way into her small kitchen.

Lana lifted the two brown bags she had in her hands and announced, "We brought Thai food!"

"And wine!"

Paula cleared off Quinn's small table, dug through her cabinets, and set out plates, utensils, and wineglasses.

The girls chatted on, whirling around the kitchen and serving up the food, while Quinn could only stand there doing a mental inventory of what she had put in her overnight bag and what might still be needed. What did one take for a sex fest?

Condoms? The guys would have those.

Lube? Again, if needed, the guys.

Toys? Not her department.

Icy Hot for aching muscles?

"Hey, what's going through your pretty little head?" Quinn's eyes focused to see Paula's face only inches from hers. "Let's eat."

They made small talk and gossiped over dinner, while Quinn just said a few uh-huhs, okays, and mmms where appropriate. She was used to the other two blathering on and on about the latest scandals, whether it was someone they knew or someone in the latest tabloids. The girls only brought Thai when they wanted to dish the dirt.

After clearing the table, Lana filled everyone's wineglasses once more before settling back into her chair. "So…"

Quinn grimaced in expectation of a possible grilling. Quinn had a feeling she was the dirt they were going to dish tonight.

"So," Paula echoed.

"Any plans for the weekend?"

"Not really."

"Seeing your parents on Sunday?"

"No."

"Quinn, you have to get out there and start meeting people. Try new experiences."

If they only knew.

"What happened with Logan Reed?"

"Nothing."

"I thought you said you were going home with him."

"Well, I ended up striking out."

"That doesn't surprise me," Lana said. "Because I did some snooping this week, and the rumor is, he plays for the other team."

Quinn lifted a brow and took a sip of her wine.

"He doesn't like women," she clarified.

"That's a shame." Paula sighed. "Another good one lost to the other side."

The wine Quinn drank went down the wrong pipe, and she choked, sputtered, and then coughed, trying to catch her breath. Paula leaned over and whacked her between the shoulder blades.

"Ouch!"

Paula gave her an apologetic smile. "I didn't want to have to do the Heimlich."

Lana was wrong about Logan not liking women. But they weren't all he liked.

Anyway, she wasn't going to be the one to verify or deny the rumor. This weekend was her little secret. The last thing she wanted was her friends to find out, even as well-meaning as they were. They were both blabbers, and before she knew it, her parents would find out. Her straitlaced, churchgoing, community-involved parents.

Quinn groaned at the thought.

She could feel their condemnation now. They would never speak to her again. They would be the laughingstocks of their country club.

Her parents had loved Peter, who worked at a very large brokerage firm. In fact, they blamed her for the breakup. In their eyes, Peter was perfect. It didn't matter Peter wasn't perfect for her; he was perfect for them, for their image.

Or more, for her mother's image. Her father was much more easygoing than Quinn's mother. *She* was the one worried about their reputation. *She* was the one who wanted to be in control. Of Quinn's father. Of Quinn.

It had always been that way growing up. They didn't have to keep up with the Joneses. Oh no. No, they had to keep up with the Roosevelts. Hell, the Vanderbilts.

And what could be better? A daughter and a son-in-law who were both successful financial analysts with their MSFA degrees, their accolades, and their prosperous careers…

But then, neither of her parents had to fuck Peanut. Er, Peter…

Chapter Five

Stones pinged off the underside of Quinn's car as she drove down the never-ending driveway to Logan's farm. Her heart pounded with nervousness, but her nipples pebbled in anticipation of what—or who—was waiting for her at the end of the lane.

She had come straight from work, and it was close to six o'clock, but the sun still burned high in the early-summer sky.

When she came around the last bend in the lane, the reflection of sunlight off the multitude of windows on the sprawling log-cabin ranch made her suck in a breath. The house was gorgeous. Like the two men who lived in it.

Quinn parked her Infiniti next to a large black SUV, wondering what the vanity plate of BB 17 meant. She didn't see Logan's truck anywhere. She was surprised, if not a bit bothered. They had wanted her here for dinner.

Maybe she'd end up on the table. Again. Served up for dinner.

She got out of the car, and when she reached into the backseat of her sedan for her bag, something nudged her in the rear. She spun around to face a large German shepherd.

The shepherd wagged his tail and *woofed* at her in what she assumed—and hoped—was a playful manner.

"Magnum, leave her alone. Hold on, Quinn. Let me get that for you."

Ty jogged down the steps of the deck and over to the car. He pulled her bag from her fingers. He had on a snug Boston Bulldogs T-shirt over long, gray, silky shorts that hung down past his knees, along with a pair of startlingly red Nikes. His red and black Bulldogs ball cap sat backward on his smooth head. Quinn's gaze was drawn back to the skin above his sneakers. He had a barbed-wire tattoo wrapped around his right ankle. His skin was so dark, it was extremely hard to see.

The dog, Magnum, nudged her hand with his wet nose.

"He wants attention."

Don't we all? she thought, rubbing the dog's large, blocky head.

Ty tilted his head toward the house. "C'mon, let's go inside. Dinner's ready."

Quinn followed him in, watching his muscular ass moving beneath the silky fabric of his shorts as he climbed the steps.

Inside, he dropped her bag in the living room and escorted her into the kitchen.

She came up short when she saw only two place settings on the table she was very intimate with.

"I don't understand."

Ty kept moving toward the stove. As he stirred something in a large pan, he said, "Logan thought we needed to spend some time alone together, to get to know each other better."

"But I don't know him really either."

Ty gave her a smile over his shoulder. "You will."

She hoped so. Okay, so she knew ahead of time she'd have to go with the flow. She was a guest here. If they wanted her to have an intimate dinner with Ty, then she would. And anyway, whatever he was cooking smelled delicious.

"We eat healthy around here. I hope you don't mind a chicken stir-fry."

"No. Sounds good." Quinn slipped into a chair, the same one from last Sunday. "It's refreshing to see guys eating well without a woman forcing—" Quinn bit off the rest of her foot-in-mouth comment. She gave Ty a sheepish grin. "Sorry."

"No, you're right. I guess being a former athlete influenced my eating habits. I made Logan change his ways. He was a beer, pizza, and chips type of guy before we met."

"You'd never know it by his body," Quinn said, feeling the heat crawling up her neck.

Ty slid a plate of stir-fry in front of her, then placed another plate across from her and settled into a chair. He plucked his cap from his head and threw it on an empty seat.

He ran a hand over his smooth scalp and chuckled. "He works hard."

"I'm sure. So you were an athlete? What kind?" She placed a forkful of veggies into her mouth and was pleasantly surprised how good it was.

Ty placed both hands over his heart and made a wounded sound. “Oh, that hurts.”

“What?”

“You really don't know?”

Quinn chewed thoughtfully but shook her head. She had no idea. Why would he think she would?

“I was a wide receiver for the Boston Bulldogs.”

She looked at him blankly.

Ty spread his arms wide, ignoring his cooling food. “The Boston Bulldogs? You know, the NFL team? In Boston? In the NFC division?”

Quinn was starting to get the feeling she was missing something, that she should know who he was. But she didn't. She didn't know squat about football. She'd never even watched a Super Bowl.

“So you were an important member of the team?”

“Shit, yeah. I was the wide receiver. That's important. I'd tell you my stats, but I don't think you'd—”

“Get it,” she finished for him. “Maybe you could teach me about football?”

“Sure, I'd like that.” He reached across the table to capture one of her hands. “But there are other things I'd rather teach you first.”

Quinn studied the sharp contrast in color between the two of them. She looked pale next to his rich, dark pigment. She had never been with a black man before; she had never really given it much thought.

It wasn't just the difference in color, though; it was the size of his hand. His was twice as big as hers. Big hands that had carried a football. His nails were neatly trimmed, and when she turned his hand over, his palm and the pads of his fingers were a light pink. Quinn ran a finger over the creases in his palm. He made a fist, capturing her finger for a moment before pulling away.

His voice was husky when he said, “Let's finish eating…”

Quickly was unspoken between them.

Quinn tried to get her mind off what was to come. “Why did you stop playing football?”

“Injury. I didn't want to be benched for the rest of my career.” And he left it at that.

Ty cleaned his plate and then waited patiently while she ate about two-thirds of her meal. She finally had to shove the plate away. She was full.

“Excellent,” she told him while he cleared the table. She followed his movements with her eyes as he carried dishes over to the sink.

He had to have the most luscious ass she'd ever seen. Even in his shorts, she could tell it was full and muscular and round. Very round. She had a sudden urge to touch it.

Should she dare? Her fingers curled into her palms. *Good* girls like her just didn't grab a stranger's ass. Well, not quite a stranger, but close enough.

But hell, she was here to push her boundaries. Wasn't that what she was supposed to be doing? It would do her no good to hold back.

Pushing her chair back, she rose and came up behind him. His back was to her as he rinsed the dishes in the sink. She stepped into him, pushing her chest into his back and sliding her hands over his rump. She squeezed slowly, testing the firmness of his flesh, kneading the muscles flexing beneath her fingers.

A dish clattered. Ty braced his arms on each side of the sink and dropped his head forward as Quinn smoothed the silky fabric of his shorts over his ass. His cheeks were solid and impossibly firm, making Quinn want to sink her teeth into them.

"How?" She didn't even realize the question had escaped her until he answered, his voice a bit thicker.

"A lot of squats, weights, and sprints."

She slipped her hands into the waistband of his shorts and skimmed her fingers along his hips, over the curve of his buttocks. There was nothing between him and the shorts; just skin and heat. She shifted closer and wrapped her arms around his waist, placing her cheek against his broad back, feeling her way around to his front.

There. There it was. It was hard to miss. Literally. His cock was caught crookedly in his shorts, and she moved it to what she thought would be a more-comfortable position. She stroked along its hard length, amazed how large he really was. Just as she had feared. She had heard jokes, of course, about black men being hung. But in Ty's case it was true. Her hand seemed miniature in comparison.

She wanted to lick him. Taste him. Suck him. See if his skin was as sweet, as decadent, as it looked.

When she murmured what she wanted, he peeled her arms from around him and shook his head. "Not here. Come with me."

Those last three words held so much meaning. She had no doubt she would be coming with Ty. Both into the room and in more-wicked ways.

He took her hand and led her into the living room. He dropped to his knees on the plush throw rug in front of the impressively large stone fireplace; all it lacked was a roaring fire—too hot for the season. He tugged her down beside him, and they knelt facing each other. He pulled his T-shirt over his head and tossed it away. Quinn's breathing became uneven when he reached for her.

"Am I your first black man?"

"Yes."

He ensnared her cotton top in his fist and yanked it over her head, tossing it in the same direction of his own.

"Are you frightened?"

"Yes."

She had on the black lacy bra she had picked up at the lingerie shop earlier in the day. She reached behind her to unsnap it, but his hands were there, brushing hers to the side. He skillfully unclipped the little eye hooks.

Her breasts, now free, peaked to hard points. Ty leaned in, but he didn't touch them. Instead he gave her a kiss that sent electric heat scorching through her body.

"Because I'm black?"

A shiver of arousal moved through her. "No. Because you're too big."

He laughed against her mouth before his lips captured hers. His teeth tugged on her lower lip, and his tongue explored her mouth. Quinn clung to him harder, her nipples pressed to the smooth expanse of his chest. She brushed the hard tips against his skin, relishing the fact that with each touch, her pussy throbbed harder.

She planted her hand on his chest and pushed him until he was flat on his back. He stretched out, still in his shorts, which tented over his erection. Quinn pushed one sandal and then the other off her feet with her toes, before—still on her knees—she shimmied out of her capris and threw them onto the nearby couch. She moved to straddle Ty's hips and sat lightly on his thighs. His arms were folded underneath his head. He had been watching her strip but hadn't moved a muscle. And speaking of muscles, Quinn couldn't help but notice the muscling throughout his upper body. He was like a piece of art, a sculpture, all hard curves and angles. Rich color, dark shadows.

He was hairless. Not a hair on his head, on his chest, even his underarms. His skin was sleek and looked quite edible. Besides the barbed-wire tattoo on his ankle, his right bicep had a white tiger that was exactly like Logan's.

He had thick black flames tattooed up the sides of his rib cage. She couldn't see where they started, somewhere beyond the waistband of his shorts. But they ran all the way up his sides and stopped just below his pectoral muscles. His pecs were firm and built, his nipples small and dark, almost black.

Quinn planted her hands on his abs and leaned forward, taking one of those hard nipples into her mouth. She swirled her tongue around it, flicked it once, twice. Ty's eyelids lowered, and he shifted his hips up against her, the heat of his meaty thighs burning her slick pussy.

She worked her lips along his ribs, pausing to lick around his navel before coming to a halt at his shorts. She hooked her thumbs into the waistband and tugged them down until his cock sprung free. She rose enough to push his shorts down to his ankles, and he kicked them off. Now he was completely naked. A dark stud against a light plush rug.

He was magnificent. In all ways. And tempting. She had the urge to touch him more intimately. And she wasn't going to fight it. Not this time.

She settled between his thighs and cupped his balls, squeezing them gently, stroking the almost black, wrinkled skin. She encircled the base of his cock with her fingers and stroked her tongue up the back side of his shaft. His cock twitched against her mouth. She looked quickly up at his face. He was watching her but hadn't moved his arms from behind his head. A slight flare of his nostrils and a tightening of his jaw were enough encouragement.

Quinn drew her mouth over the mushroom top of his cock, tasting his salty precum. She licked the head clean, dipping her tongue slightly into the slit at the end. With one hand cupping his balls and the other squeezing the root, she sank his cock as deep as she could into her mouth. She licked and stroked and sucked hard against the steely silk of his skin. Her lips nibbled along his length for a moment before taking him deep between her lips again.

Still, he said nothing. Did nothing. Until she started a rhythm with her mouth and her hand.

He was fast. Without warning, he had his fingers shoved deep in her hair, and he lifted his hips in time with her mouth. Quinn sucked harder with each upstroke.

"Turn around. I want your pussy at this end." Ty's voice slid over her like melted chocolate.

Without releasing his throbbing cock, she spun her body around and straddled his rib cage, shoving her pussy toward his face. The cute little matching panties she had on were soaked. And when she felt his finger tracing around the edge of the elastic, she let out a tortured moan around his dick.

He poked and prodded and teased her pussy while she sucked harder, farther down his length.

He did just enough to drive her crazy. Not entering her. Not licking her. Not even touching her fully. If he did, she might just come instantly. She ran her tongue around the crown of his cock and began to palm him, her saliva and his precum making him slick enough so she could do it harder and faster.

She felt hot breath against the wet nylon of her panties, and she cried out when his lips found her heated flesh. The only barrier was the fabric between them. Fingers pulled the narrow crotch to the side, and she felt something hot—his tongue—plunging in and out of her pussy. Her thighs quivered, and she buried her head in his lap, capturing his sac between her lips and rolling his balls over her tongue, struggling not to bite him when waves of ecstasy went through her. She stroked him with both hands and suckled his balls, letting out little mews of pleasure as his tongue worked magic on her. When he caught her clit between his lips and tugged, she shuddered and collapsed, gasping as the ripples of orgasm ran through her.

She tried sucking in a breath, but she couldn't. Her cheek was pressed against his thigh, and she had all her weight on him, too weak to move. Finally her heart slowed, and her breathing became easier. She tried to shift her weight off Ty, but he held her in place with hands on her ass, his arms wrapped tight around her thighs.

She needed to finish him off. She had left him unsatisfied, and that wasn't fair.

She pushed herself up off his legs and…

Looked straight at Logan.

Across the room, Logan was sprawled in a leather love seat; his jeans unfastened and pushed down a little. Just enough so he had his cock in his hand, and he was stroking himself, tilting his hips up, shoving his cock deep into his fist.

Quinn could only stare. She didn't know how long he had been there. How much he had seen. Enough, apparently.

Ty extended a hand to Logan. A silent invitation for him to join them. Logan locked his gaze with hers and stood, his cock hard and sticking straight out from his body, framed by the denim.

A fleeting thought of *this is it* went through Quinn's mind. This was what she had come here for, and she was not going to chicken out now. Something about these men made her want to just let go and enjoy. All her life she had done what was expected of her. But now… Now she just wanted to break the rules. Throw caution to the wind. Just do something for herself. Do something unexpected, daring. Logan and Ty seemed to be making that easy for her.

She didn't want to be afraid of what people thought of her anymore. She didn't want to care. Maybe this weekend was a start.

Without breaking their gaze, Logan unbuttoned his shirt and peeled it off his shoulders, then kicked off his boots and shucked his jeans. As he pushed the denim down, vibrant color caught her gaze. Something she hadn't noticed before… A coral snake, larger than life, but just as beautiful, wrapped around his narrow hips. Once naked, he moved closer to them, drawing her attention to the man, not his ink.

Quinn felt a little silly still sprawled over Ty, so she tried to move away again, and this time he let her go.

She slipped to her knees on the rug. She was the only one still with anything on—her lacy black panties.

She felt helpless. She didn't know what to do. How this worked. What was expected of her.

Logan reached down to tilt her face up to him. "Stop worrying."

Quinn released her lower lip from between her teeth and let out a breath. Logan sank to his knees in front of her. He brushed a lock of hair away from her face. He shared a quick look with Ty when the other man rolled onto his side and laid a hand on her back. The larger man's fingers stroked along her spine; it was soothing, but it brought her nipples to points once again.

Logan's fingers drifted from her face down to her breasts, brushing against one nipple, then the other.

"We're going to take this slow."

Quinn's breathing quickened with one man's fingers teasing her nipples while the other stroked along her back and down around the top of her panties. Ty suddenly wrapped an arm around the front of her shoulders and pulled her until she was lying on her back next to him. Logan ran his hands down her sides.

"Let's get you out of these," he said while tugging her panties over her hips and thighs. He carefully lifted one of her legs and then the other, slipping the black panties over her feet. The whole time his hands skimmed along her skin, caressed a hip, touched the sensitive skin behind her knee, circled her heel. He raised one foot and placed a kiss on her instep. He lowered it and ran his hands up her calves, and when at her knees, he nudged them apart.

"I want to see you." Again, Logan gave Ty a look, but Quinn couldn't figure out what it meant.

Ty sat up and shifted Quinn in between his legs. Her back to his front, his cock nestled along her spine. Hard, hot. She could feel the vein throbbing. Ty wrapped his arms around her waist and placed his lips against her neck. Against her pounding pulse.

At the same time, Logan was pushing her knees up and out, exposing Quinn to his sight. His touch.

Ty breathed against her ear. "So pink."

Quinn felt a tickle between her pussy lips and realized it was her own juices. She was so wet, so ready. Waiting.

Logan moved onto his stomach between her legs, while Ty shifted her into more of a sitting position against him. The perfect position to watch what Logan was about to do.

"I missed dinner," Logan said softly, not raising his gaze from her pussy. "I'm very hungry."

Quinn dropped her head back against Ty's chest. He nuzzled her neck, his hot breath giving her goose bumps. "Watch him."

She did.

Logan slipped his index and middle fingers between her plump lips in a V, spreading her open to him. His head dipped, and she felt the first warm stroke of his tongue along her folds and up to her clit. He circled and licked and suckled. Quinn gasped and tilted her hips to give him better access.

Ty pinned her arms to her sides but caught both her nipples between his fingers, tugging, twisting, and plucking the hard tips. His breathing deepened against her neck, his cock twitched against her back, and his testicles felt like little balls of fire against the base of her ass.

Logan shifted the V of his fingers up until it framed her clit. His lips opened, and he sucked on her hard. Quinn cried out and tried to twist her body. The pleasure was too much. Too intense. He plunged two fingers into her pussy.

"How many fingers can he get in there…?" Ty whispered against her skin, his teeth grazing her shoulder as he pinched her nipples harder. He rocked against her, his cock almost painfully hard against her spine, his precum making her skin slippery.

Logan played along the hard nub of her clit and the slick folds of her pussy and slipped a third finger into her. He thrust the three fingers in and out of her at a torturously slow pace.

Quinn arched her back, pushing her breasts against Ty's hands while thrusting her pussy toward Logan's mouth. She struggled to free her arms, wanting to desperately grab Logan's long hair and shove his mouth tighter against her.

Logan's tongue replaced his fingers, thrusting in and out of her as his thumb circled her clit this time.

Quinn let out a low wail as his head made jerking movements between her thighs.

Ty's tongue stroked along the outer shell of her ear, and he sucked on her earlobe, never stopping the constant rolling of her nipples. They were swollen and tender, and it hurt so good.

Again, two fingers were in her, slipping in and out as Logan softly kissed her inner thighs.

"Logan."

The deep voice startled her out of her sex-induced daze.

"Let me taste her."

Logan smiled at Ty's request, and with a last long stroke over her pussy, he rose to his knees, his lips glistening with her juices.

Quinn expected them to switch, but they didn't.

Logan pressed his chest against hers and met Ty's lips over her shoulder. Their lips opened, and Ty's tongue traced along Logan's lips before dipping in between them. Their eyes closed, their mouths angling, and they deepened the kiss. Logan's cock pressed against her lower belly, where it left a streak of slickness of its own.

Quinn should have felt left out. The passion, the love, between the two men was unmistakable. But she didn't.

She felt fortunate to be a part of it.

And she wanted one—or both—of them inside her.

During the kiss, Ty freed her arms. She reached between them to capture Logan's cock in her hand, using the precum to lube her palm as she stroked him. She reached behind her and grabbed Ty's already-lubricated cock and stroked it with the same rhythm as they continued to kiss over her, sandwiching her between them.

Their kiss broke, and Logan brushed his lips against hers before Ty took his turn, giving her a short, deep kiss.

"Lie back," Logan told Ty, who obediently shifted back to the center of the plush rug and went supine, his cock still hard and bumping against his hip.

"Now you," Logan said to Quinn, taking both her hands in his and moving her to straddle Ty's hips. He leaned over and sucked one of her nipples into his mouth, nipping the tip, making Quinn cry out. He released it and did the same to the other one. Quinn sank her fingers into his hair, but Logan grabbed her wrists firmly and pulled away.

He gave her a reassuring smile. "Sit."

Quinn looked down. She was facing Ty's feet. Did Logan want her to mount Ty backward? She wasn't sure if he'd fit normally.

"Logan, I—"

Logan placed a finger against her lips, halting her protest. “Don't worry.”

He held her arms so she didn't fall, and said, “Sit,” again.

Holding on to him, Quinn lowered herself down, planning to settle over Ty's belly and work him in slowly. But it wasn't what Logan wanted. He pulled her by her arms until her pussy was directly above Ty's cock. Ty had a grip on his cock, keeping it steady, already enshrouded in latex.

When her slick cleft met the thick head of his dick, Quinn let out a shaky breath. She fought the urge to sink down on him and ride him hard. But she knew better. Logan held up most of her weight as she poised above Ty, the head of Ty's cock nudging her folds wider.

Quinn felt some trepidation, fearful but excited at the same time. Logan's cock was inches from her mouth, and before she could think twice, she captured it between her lips, swirling her tongue around the head. Logan grunted and almost let her arms go, but shifted for a better grip. She sucked his cock deep, pulling hard with her mouth. Her pussy pulsed, needing something, someone deep within her. She wiggled her hips and found the perfect position for Ty's cock as she slid herself farther onto his throbbing rod.

“Jesus Christ, she's too tight, Lo.”

Ty was barely in her, but Quinn moved up and down in time with her sucking of Logan's cock. Every time she came down, Ty went in her a little more. A little deeper. A little farther, stretching her, filling her to the point that she thought she would burst. It felt so good.

Ty's cock bumped against her cervix, and she gasped as a tremor went through her inner muscles, squeezing him even tighter. She heard a hissing breath behind her.

"*Fuck.*"

Quinn released Logan's cock from between her lips as he leaned her back until she lay on top of Ty, her back to his chest. Her body rose and fell with his breaths. Every time she rose with his chest, his cock twitched within her. He pressed his hips upward, moving just enough to make her want more.

Logan moved around to the top of Ty's head and leaned over them, running his hands down Quinn's sides, over Ty's sides, smoothing his palms over their heated skin. He shifted his weight until he was over Quinn, his thighs pressing against her shoulders as he balanced himself over her, stretching out his body above the both of them.

By doing this, he had full access to her mound, the place where she and Ty were joined. He gave her small kisses and long strokes with this tongue over her lower belly. Quinn sucked in a breath as Logan placed his mouth over her clit and suckled. Ty continued to shift his hips, sheathing himself deep within her pussy, the stretching sensation a painful pleasure.

Logan's position gave her easy access to his cock, which brushed against her cheek. Turning her head, she licked along his length. Ty lifted his head and sucked Logan's balls into his mouth.

Logan tensed above her and blew a hard breath against her clit. "Shit."

Ty continued to roll Logan's sac in his mouth while thrusting up against Quinn. She was slick but tight, and the tug of his cock within her, along with the motion of Logan's lips, made her squirm. She licked at Logan's cock more furiously, from the root to the head, before circling and working her way back down.

Quinn wanted to sit up, but she couldn't. She wanted to ride Ty long and hard. But their position kept her powerless. The lack of control drove her close to the edge.

Ty's hand found her breast, squeezing and kneading. His other hand slipped up and over Logan's ass.

Quinn could only guess what he was doing to Logan as Logan groaned against her pussy.

"Tyson." Logan groaned as he jerked forward a bit, his cock throbbing even harder, if possible, in her mouth.

Logan rocked a bit above her, while Ty rocked his hips against her, burying his cock deep within her with each thrust.

"Ty, I'm gonna come," Logan cried out and pulled away from Quinn's mouth. Ty released Logan's ass and grabbed Quinn's breasts, pressing them together. Logan shifted his weight enough to plunge his cock between her breasts, while Ty once again pinched her nipples. Logan surged against her, fucking her tits as he bore down against her clit with his mouth. Ty surged up, pushing his cock deep within her.

Quinn felt the clenching of her inner muscles begin. "Oh, *fuck me*." Her orgasm pulsated from the center out, and she opened her mouth to scream. Nothing came out but a squeak.

Ty grunted from beneath her, pounding into her twice more before tensing. He stilled, gripping her breasts harder as Logan thrust a few more times. Then she felt the jerk of Logan's cock and the hot spurts of cum landing on her belly.

Logan rolled off them and collapsed bonelessly onto the rug. His chest rose and fell with his hard breathing, almost in time with Ty's breathing beneath Quinn.

Ty's hand drifted over her belly, drawing circles in the ejaculate covering Quinn's skin. He let out a large sigh, and she attempted to extract herself from him, but he held her close, his cock still within her, still twitching occasionally. He was probably doing it on purpose, she thought, and she couldn't help but laugh.

Logan rolled onto his side and propped his head in his hand, giving her a smile.

“Something funny?”

Ty flexed his penis again in her, and he joined in her laughter. If he kept doing that, she was going to come again. It wouldn't take much; she was oversensitized as it was. The vibrations of his laughter definitely didn't help.

Chapter Six

Ty stretched his muscles and, doing so, moved enough to dislodge Quinn. Logan climbed to his feet and helped her up.

"We need a shower," Logan said, grinning at the mess on Quinn's stomach.

Ty definitely needed a shower. This had gone a lot better than he'd thought it would. It was amazing Quinn had adapted to the both of them so well, so quickly. Yes, they were taking it *slow*, as Logan wanted. But Quinn seemed very open-minded and supersensual. He had no doubt she would be up to more.

But then, he didn't want to overwhelm her and scare her away either. This last week, he and Logan had been on eggshells wondering if she'd dare show up. She had. She seemed the perfect complement to the both of them. Although it was early yet.

And they didn't know her very well. Nor she them…

"Ty?" Logan's rough voice shook him from his thoughts. Quinn and Logan both stood staring at him, naked. Quinn still wore the evidence of their escapade.

They definitely needed a shower.

Without hesitation, Ty scooped Quinn up in his arms, causing her to yelp in surprise. But she laughed as they trooped down the hallway into the large master bathroom.

Logan turned on the shower jets, adjusting the temperature, as Ty let Quinn slide down his body.

"Are you okay?"

Quinn licked her bottom lip before saying, "Yes."

"Sure?"

She nodded her head and gave him a slight smile.

"No regrets?"

Her smile widened, bringing him a little relief. "None."

Logan came behind her and laid a kiss on her shoulder. "Good, because that was only the beginning."

Quinn snaked an arm back around Logan's neck and head, tilted her head back, and pulled him into a kiss.

A little bite of jealousy hit Ty before she reached out blindly for him. He stepped into her, her fingers curling on his chest.

Logan broke the kiss and said, "Shower."

He snagged her hand, along with Ty's, and pulled them into the oversize shower stall. It was surrounded with frosted glass and had side jets as well as the wide showerhead. Ty loved this shower. Though he should; he had picked it. As well as the large Jacuzzi tub and the double sinks. Well, just about everything in the bathroom had been his idea.

Ty shut the glass door behind him and stepped in front of one of the jets, enjoying the pressure of the water shooting against him. The water was hot and stinging, but it felt good on his muscles.

Logan grabbed a loofah sponge and poured shower gel onto it, squishing it until it foamed. Ty was entranced by watching the warm water traveling down Logan's body. He had seen it plenty of times. They loved fucking in the shower, but tonight, for some reason, he seemed more sensitive to watching his lover. Maybe because he had to share.

Not that he minded. *Yet.*

He glanced at Quinn, who was brushing her hair, a dark gold now it was wet, out of her face. She was beautiful. Her skin was fair, her hair blonde, which was her real color. Water trickled over her golden curls at the apex of her thighs. Her legs were long enough and shapely. He was pretty picky when it came to women. During his pro football career, he had had plenty of opportunities, way too many groupies. But he had no bones to pick with Quinn.

Maybe that's why Logan had brought her home? Because he knew what Ty liked?

Maybe. But the attraction between Logan and Quinn was unmistakable, if not a little disturbing. He loved Logan. He didn't want anyone coming in between them.

Join them? Possibly. Split them apart? No.

Logan handed him the soapy loofah and grabbed a washcloth off the shower rack and soaped that up too. He started to scrub Quinn's back, and Ty took the hint. He swiped the loofah over her chest and stomach, gently washing away the remains of their sex. He dropped to his knees and soaped up her legs, while Logan did her arms and neck. Ty watched as Logan followed the flow of water over her skin with his lips, noticed his lover was already getting hard again.

Ty stood and stepped behind Logan, moving the loofah over Logan's skin. He reached around between Logan and Quinn and washed Logan's chest, making sure he tweaked Logan's nipple ring. Ty's cock twitched in anticipation. He smoothed a hand over Logan's wet ass and dipped between his ass cheeks.

Logan spun around and snagged Ty's arms, pinning them behind his back. He shoved Ty into the tile wall and buried a knee between Ty's thighs. Logan's expression looked fierce as he took Ty's mouth, ravishing Ty's lips with his own. Ty gasped into Logan's mouth, loving it. He loved when Logan took control, even though Logan was the smaller man.

Logan broke the kiss. He snagged Ty's earlobe between his teeth. "Jealous?"

Ty couldn't answer. Now extremely hard, his cock butted up against Logan's hip.

"If you don't like it, I will tie you up and make you watch me fuck her."

His murmured threat in Ty's ear sent a shot of lightning down Ty's spine. Ty only nodded slightly, very aware of the grip Logan's teeth still had on his lobe.

Logan suddenly let him go, and Ty's pulse slowed a fraction.

His lover returned his attention to Quinn, who was concentrating on washing her hair. She had ignored the little show of male dominance, though Ty was sure she wasn't as comfortable about it as she appeared.

If there wasn't going to be any sex in the shower, he was getting out. Ty stepped out the shower and snagged a towel from the heated towel rack. Another feature he had insisted on in the bathroom.

He dried his hairless body, looking at himself in the mirror. He spent a lot of time keeping in shape, taking care of his personal grooming. He did it not only for himself but for the man who was in the shower right this minute with a woman. Another lover.

They had previously discussed bringing in a third person at great length. But now that it may become a reality, he didn't know if he could get used to the idea. He didn't know if he wanted to.

He liked Quinn so far. And except for not knowing anything about football, he hadn't found anything about her to dislike. But would his and Logan's relationship survive a third person?

"Ty."

He started and realized he'd been rubbing his cock, which wasn't as hard now as when Logan had him pinned against the wall, over and over with the towel. The mirror's reflection showed Logan peeking his head out of the shower. Sometime during his daydreaming, the water had been shut off.

"Hand me a towel, T."

Ty did so, and Logan and Quinn stepped carefully out of the shower. He held open a towel for her, and Quinn stepped right into Ty's waiting arms. He wrapped it tightly around her, securing the corner by tucking it along the top.

She smiled up at him. “Thanks.”

Ty reminded himself again, it wasn't Quinn's idea to be there. It was Logan's. He loved Logan and had to respect his decisions. Quinn didn't seem to have any ulterior motives. At least that he could see.

Ty handed Quinn a smaller towel to dry her hair. And when her hair was only damp, he directed her into the bedroom, where Logan was waiting with a towel wrapped around his waist.

Ty hadn't even bothered to cover up; he was still naked, his cock more relaxed, his damp towel in his hand. A wicked thought crossed his mind, and he rolled up the towel. Logan wasn't paying attention; he was digging in one of the dresser drawers.

He snapped the towel, cracking it against Logan's ass.

Logan yelled and flinched, his own damp towel not much protection against the stinging lash. “You fucker.” With a laugh and a flick of his wrist, he pulled off his own towel and quickly rolled it up.

Ty scurried around to stand on the other side of the wide bed, hoping for some sort of protection with the distance between them. Logan lunged toward him, the crack of his towel catching Ty on his bare hip.

“Shit!”

“Hurts, doesn't it?” Logan laughed and spread his legs into a fighter's stance. “C'mon, give it your best shot.”

Ty felt the laughter rolling up through his belly. He loved moments like this with Logan. Horseplay had been the norm in his team's locker room, but he enjoyed the horseplay he had with Logan better. It usually ended better too. With one of them deep within the other's—

Snap.

Logan got him again. Ty rubbed his smarting skin. This time the target was his nipple, and Logan had hit a bull's-eye. He'd had it!

Ty lunged and tackled Logan to the bed, pinning him down onto the quilt. He snagged the smaller man's wrists, holding them to the mattress in a firm grasp, and straddled Logan's naked hips.

"I got you."

Now they were both fully erect; their cocks smashed against each other. Ty shifted his hips and rubbed the length of his cock against Logan's. Logan's eyelids lowered, and a muscle twitched in his jaw as Ty did it again. And then once more.

A mix of a groan and a curse escaped Logan's parted lips. His breathing became shallow, and he let out a rush of air.

Ty leaned over to kiss him, their breaths mingling and then their tongues.

"God, I want to fuck you," Ty murmured against his lips. With Logan's arms still captured, Ty moved down to Logan's chest, brushing his lips against the light golden skin. "You want me. You want me in you." He snagged Logan's pierced nipple in his mouth and tugged the ring with his tongue.

Logan lifted his hips off the bed and, with a strength that always surprised Ty, twisted his body and suddenly had things reversed. Ty was now the bottom, and Logan was on top.

Ty knew he was the stronger man. He knew it. But Logan always seemed to get the upper hand.

He lay placid for a moment until Logan let up a bit. Then, just as quickly as Logan had done, Ty broke free and tackled Logan to the mattress, flipping him over and putting his weight on him to keep him in place. He automatically reached for the tube of lube that was on the nightstand, and gripping Logan's ass, he spread his cheeks.

"Tyson."

The tone was low and authoritative. But Ty didn't care; he was enticed by the pucker of Logan's hole, and he wanted nothing more than to be buried deep within his lover at that moment. He popped the cap on the lube and squirted lube into the crease between Logan's cheeks and on his own cock.

"*Tyson.*"

Ty wrapped his fist around his cock, stroking it a couple of times to spread the lube, pressing it against Logan's tight rim.

"Tyson!"

Logan's tone this time stopped him cold. He gritted his teeth against the powerful urge to just drive it home in Logan's ass.

"Fuck! What?"

Logan's upper body was turned enough to let Ty see the mix of emotions on Logan's face.

Logan wanted him to fuck him. Logan wanted him to stop. But why?

Shit.

Ty had forgotten all about Quinn. She was sitting on the edge of the bed, the towel still wrapped around her, and she had a look—

It wasn't disgust. She wasn't disgusted two men wanted to have sex with each other. No, Ty could only guess it was desire he saw in her eyes. Excitement. The draw of forbidden pleasures.

She sat at the edge of the bed, her hand gripping the towel around her, her blonde hair draped around her bare shoulders in long, damp waves. Free of any makeup, she was still beautiful. Natural. Ty liked that.

Ty put a hand on the small of Logan's back and pushed himself away slightly, but not breaking contact completely.

Quinn's breasts heaved under the fisted towel, her breathing more choppy than normal. She suddenly went from an innocent watcher—a simple bystander—to the target of their attention.

Her voice broke as she spoke. "Earlier you guys shared only me, you didn't share each other."

Ty felt the vibration of Logan's voice beneath his palm. "Like I had said, we are going to take this slow. We didn't want to—"

"Shock me?"

"Shock's a bit dramatic." Logan tilted his upper body to look at her more fully. He licked his lips before saying, "Quinn, have you ever seen two men together?"

Logan's words made Ty suck in a breath. His muscles clenched.

"Fucking?"

"Yeah, okay. *Fucking.*"

"In a porno at college."

Ty laughed, breaking his own tension. "Why don't we show her how we do it? See if she can take it."

Ty knew she'd be able to handle it. He just wanted an excuse…

Logan propped himself up on his elbows and peered around to give him a look. "And you think you'll get to be the top?"

Ty slid his lubed cock between Logan's ass cheeks in one long, teasing stroke. "I don't think. I know."

Logan clenched the muscles in his ass, tightening his cheeks around Ty's cock. He wanted Ty in him bad. But Ty was a large man, and it had been a while since he'd been the bottom.

A long while.

Until this moment, Ty had been happy to be on the receiving end. Tonight, things were shaken up. Probably due to Quinn's sitting there watching them, entranced. He imagined her plump lips wrapped around his cock while Ty pounded him.

Logan flexed his hips and shifted back at the moment the head of Ty's cock slid over his hole. Logan pushed against him, and he felt the press of the large crown against his tight rim. He made himself relax, and he pressed his forehead against the quilt for a second and let out a long breath.

"Quinn?"

He didn't want Quinn to feel left out. Her gaze was locked on what Ty was doing, and she only nodded her head slightly. He had to assume she was giving her approval, that she didn't mind what they were about to do. The fact that she couldn't find any words might have been a good thing. Maybe it meant she was excited about the prospect of Ty fucking Logan's ass. Maybe as much as Logan was.

The thought of Ty fucking him excited him. The thought of Quinn watching excited him even more.

Logan nodded his head in resignation. Ty was going to be the top tonight. He wanted to tell Ty to be easy with him, take it slow. But as the dominant in the relationship, Logan couldn't make himself say the words. He would take whatever Ty gave him. Hopefully, without one whimper.

Logan's cock leaked a little more onto the quilt. He shifted his position slightly, his buttocks higher, giving Ty better access.

Ty grabbed the lube and squirted more of the cool lubricant around his hole. He snapped the lid shut and tossed it to the side before sliding a slick finger around Logan's rim. The more Ty circled his hole, the more Logan wanted him to just shove it in deep and fuck him fast and hard. One finger pressed against the hole, and Ty dipped it in. Logan groaned; it was only a taste of what was to come.

Ty slid the finger all the way in, then slipped in another; he thrust a little, trying to loosen Logan up. Logan let out a shuddered breath but still kept silent.

"Baby, you're so tight. I don't know, Lo. It's been a while."

Logan refused to answer. Ty added a third finger, and he fucked Logan slowly with them, the pulling and pushing sensations making Logan's cock throb even harder.

Ty suddenly pulled his fingers out, and Logan let out a hiss. He couldn't look behind him; he didn't want to know when. He just wanted to know.

The press of Ty's head against his puckered hole made him tense for a second. But he forced himself to relax. The pressure was intense as Ty pushed against him, waiting for his cock to break the ring. Then it did. It was tight and painful, and Ty slowly pressed onward, burying his shaft into Logan's narrow canal.

Ty's fingers buried painfully into Logan's hips, holding Logan still while Ty went deeper. The farther he went, the wider Logan was stretched, the more it burned. And then Ty hit it. That magic spot.

It was just a bump, but Logan gasped and thrust back against him until Ty was completely sheathed within him. Ty stilled, and there was no sound in the room besides the two of them breathing hard. Logan closed his eyes and just enjoyed the fullness within him.

This was when the two of them became one. This was when they felt totally connected. This was when they were lovers and not just a couple.

Ty pulled back. Just a little. Then he was fully seated once again. He pulled back a little more and thrust forward until he was fully inside Logan. The third time he pulled back until the crown of his cock was just inside the edge of Logan's tight ring. Then he buried himself deep once more.

Logan could feel Ty shaking, his fingers digging deep into Logan's flesh. Logan had kept something precious from Ty for a long while. Logan had taken control of their relationship, and though they both had enjoyed that, it resulted in Ty missing out on this part of the intimacy.

Logan swore to himself he'd make up for it. Plus, Logan had forgotten how good it felt to have Ty sheathed within him.

The next time Ty pulled back, he pulled out completely, squirted more lube on his cock. Without hesitation, he shoved it deep.

Logan bucked against him, letting out a loud groan. Ty reached a hand between them and grabbed Logan's balls, circling his thumb and forefinger around the base of Logan's cock and sac. He squeezed, cutting the blood off from Logan's erection—an instant cock ring that made Logan even harder.

Logan felt something brush against his ribs, and he opened his eyes to see Quinn had moved up close to them, staring at where they were joined. Watching Ty's thrusting motion in fascination.

Ty slowed his pace a fraction when Quinn reached out and ran a hand over Ty's chest, down his belly, over Logan's ass, up his spine.

Watching them had turned her on. Her eyes glazed, lids lowered, lips parted.

"What do you want, Quinn?" Logan asked through his clenched teeth.

His question caught her attention, and she looked at him.

"What do you want?" he asked again.

"I don't know."

"Ah—" Logan gasped as Ty continued his rhythm, his hips against Logan's ass. "Do you…want to join us?"

She bit her lower lip and after a moment nodded her head.

"Towel off."

She unhooked the corner from the top and unraveled the towel from her body. As she did so, she slipped a hand between her legs and pressed her fingers against her clit.

"Condom." Logan's command came out more breathless than he would have liked, but of course, he was in the midst of being thoroughly reamed by his big black lover.

He sucked in air through his flared nostrils, trying to concentrate on what Quinn was doing.

She crawled around them, over the mattress, to the nightstand, and found a condom in the drawer.

"Put it on me."

She ripped the package open with her teeth and took out the latex disc. She shuffled herself back next to them and reached beneath him. She pressed the condom to his throbbing head and rolled it down his length.

Logan cursed and bit the inside of his cheek to keep from coming. Ty continued to thrust deeply. Every few strokes he changed the angle to brush against Logan's prostate.

Logan took a couple of deep breaths before he could speak. "Get under me."

Logan lifted one arm and let her slide underneath him into the missionary position.

"Spread your legs."

She did. She was directly underneath him now. Looking up into his face. Her lips were parted, and her breathing came out in quick pants.

Logan realized he was panting too.

"Spread your pussy with your fingers."

She reached down with both hands, separating the folds of her pussy with her manicured fingers.

Logan lowered himself slowly, not wanting to dislodge Ty, who had paused his movements until Logan got settled.

Logan's cock nudged against Quinn's pussy, finding the right spot.

"Slide down," he ordered.

And she did, sliding him deep inside her. She was wet enough that there was no resistance. Logan had never felt anything so good in his life. His cock was buried in hot, tight pussy while he had his lover deep within his anal canal.

He could stay like this forever.

Ty had different thoughts. He grunted and thrust against him. Every thrust pushed Logan deep within Quinn.

Quinn squirmed beneath him, crying out with each thrust Ty made. Her hands fluttered aimlessly.

"Pinch your nipples," Logan directed.

She squeezed her breasts together, kneading them, her fingers twisting both of her nipples. Her hips tilted, bringing Logan in farther, and she thrust against him. Logan stayed perfectly still as Quinn fucked him from underneath and Ty fucked him from behind.

Logan dropped his head to Quinn's shoulder; he was having a hard time holding his weight off her. His arms started to shake. He licked her skin along her collarbone and up her neck. He found a tender spot and nipped her. She threw her head back and arched up against him, grinding her clit against his groin. Logan's balls tightened, and he just wanted to let go.

Quinn sank back to the mattress, and Logan put his forehead against hers.

"Quinn," he whispered.

She opened her eyes and met his. Then, at once, her eyes widened. She arched her back again and cried out. He felt the tremors around his cock as she came. Never once breaking their gaze.

Logan let go, a guttural groan escaping from deep within him. He spilled his seed, his cock throbbing within her.

A second later Ty grunted loudly and pressed against him tightly, making small, deep thrusts as he shot his cum deep within Logan.

They were damp, sticky, and satisfied, but too tired to move. Finally Ty did, releasing Logan, his spent cock slipping out. Ty bent over and laid a kiss on Logan's ass.

Logan collapsed to Quinn's side, careful not to crush her. He let out a long breath.

"Damn," was all he could say.

"Damn," Quinn said, her eyes shut, her body relaxed, but still in the position where Logan left her.

Ty fell to the mattress on the other side of Quinn. "Damn. Next time I want to be in the middle."

The bed shook with their lazy laughter.

Chapter Seven

What could be better than waking up next to a hot guy? Waking up sandwiched between two of them.

After gathering some energy the night before, they had showered—again—before collapsing into a pile on the bed like a litter of puppies. All tangled arms and legs.

After a hearty but healthy breakfast, Ty disappeared, and Quinn helped Logan clean up the kitchen.

Logan scrubbed the dishes. Quinn rinsed and stacked them into the dishwasher. The kitchen was enormous and had every appliance anyone would ever need. And then some.

When they were finished, Quinn sank down into one of the kitchen chairs and wrapped her hands around a mug of coffee. She took a cautious sip.

The woodworking in the kitchen, along with the rest of the house she'd seen so far, looked like it was handmade. The cabinets were beautiful, almost works of art. The natural grain of the wood had been brought out by the stain that had been used.

"Ty and I built this house."

Logan's comment drew her gaze away from admiring the handiwork and onto him. "Just the two of you?"

His hair was loose around his face, a little wild, and his beard a bit longer, as he hadn't taken the time to trim it that morning. He leaned back against the counter, crossing his arms over his chest. His jeans fit him well in all the right spots, and his worn black Johnny Cash T-shirt hugged his muscles, the sleeves not long enough to hide his ropy biceps. They were very nice, but definitely not as big or as defined as Ty's.

"Mostly. We had some subcontractors here and there. Electrical, concrete, stuff like that. Ty's good with his hands."

"Yes, he is." Quinn felt the heat rush up into her cheeks when Logan laughed. "Well, anyway, it's a gorgeous home."

Logan tilted his head and studied her. "I like how you said *home* and not *house*."

"Well, it feels like a home. Not just a shelter."

Logan didn't say anything for a moment. He just stared at her.

Suddenly feeling uneasy, Quinn rose and moved in front of the French doors, which opened up to a huge wooden deck. The sunlight through the glass warmed her face, while the coffee she sipped warmed her shaky insides.

Quinn felt Logan move up behind her and watched his reflection in the glass. He reached past her to flip the lock on the door and pulled it open.

"C'mon. Let's go outside. It's really nice out."

She followed him out onto the deck, stepping carefully so her bare feet wouldn't catch a splinter. She walked to the far end of the deck and leaned against the railing. Logan stepped into her, wrapping his arms tightly around her, and pulled her back against him. She leaned into his chest, stilling enough to feel his heartbeat against her shoulder blade. It was slow, steady, and soothing.

She looked out over the fields surrounding the house. The land was mostly flat, and there were acres and acres of grass, as far as her eyes could see. All well maintained. It was what a well-manicured lawn would look like for a giant's home.

"You have a beautiful place here."

He rested his chin on her shoulder and murmured, "Thanks."

"What made you become a sod farmer?"

"I don't know really. I sort of just fell into it, I guess. My uncle, who lives in Kentucky, manages a sod farm there, and I visited him one summer when I was in high school. He put me to work, and I thought it was an easy way to be a farmer. A lot easier than cows or pigs."

Quinn chuckled. "That was your only option? To be a farmer?"

He shrugged against her. "Well, it was either grow legal grass or grow illegal grass. My uncle kinda set me straight on that too."

Quinn turned slightly, trying to see his expression, but Logan held her tighter and kept his chin on her shoulder.

"My mom sent me away that summer because I was becoming a bit of a handful for her. She was a single mom, and I was starting to run with the wrong crowd."

Quinn kept silent, waiting to see if he'd reveal more. He didn't. She had a feeling there was much, much more.

"Did she know you were gay back then?"

Logan stiffened. He let her go and stepped back from her. "I'm not gay."

Quinn turned and opened her mouth to argue, but quickly shut it. His expression was dark and closed. He had curled his fingers into fists, his arms stiff by his sides.

"If I were gay, I wouldn't like women. I love women." He shook his head, his hair sweeping against his face. He closed his eyes, took two breaths, before opening them again. Quinn could see him visibly relax once more; his fingers uncurled, and his shoulders lowered.

"Quinn, I can see how you'd think we're gay. But in reality, we're bisexual."

"Sorry." She looked down at her bare toes. "I didn't mean to upset you. This is all new to me." That was an understatement.

Within two strides he had a hand under her chin and an arm wrapped around her back. He tilted her face up. "No, I'm sorry. I've lived with that stereotype for a long time."

He leaned in and brushed his nose against hers. An Eskimo kiss.

"I'm glad this is all new to you. I want you to enjoy this weekend and experience things you've never experienced before."

He took her mouth then. He possessed it for his own, kissing her thoroughly enough that Quinn shivered and pressed her thighs together. Her pussy pulsated and slickened. He slid a hand into her hair and bent her head back, deepening the kiss, sliding his hand down to grasp her buttocks and pull her into him, against his already-hardening cock.

Without a warning, he stepped back, breaking the kiss, breaking the contact. His lips were shiny, her cheeks burned from his beard.

Quinn curled her toes and closed her eyes, willing her heart to stop pounding so hard. She swallowed hard. After a moment she looked at him.

He extended his hand to her. “C'mon, I'll give you a tour of a real, honest-to-goodness sod farm.”

* * *

They rode in the cab of a monster tractor. More like a lawn mower on steroids. It was a scary piece of machinery, and Quinn wondered if a special license was needed to drive it. It had all sorts of levers she was careful to avoid bumping into.

That was the last thing she needed to do—drop the mower down and ruin one of his perfect fields. It'd be like taking a pair of clippers and accidently bumping them against someone's head, giving them a nice bald spot where there wasn't one before.

No. She was keeping her hands to herself as she rode on Logan's lap, both of them bouncing on the super-springy seat. Luckily the cab was air-conditioned; it had turned out to be a very warm day. Logan even had a stereo in the thing, one he could plug his iPod into. Popular country music played in the background as he strummed his fingers along her denim-clad thighs.

They went out to a far field, and Logan demonstrated how the equipment was used as he drove up and down the field in an organized fashion, trimming the grass to a perfect length to promote thickness.

She learned the groundhog was not the sod farmer's best friend. Nor were deer. She didn't ask how he got rid of the pesky critters, but there was a shotgun hanging across the back of the cab. She was fortunate they didn't run into any unwanted guests while they were driving around. She was not in the mood to watch him blow the head off Punxsutawney Phil. Not that she gave a crap about overgrown rodents…

His hand, when not needed for shifting, drifted up along her ribs. His thumb brushed back and forth, almost without thought, along the bottom of her breast. Quinn was fully aware of it, though. Her nipples pebbled under her halter top. She wanted more than the occasional shifter hand on her, but the other was needed to steer.

He made long passes back and forth through the field as he mowed, the smell of fresh-cut grass permeating the sealed cab.

"Smells good," she finally said, breaking their comfortable silence.

He nuzzled her neck for a moment. "Hmm. Sure does."

Quinn slapped his arm lightly. "No. The grass."

"Grass is an aphrodisiac," he said, turning his head to make a tight turn for another pass along the field.

"It is?"

His chuckle vibrated against her. "It is for me."

She softly slapped his arm again. He was so full of shit. “Very funny.”

“Slap me again and I'll stop and put you over my knee.” His eyes darkened, and he returned his hand from the shifter knob to her waist.

Quinn's heart rate increased as she pictured his threat. Her pussy pulsed against his hard thigh.

“I felt that.”

“And I feel you,” she countered. His cock was hard against her hip. She rocked her hips slightly. “I guess I could take advantage of you while you are busy mowing.”

“You could.” He gave her a heated glance. “But that might be dangerous.”

Quinn smiled and ran a hand up his chest. She fingered his nipple ring through his thin T-shirt.

“Quinn,” he warned, his thigh flexing beneath her rump.

The tractor sputtered and jerked them forward, making Logan quickly shift to a lower gear to smooth out the speed.

“See?”

“Maybe we need a break.”

“You're bad. But I have a break planned soon enough.”

Quinn tilted her head and looked at his profile. His hair was pulled back into a tight ponytail, which was tucked through the back of a baseball cap bearing Logan's company's name. If it weren't for the ponytail, he'd look like every other country hick who ran around in oversize tractors. She brushed a knuckle against his rough beard.

She smiled when his jaw flexed. "You like to be in charge, don't you?"

He didn't answer her, just concentrated on keeping the mower in a straight line.

"You do. You wouldn't like it if I went against your plan and straddled you right now, would you?" Her voice was low and teasing.

"I'd wreck."

"No, you'd have to stop the tractor."

"I told you we'll be taking a break soon."

"But not right now."

His jaw tensed. "No."

"But if I slapped you again, you'd stop, put me over your knee, and spank me." It wasn't a question. She knew he might do it. She was tempted to test him. She remembered the sting of her skin when he had spanked her last time. She begrudgingly admitted to herself she had liked it.

Nothing wrong with playing a little slap and tickle out in the middle of nowhere.

He still hadn't looked at her; he kept his eyes focused straight ahead. His lips pressed into a thin line. She couldn't tell if it was with anger or desire. His cock was still as hard as steel against her, making her think it was the latter.

With a wicked grin, she reached out and tugged his nipple ring through the shirt. Hard.

"*Fuck*!" He slammed both feet on the clutch and brake pedal, bringing them up short. Quinn lost her balance and fell forward, banging her thigh against the gear shift before landing in a heap on the floor. There wasn't much room in the cab, and she ended up wedged between the floor and the dash. All the air whooshed out of her lungs, and she let out a painful groan.

"Shit." Logan yanked up the emergency-brake handle and stood up. He grabbed Quinn's outstretched hands, pulled her up, and settled her into the cab's single tractor seat. He went to one knee in the tight quarters, looking her over. Concern crossed his features. "Are you okay?"

Quinn nodded her head, a little shaky. She was okay, wasn't she? She mentally did a body check. Besides a scrape on her elbow and an ache in her hip, she was fine. No blood gushing, no broken bones, no major bruising.

Just a little bit of a bruised ego.

His relief quickly turned to anger. "That was bullshit, Quinn. You could have been seriously hurt." He stood and unbuckled his belt and slid it out of the loops. The sound of soft brown leather sliding against the rougher denim sent a shiver down her spine.

Quinn's eyes widened. Was he angry enough to spank her with a belt? That was just crazy. "Logan, I'm sorry—"

"It's too late for that. Do you know what happens to bad girls who can't keep their hands to themselves?"

Quinn opened her mouth, but nothing came out, since she was picturing some options in her head. Some excited her; the others just scared her.

"Give me your hands."

"Logan…" Her breath caught in her throat.

"Give. Me. Your. Hands." His command was slower the second time, more forceful and in a much-lower tone. A tone that said, *Don't fuck with me.*

She held out one hand. He shook his head.

"Both."

She added the other one. Somewhat reluctantly.

"Put them together."

She did, pinning her wrists together. He grasped them in one large hand, looped the belt around them, and tightened it. He pulled the free end up to the roof of the cab and slipped it through a hand grip there, tying the loose end into a secure knot. He tugged, testing it. Her arms were bound and stretched to shoulder height.

It wasn't uncomfortable. But it definitely put him back in control.

Just how he liked it.

He moved her off the seat, slid underneath her, and settled her back into his lap. Quinn's fingers wrapped around the leather.

"Now I can get my work done."

Quinn saw no point in begging him to release her. He had a determined look about him, and he avoided her gaze when he pushed in the clutch, released the brake, and shoved the shifter into first gear with a little more force than was necessary. The tractor lugged forward, and soon he was back to his routine.

The silence stretched between them. Quinn rode on his lap, and Logan drove the tractor.

His confidence on how he lived his life and what he wanted and how he got it emanated from him. He was strength and power. And stubborn. That was becoming clear to Quinn quickly.

The realization she actually liked that in a man made her pause. Tyson was the larger man physically. But it was Logan who was the dominant in the relationship. And since she was only there for one weekend, she could deal with his taking control over her. It was only until Sunday. After this weekend, they might never see each other again.

Her brows furrowed, and she grimaced. She couldn't expect anything more. Just one weekend of fun and exploration. It was just a dare.

Logan turned the tractor onto a dirt track leading along the edges of surrounding fields. Some of the fields were Kentucky bluegrass, some zoysia, others a blend, or hybrids, as he called them, depending on the sod's intended use. He had told her other facts too, but there was too much to remember. She never would have guessed sod farming was so involved.

The tractor bumped over the rough path, jerking the belt against her wrists, reminding her of her restraint.

Sick of the silence, she said, "Am I being grounded or what?"

Logan finally grinned and gave her a quick glance. "It's called being punished."

"Am I done being punished yet?"

"Have you learned your lesson yet?"

"You mean the lesson of not pulling your nipple ring when you're driving?"

He arched a brow. "Is that the lesson?"

She didn't know, was it? Quinn worried her bottom lip between her teeth. "I think so."

"Since you don't know for sure, the punishment hasn't been effective enough. I think I require some help for the punishment."

Help? What was he talking about?

The tractor lurched to a stop next to a beat-up, primer gray truck. Logan set the brake and shut down the machinery. He reached up and untied the leather knot from the hand grip, and when Quinn shoved her bound hands toward his chest, he shook his head.

"Not yet. Let's go."

They climbed out of the cab, Logan helping her down, one hand gripping the belt like a leash.

As they approached a ditch, she realized Ty was there digging, while Magnum lounged between the farm truck and the dirt hole. The dog thumped his tail in greeting but didn't move out of the cool shade of the vehicle.

Ty was bare chested and had a blue bandanna wrapped over his head, soaked with sweat. His skin glistened like a sculpture made of obsidian. His muscles bunched and rippled as he swung a pickax over his head and into the hard ground. His jeans had slid down low with the exertion, barely catching on his hips; his dark blue boxer-briefs were the only thing covering the top of his butt cheeks. Even those were soaked in sweat.

Ty stopped swinging when they approached. Quinn didn't miss the glance he gave her bound wrists and the questioning look he shot Logan.

Logan just lifted one shoulder and said, “She needed a lesson.”

Ty accepted his statement as if it answered everything. And maybe it did. Maybe this wasn't an unusual occurrence for them. Maybe they had a different woman—or man, even—join them in sex play every weekend. What did Quinn know? She could be one of many.

The thought didn't sit well in her stomach.

Maybe she would get a text message on Monday stating *We've found someone new...*

“How come you always get the cake job and I end up working my ass off?”

Logan peered down at Ty's cotton-covered ass. “It's still there.”

Ty picked up a clump of dirt and threw it at Logan. The clod exploded against his thigh into a cloud of dust. They both laughed companionably.

Ty extended his hand, and Logan grasped it, helping him out of the ditch.

“How's it coming?” Logan asked him.

“Slow. This irrigation system needs some improvement. Preferably replaced, if we had the money.”

“Yeah, I know. But we'll just have to fix what we have for now.”

Ty snagged his discarded T-shirt off the hood of the truck and wiped the sweat off his face. “That's what I'm doing.”

“I see.” Logan pulled the now-damp and dirty T-shirt out of Ty's hand and tossed it back onto the truck's hood. He wrapped one hand around the back of Ty's neck and pulled him into a deep, intimate kiss while Quinn just stood there, helplessly bound by a belt, feeling like a dog on a leash.

When they did stuff like that in front of her, she felt like she was intruding. Almost like a voyeur, peering into a neighbor's window as the couple made love.

She reminded herself she wasn't a part of their relationship. She was just a visitor.

Logan ran a hand down Ty's damp chest before tweaking one of his nipples, causing Ty to gasp. That ended the kiss, and they stood inches apart, looking into each other's eyes for a moment. She was jealous of the closeness and the passion they shared. These two men had more going for them than most married heterosexual couples she knew. No wonder the divorce rate was so high.

“You need to cool off,” Logan told Ty before planting another quick kiss on his lips and putting some room between them. He tugged on the belt, making the leather bite softly into her wrists.

Logan forced Quinn to follow him over to a water pump, only feet away from where Ty had dug the ditch. There was already a hose threaded onto the pump's spigot, and on the end of the hose, a garden-hose sprayer. He flipped up the pump handle and squeezed the sprayer's trigger, shooting water all over Ty.

Ty yelled and ran around to the back of the truck.

"That's fucking cold, Logan!"

"That's the point. C'mon. You need to rinse off as well as cool off. Don't be a wimp."

Ty yelled, "Fuck you!", but Quinn could see him, kicking off his boots, pulling off his jeans, peeling his damp boxer-briefs off, and throwing them all into the truck bed.

He came from around his shield and stood there gloriously naked in the hot sun. His skin and tattoos shone from a combination of sweat, sun, and the cool water Logan had squirted him with.

He spread his arms out and stood with feet wide apart. "Go ahead. I'm ready this time. Do your worst."

Logan raised the hose up once more and sprayed water all over Ty. This time Ty laughed and rubbed the cold water over his head and face and chest. His hands moved over his belly down to his cock. "Don't mind the shrinkage. I'm cold."

Shrinkage? Quinn noticed no shrinkage on the man. He was as magnificent a man when he was soft as he was when he was hard. Seeing him soft made her want to take him into her mouth. It would be the only time she could take him in completely; when he was hard, it was impossible. He was too much.

She came up short when she reached the end of the leather belt, not even realizing until that moment she had moved toward Ty.

Logan turned the hose on her. "Is T getting you all hot and bothered also?

Quinn gasped when the cold water hit her. Water went into her mouth, and she coughed. She shivered as he drenched her shirt and her jeans became a second skin.

Her nipples pebbled, and goose bumps broke out all over her body, which didn't go unnoticed from either of the men.

Ty reached out and said to Logan, "Let me have her."

Logan threw the hose down and tugged her "leash" until she was close to Ty. He handed the end over to the larger man.

Quinn only hesitated a moment, then fell to her knees in front of Ty and took him into her mouth before either of them could stop her. If they even wanted to stop her.

She had never enjoyed giving a man oral sex before meeting these two, but now, she enjoyed it. Craved it. Wanted nothing more than to give Ty, and Logan, pleasure.

She took him deep, knowing his soft cock would soon be larger than she could handle. The skin was velvety soft and hair free. She wanted to cup his balls, but she was still restrained. She sucked him harder and felt him grow and harden. He tasted saltier as his precum leaked at the back of her throat. She relished him like she was a starved woman, one who had never had a man in her mouth before. She sucked him frantically, and finally he was so hard she could only get her lips, her mouth, around a portion of him. She licked the thick knob, capturing his precum on her tongue. She ran her tongue up and down the throbbing vein that ran along his length.

Hands dug into her hair, almost to the point of being painful...but not quite. She was forcefully pulled away from Ty's groin. It was Logan, standing with his jeans and boxer-briefs pooled around his knees. His cock bobbed at the same height as her face.

She looked up at him from on her knees in the wet dirt. His expression was pensive, a bit distant as he slipped his thumb between her lips. He pushed down, opening her mouth and holding her head in place by her hair. He pushed his cock in deep. Deep enough, the head bumped the back of her throat. She fought her gag reflex and forced herself to relax her muscles, swallowing him, her saliva slicking up his skin, making it easier for him to slide in and out between her lips.

Ty still had ahold of the belt, and Logan her hair. A thrill went through her. She felt as if she were a captive, her future unknown, her freedom and her life in their hands.

Ty moved closer to Logan, and they stood facing each other. One dark, one light. One clothed, one naked. Logan pulled his hips back, but her feeling of loss was short-lived as Ty entered her mouth again, thrusting his hips slightly, careful not to hurt her.

She stayed on her knees until they ached; her two temporary lovers took turns with her mouth, making her wet. Making her ache. Making her want them both deep inside her. At the same time.

After seconds, minutes, hours—she didn't know, she lost track—Quinn felt pressure on her wrists, and Logan pulled his cock out of her mouth.

He said to Ty, "Let's tie her down."

"Where?" asked Ty.

"The hood?" Logan shook his head. "No, too hot."

He looked around the site, his gaze bouncing off the exposed pipes, the water pump, and the tractor before landing back on the truck. He went to the passenger-side door of the truck, opened it, and motioned Ty over. Quinn had no choice but to follow as the belt tightened. Blood rushed through her veins, and her heart pounded loudly in her ears.

Logan took the loose end of the belt from Ty and placed it at the top of the doorjamb, pulling it until her arms were stretched above her head before effectively slamming it shut.

Quinn closed her eyes and attempted to slow her breathing. She should be panicked; she should be screaming for help. But she didn't want to. They hadn't hurt her yet; in fact, everything they had done in the past two days had been extremely pleasurable. She had no reason to distrust them. None.

"Strip her."

Again, a flicker of insecurity went through her, unsure if she was as comfortable at being naked out in the open as Ty was. But she was so hot—both from the sun beating down on them and from having had both men in her mouth. Removing her clothes might help her body temperature, but only the boys—*her* boys, she would like to think—would help cool the desire burning inside of her.

Logan pulled at the snap on her jeans and drew the zipper down. The denim was still wet, and he struggled to roll it down her legs. Her panties clung to the soaked denim, leaving her naked from the waist down.

He left them wrapped around her ankles, effectively hobbling her. She couldn't kick them off; between the wet fabric and her boots, it was impossible.

And she liked being at their mercy.

As Logan rose, he ran his hands up over her calves, knees, then thighs. He rubbed his fingers along the outer folds of her pussy, feeling the proof of how ready she was. As he straightened, he caught the bottom of her shirt in his fingers and pulled it up and over her chest and arms until he got to her bound wrists. He knotted the shirt there, out of the way, apparently not even willing to undo the binding to undress her. He left her in her bra only; part of another lingerie set she had picked up at Victoria's Secret on Friday. It had pink cups, half-satin and half-lace, and it showed her breasts off at an advantage. The set had cost her a small fortune, and she hadn't expected the panties to end up in the dirt.

Logan suddenly disappeared, and Ty was there, pulling her bra down, baring her breasts to the sun, the elements, and both men. Her bra shoved her breasts up, her nipples hard and puckered, waiting for fingers, a mouth, anything.

Logan reappeared from around the truck and leaned over her chest, taking one nipple in his mouth. Quinn cried out. Hidden in his mouth was a piece of ice from the cooler he had dropped near her feet. He flicked her nipple with his cold tongue and sucked it deep again, the ice cube drawing her nipple to a hard point, contracting it painfully. Painfully sweet. Quinn dropped her head back and groaned. Logan grasped her other breast in his roughened palm and kneaded it, sending a bolt of electricity to her toes.

Ty appeared behind him with another ice cube in his fingers. He brushed it against her other nipple, making that one as hard as the first.

"Do you like that?" he asked.

Not waiting to hear her answer, he circled the cube around her areola, leaving a cool, wet trail in its wake. He slid the melting ice between her breasts and down her belly. Quinn sucked in her stomach, automatically withdrawing from the unusual coolness against her heated skin. Logan continued to suckle her nipples until the cube in his mouth melted to liquid. He pulled away long enough to crack open the small cooler and pop another cube in his mouth.

"Oh, she likes it. She's liked everything we've done to her, and this is only the beginning." Logan sounded so sure of himself.

Quinn quivered at Logan's words. She watched his movements in anticipation. His head ducked, and he caught her lips with his, the ice cube between his teeth. She ran the tip of her tongue against it and snagged it from his mouth. As he deepened the kiss, he stole it back, swirling it along his tongue and hers.

Ty drew a line down her belly and around her navel, the cold making her shiver. But it wasn't just the cold causing goose bumps. He slid two fingers between the folds of her pussy and followed with the ice cube, brushing it against her clitoris, making her body jump from the shock.

Logan broke the kiss, gave her a heated smile, and disappeared again.

Ty stroked the ice along her cleft, and she moved her hips enough to push against his fingers. She wanted more than his fingers in her, but they would do for now.

Except Ty resisted. He teased her with the ice cube, staying just on the outer edge, not breaching her when she wanted to be thoroughly breached.

Logan returned to her field of vision, this time as naked as Ty. The sun caught his nipple ring, making it shine against his golden skin and light pelt of hair. The light caught the vibrant reds in the coral snake tattoo that wrapped around his hips. His cock was rigid, the head engorged, ready to play.

He gave her a wicked smile. “One of these days, we are both going to be inside you. Filling you up until we can't fill you any more.”

One of these days.

It didn't sound plausible. The act itself and the timing.

She was leaving tomorrow. Sunday.

They had dared her to come.

And she had.

She had come to them, and she had come with them. She didn't expect anything more.

She wanted them both inside her now, because now might be all they had. She wanted to be a part of them both.

Ty traced his tongue around the shell of her ear and sucked on her lobe before asking, “What are you thinking?”

“I want you to fuck me,” she answered him.

He let out a breath, the warmth tickling her ear. “I'm going to fuck you.”

Quinn caught Logan's gaze. “I want you to fuck me too.”

“I will.”

She shook her head slowly. “No.” Her heart thumped. She couldn't believe what she was about to say. “What you just said. Both of you filling me up.”

It was Ty's turn to shake his head. He licked along her bottom lip and said, “You're not ready.” He brushed his lips against hers and leaned away.

“Get me ready.”

Ty gave Logan a look, and Quinn followed it. Logan's brows furrowed in thought.

Anticipation shot through her. He was considering it.

Logan finally asked Ty, “Did you bring what I told you?”

“Yeah.”

Within two strides, Logan was opening the passenger door, releasing the hold on Quinn's restraint. He picked her up and laid her down on her stomach on the truck's bench seat, bending to strip her of the boots and the jeans tangled around her ankles. He reached past her, opened the glove box, pulled out a strip of condoms and a tube of lube, and threw them onto the truck's dash.

They'd had something planned all along. Why else would they have lube and condoms in the glove box? From the beginning Logan had planned on meeting Ty out here.

“Lo, she's not ready.”

“We'll get her ready. Is this what you want, Quinn?”

The fabric of the truck's cloth bench seat was rough against her swollen nipples. “Yes. I want this.”

Ty grabbed her thighs and pulled her back until her legs hung over the side of the bench. His fingers spread her, and he dropped to his knees. He pressed his mouth against her, making Quinn cry out. She lifted her hips as his tongue stabbed her heated core, his lips crushed against her. He plucked at her clit while sliding two fingers deep within her, thrusting slowly in and out.

Logan climbed over her and straddled her waist, facing Ty, careful not to put his weight on her. She felt the heat of his sac against her back. He grabbed the lube and spread her ass cheeks. He squirted the cool lube between her crease before tossing the tube aside. His slick fingers played along her heated skin, rubbing between her cheeks, squeezing, then spreading.

Logan's fingers traced around her tight hole as Ty continued to stroke and lick her clit, alternating his tongue and fingers along that tender spot, making her whimper and press back as much as they'd allow her.

Logan pressed a thumb against her rim, making her jerk slightly with the unfamiliar sensation. He teased along the seam between her anus and her pussy, circling her tight hole once more, pressing again slightly, not pushing past the ridge, but just against it.

Quinn thrust her hips back against Ty's onslaught. His mouth worked wonders on her, and she felt the slow buildup of an orgasm. She wanted someone in her. She didn't care who. She wanted someone to fuck her hard and fast and deep. And she wanted it now. She thrust harder against his fingers, ground against his tongue. Until the tremors within her began.

"I'm..." She gasped. "I'm...coming."

As her body jerked against Ty, Logan slipped his thumb past her tight ring.

"Oh God," Quinn cried.

Ty didn't stop caressing her with his tongue, while Logan pushed his thumb in and out of her tight canal.

"That's it, baby. Feels good, doesn't it?" Removing his thumb, Logan shifted forward, sliding his cock between her lubed cheeks. He squeezed her ass together and pumped between it, the shaft massaging her rim.

"God, yes."

"Want more?"

"Yes. *Please.*"

Logan pulled back and pressed two fingers against her hole. He then grabbed the lube and squirted more on his fingers and on her crease. He massaged the lube around and slowly pushed two fingers in her. Quinn clenched down.

"Shh, baby, relax. You have to relax."

Quinn bit her bottom lip as the strange stretching sensation took her mind off Ty's actions.

Ty moved away for a moment. She heard the ripping of a foil pack and a moment later his cock pressed against her pussy. He drove forward, separating her folds, sheathing himself within her. He pressed as far as he could before stilling, buried deep. He gyrated against her.

"Oh man, she is so fucking tight."

Ty worked himself in and out of her pussy, while Logan fucked her ass with his fingers, loosening her up. The sensation of the two of them in her sent another jolt of electricity through her, making her nipples pucker. She bucked against them.

"She's tight back here also. She's got a sweet virgin ass. But not for long. It's gonna be mine."

Logan moved off her back, creating a weird pulling sensation as he disengaged his fingers from her. He sat back on the driver's side and rolled on a condom as he watched Ty drive into Quinn over and over. Logan's eyelids were heavy, and he stroked himself a couple of times before moving back toward Quinn.

"Okay," was the only thing Logan had to say to make Ty pull out, step back, and rip off the condom. Ty lifted Quinn out of the truck and into his arms as Logan moved to sit on the edge of the bench seat, his legs hanging out of the passenger side of the truck.

He lifted his arms, and Ty handed her to him backward. They wanted her to sit in his lap, facing Ty. She did; Logan's rigid cock twitched against the small of her back. She felt the cool lube along her butt cheeks as Logan applied it liberally to her and his cock. When he was done, he reached around her and cupped her breasts, circling his thumbs around her pointed nipples. Quinn gasped and pushed back against him, lodging his cock between her buttocks.

Outside the truck, Ty moved in to stand between their legs and leaned into the cab. He caught her jaw in his fingers and made her look at him. "Are you sure?"

Quinn nodded. She was sure. She had come here on a dare, and she wanted to be daring. She wanted to experience things she had never experienced before. But not just with anybody. Not just anyone. Only with these two men…

And…*oh…*

Logan and Ty lifted her up by her hips and lowered her gently. Logan grasped his cock, lining himself up with her hole, and pressed.

No. No, he'd never fit. This was going to be extremely painful. It was impossible…

With his feet braced against the door jamb, he pushed upward as they lowered her, the tip of his cock stretching her tight ring. It burned. He pushed onward, his cock slick with lube. She held her breath, unable to breathe. Once he breached the tight ring, he slid in farther, filling her, impaling her. Taking her completely.

Logan's breath against her neck was ragged and rough. His weight against her back pushed her toward Ty, whose cock throbbed against her sternum as he helped hold her. Ty's expression was dark as he studied her, making sure she was not in any extreme pain. There was pain; oh yes, there was. But it was a different type of pain, a pleasurable pain. One of stretching and pulling. She told herself not to tense, but to relax.

In fact, it was what Ty was whispering to her. "Relax. Relax." Over and over. A soothing rhythm. Suddenly he let her go. He no longer held her, and she looked up in surprise. She was sitting on Logan's lap; he was completely sheathed within her.

She moved a bit and groaned. So did he. Logan hugged her against his chest, and he only had to shift slightly to make her feel him, his whole hard length buried within her.

"Ty," he moaned. Ty leaned forward and kissed him, their lips angling. Logan's grip on her tightened, and he moved his hands up to capture her nipples, pinching and twisting them.

Ty broke the kiss with Logan to kiss Quinn, crushing her lips under his, tangling his tongue with hers. He kissed her as Logan shifted his hips under her, making small thrusts against her.

"Ty," he moaned again. "I'm not going to last long." He released Quinn's nipples to grab a condom, rip open the package, and reach around Quinn to roll it over Ty's cock. He stroked Ty's hard length as the darker man deepened the kiss with Quinn.

"Are you sure?" Ty asked against her lips.

"I want you in me too," she answered, a bit breathless, a bit anxious about how this would all work. Would it work? Was it actually possible to have both her men at the same time?

Logan guided Ty's cock to Quinn's slick opening. She kissed Ty more frantically, again trying not to tense in anticipation. Logan stilled her hips with his hands as Ty pressed forward and entered her slowly.

He stopped when he hit resistance. He had said she was tight before, but with Logan in her, she felt even tighter. She didn't think he could fit at all now. But he surged forward, stretching her impossibly. And when he couldn't go any more, he paused.

Ty stared behind her, and she could only imagine the boys were making eye contact. Communicating with unspoken words. She wanted that. She wanted to feel their love.

Ty pulled back and then moved forward, slowly sinking into her and then withdrawing. He moved his hips in a slow rhythm, and Quinn dropped her head back against Logan's shoulder. Logan placed his lips against her throat and nipped at her tender skin. His fingers once again found her nipples, and he twisted them gently as Ty thrust.

Logan sat still, she could only guess to not hurt her. But he was breathing hard, watching Ty thrust against her, against him deep within her. Both their cocks buried inside her with only a thin wall of flesh between them. He kept one hand on her breast, and wrapped the other around the back of Ty's head, pulling Ty to him.

Their lips met again over her shoulder for an instant, before breaking apart. Ty moved back a bit and whispered, “Lo, I love you.”

“I love you too.”

And in that moment, Quinn loved the both of them. They had brought her into their world. Made her a part of them, if only temporarily, and she felt loved.

Logan brushed his lips along her shoulder, while Ty took her mouth, thrusting a bit harder, a bit faster.

Quinn wanted to grab his ass, pull him closer, pull him into her farther, but her hands were still bound, pinned between their bodies. Logan pressed a hand between them and traced circles around her swollen clit.

"Oh God—" She whimpered, grinding herself against Logan's lap.

He stiffened and sank his teeth into her shoulder as he lifted up slightly. He shuddered beneath her and grunted against her skin as he came.

His coming put her on the edge. She ground harder against him as Ty thrust deeper. Logan's cock softened slightly, giving Ty more room within her. Every little bit Logan gave up, Ty took. And he took it hard, gripping her hips roughly with his fingers, pounding against her until he tensed and blew his breath between gritted teeth.

Logan circled her clit faster, pushing against the hard button until she shattered, screaming nothing, everything, words that made no sense. Ty's hips pinned her tight against Logan as he rammed her one more time and stayed deep, his cock pulsing within her, the silky-soft sacs of both men's testicles brushing against her.

She leaned back against Logan and gave a satisfied sigh as Ty withdrew, wiping the sweat from his forehead.

He gave her a concerned look. "Are you okay?"

As Logan slipped from her, he wrapped his arms around her and hugged tightly.

She looked at Ty, then at Logan, and said, "Wonderful. But I'm not sure if I'd want to do that every day."

Logan's chuckle rumbled against her back, and he laid a quick kiss where he had bitten her.

"You'll be sore later," Ty said as he walked away to the back of the truck. He returned a moment later, the condom gone and a towel in his hand. He handed it to Quinn.

Before she could take it, Logan grabbed it and wiped the perspiration from her face and body gently, especially careful around the tender spots. He wiped the sweat off his own brow before tossing it aside.

"Can you untie me now? I think I've been thoroughly punished."

"I'd say," Logan answered. He unstrapped her wrists and rubbed her skin where it was a bit tender from the leather. "You'll have to get in trouble more often."

Chapter Eight

Logan stayed behind to work on the ditch for a couple of hours, and Ty took Quinn back to the house in the tractor.

Quinn ended up in the oversize Jacuzzi tub, soaking her sore body. As she lay back in the warm, soapy water, she thought about all that had transpired in the last two days.

She was leaving tomorrow, and she didn't know if she was ready to go.

After a few minutes, Ty came in and joined her, adding more hot water and more bubble bath. And between playing footsie and stray brushes of fingers and toes, they discussed the sod farm and who Ty and Logan's clients were and the trials and tribulations of owning their own business.

Ty told Quinn that Logan had started the business years before meeting him. They met each other at the Boston Bulldogs stadium right after Ty was injured and was forced to retire. Logan's company had been resodding the football field. Logan had let Ty buy into his business, giving him something to do with his life and helping Logan out by improving his business economically. They were a great team and worked well together.

Quinn listened and heard the love Ty had for Logan in his voice. She wanted to have that type of love with someone. She wanted someone to desperately want and need her. To love her completely.

When Logan came back to the house, he made them both get out of the tub, because their hands and feet were wrinkled and waterlogged. He took a quick shower, and they threw together a late meal.

With her physical hunger and sexual hunger satisfied, it didn't take Quinn long to start drifting off when they settled in the living room to watch a movie.

Logan carried her into bed and tucked the sheets around her snugly, laying a kiss on her forehead.

Quinn wasn't sure if they'd expect to have sex with her once more that night, but Logan told her to go to sleep; she needed to recover from the afternoon's adventure. She wanted to protest, but as soon as she closed her eyes, she was out.

She wasn't sure how long she had slept before movements in the bed woke her.

* * *

Quinn had been put to bed two hours earlier when Logan finally talked Ty into also hitting the sheets. They had finished the movie and a couple of microbrews each when Ty also started to lose the battle with sleep. Logan shut off the TV and returned to Ty, who had his head back on the cushion and his eyes closed.

“Ty,” he whispered, running his fingers down the larger man's T-shirt-covered chest.

Ty's eyelids lifted a bit, and he gave Logan an answering grin. "Was I snoring?"

"No." Logan extended a hand to pull him up, and Ty grabbed it. Logan grunted at Ty's weight. "Shit. Between your workouts and you digging at the ditch, you certainly aren't losing any muscle."

Ty rose up, reminding Logan of how much taller Ty was than him. Logan wrapped his arms around Ty's waist and pressed his hips against him.

"You like my muscles."

Logan scraped his teeth along one of Ty's nipples. "I freakin' *love* your muscles."

"See?" Ty grabbed Logan's ass and squeezed. "I love that tight ass of yours."

Logan nuzzled the dark skin of Ty's neck, tasting the saltiness with his tongue. "Well, you won't be getting it tonight," he murmured against his neck.

Ty's laughter rumbled against him. "No?"

"No. Just because you got a little taste of being the top last night doesn't mean it's going to stay that way."

Logan's fingers splayed along the larger man's back, moving down until he clutched Ty's butt, which was snugly hidden in his jeans.

"What are we doing, Lo?"

Logan knew what Ty was getting at, but really didn't want to talk about it. "What do you mean?"

"You know what I mean. About Quinn."

"Just having some fun."

"Is that all it is?" Ty leaned back in Logan's arms and looked down, searching his face.

Logan was careful not to give anything away. "What else would it be?"

"I dunno. All I know is I don't want anyone coming between you and me."

Logan didn't know what to say to Ty. He had never heard his lover be insecure, and it was unmistakable at the moment.

"She's leaving tomorrow," Ty reminded him.

"Yep."

"How're you gonna feel about that?"

Logan shrugged. "It was expected. It was the deal…or dare, I guess." He hugged Ty closer. "I have you."

"Am I gonna be enough after this weekend?"

Logan pulled away roughly, slamming his hands on his hips. "Ty. Knock it the fuck off."

"Hey, I'm calling it as I see it. I like her too, you know."

"Ty," Logan growled in warning.

"She's smart. She's gutsy. She's sexy as all get-out…"

"And your point?"

"Do you want it to end tomorrow?"

"Will you get to the fucking point?"

"Why don't we ask her to stay for a while? See where this goes."

Logan shook his head in frustration. "And here I thought you were worried about her coming between us."

It was Ty's turn to shrug. “All I'm saying is, I'm willing, if you are, to explore what this is. If our relationship can't handle her being a part of it, then there's a reason.”

Ty's gaze was serious. A little too serious for Logan's taste. He loved Ty and believed their relationship was strong, but did he want to risk it?

He didn't know.

His anger drained away quickly. He wasn't pissed at Ty; he was mad at himself. For not wanting to admit he *might* have feelings for Quinn.

He was too tired, and it was too late for this discussion. He extended his hand to Ty. “C'mon, let's sleep on this.”

Ty gripped it and gave it a squeeze. Logan led him into the bedroom, where Quinn was curled under the sheets on one side of the oversize bed.

Ty placed a finger to his lips and pulled Logan over to the other side. They helped each other remove their clothes, Logan just wanting to toss them in the corner, but Ty folding everything neatly.

Logan watched Ty's muscles ripple as he put the clothes on the dresser and pulled the bedcovers back. Logan's balls tightened, and he was hard by the time Ty straightened up and turned back to him.

Logan grabbed his own cock, drawing Ty's attention. He squeezed the root before fisting it to the tip.

Ty sank on the edge of the bed and patted the mattress. But Logan didn't obey. He was the top, and after yesterday, Ty needed a little reminder. He stepped between Ty's knees, wrapped his fingers around the back of Ty's smooth head, and pulled him forward until his cock butted up against Ty's lips.

Ty opened his mouth at the same time one of his hands grabbed Logan's sac and the other snaked around to grab his ass cheek, making Logan throw his head back and bite back a groan. Ty's hot mouth swallowed him deep, sucking and licking along his length. At the same time, his other hand stroked along Logan's crevice, fingers teasing his anus, circling the tight hole. Then Ty palmed Logan's sac, tugging softly, then kneading.

Ty sucked harder, his cheeks sinking in with each stroke of his mouth. The only thing Logan wanted more than to let his load go in Ty's mouth was to fill Ty's ass up with his hot seed—a reminder that Ty was his.

Logan tilted his hips and thrust. Ty had no problem relaxing his throat and swallowing his length. Over and over, until Logan had to push away, breaking the contact. Ty's lips shone with saliva and precum. Logan leaned down and captured his bottom's mouth, tasting his own essence along with Ty's.

He groaned into Ty's mouth, shoved him back on the bed, and covered him quickly with his own body. Their cocks met, and Logan ground against him. He held himself up long enough to grab the lube on the nightstand, and he liberally squirted it between them, making their cocks slippery. Ty reached a hand down and grabbed both of their rods and stroked them as one.

Logan traced his tongue along Ty's abs and around a dark nipple. He captured one between his teeth and nibbled carefully. Ty arched his back, sliding his hand faster up and down their joined cocks. Logan's tongue swirled around the pebbled nipple, licked along his pecs and up to the apex of his neck. He sank his teeth into the tender skin where Ty's neck met his collarbone and thrust harder into Ty's fist. Ty loosened his grip, allowing Logan to slide his sac up Ty's hard length.

Logan reached between them and pushed Ty's erection between Logan's legs, so it slid along his tender seam. Logan squeezed his thighs together, keeping a tight hold on Ty's cock as Ty thrust up against him, throwing his head back and exposing more of his throat to Logan.

And Logan took advantage of it.

He nipped along Ty's jugular and then snagged his earlobe before pressing his lips against Ty's ear.

"Turn over," he ordered softly.

At first Ty didn't move. Logan knew he resisted on purpose. It was all a part of their play.

"Turn over and give me your ass."

Ty turned his face away and closed his eyes.

"I'm going to fuck your ass…" Logan thrust against Ty's lower abdomen. "Hard. Deep. I'm taking what's mine."

Ty turned back to him, his smile broad. "You want it; you take it," he said, low enough not to wake Quinn.

Logan didn't think he could get any harder at that moment. He was in the mood for roughness, for conquering, for taking what was his. But he was still fully aware of Quinn sacked out nearby.

"Do it. Take me, then." Ty reached up and flicked Logan's nipple ring before catching it between his fingers and twisting it a bit. Enough to make Logan grit his teeth.

The pleasure was intense, and he wanted—needed—to bury himself in Ty. Soon.

He decided not to wait for compliance. He slipped to Ty's side and pulled Ty to him, pinning Ty's round, muscular buttocks against his throbbing cock. He grabbed the lube once more and prepared himself. He wrapped an arm around Ty and pulled him even closer as his cock probed for Ty's opening. Logan reached down and found it and guided himself to just the right spot.

He thrust hard.

Ty was ready. He had relaxed his muscles, and Logan met no resistance as he pushed past the ringed muscle. He sank into his lover, buried himself balls-deep. He stilled for a moment and caught his breath. They lay on their sides, Logan spooning the man he loved as he took him completely. He let out a shaky breath, while Ty hissed his breath between his teeth.

Before Logan could gather his bearings, Ty ground back against him, making Logan not able to wait; he met every tilt of Ty's hips with one of his own. He nudged a leg between Ty's and reached around to capture Ty's cock. He swirled his thumb around the slick precum and used it to lube his fist as he stroked Ty's cock in rhythm with his thrusting. Ty arched his back, shoving his ass into Logan's lap, and he reached up and entwined his fingers into Logan's loose hair. Ty's hands curled into fists, and Logan felt the pull against his scalp. It made him thrust harder, his thighs slapping against the smooth, dark skin of Ty's ass.

Logan had a distant thought that they were being too loud, moving too much, causing the bed to shimmy. But he couldn't stop. He didn't want to stop.

He angled his hips a bit, making sure he hit Ty's sweet spot, and he knew he'd found it when Ty yanked on his hair and cried out. Two more deep thrusts and Ty was coming in ropy spurts over Logan's hand, over his own belly, all over the sheets.

Logan used his weight and flipped Ty to his stomach and wrapped an arm under Ty's hips to lift them just enough. Just enough so he could pump harder and faster into Ty's ass. Logan threw his head back and panted as his balls tightened with every stroke. Ty's tight ring squeezed his cock until he couldn't hold back any longer, and he grunted as his cock twitched deep within Ty, spilling his seed into his man. His lover.

He stayed buried to the hilt until the last drop was milked from his cock. He slowly withdrew with a long, satisfied sigh. He laid a kiss in the small of Ty's back and gave his ass a playful smack.

They were going to have to change the sheets.

Shit.

Logan looked over to where Quinn *had* been sleeping and nudged Ty. She was sitting up with the sheet tucked under her armpits, and her eyelids were heavy as she watched them. Her hair was spilled around her face, her bottom lip looked swollen, as if she had been worrying it between her teeth, and she had a flush blossoming from her chest to her cheeks.

Logan didn't think she was red from embarrassment.

Shit.

Ty moved first, dislodging Logan from their contact. “Sorry, Quinn. We didn't mean to disturb you.”

“It's all right.”

Her voice was low and husky, causing Logan's gut to twinge. She had definitely been affected by what she had seen. Logan sat up, gathering a corner of the sheet over his lap.

Ty stood up. “I'll go shower now.”

He quickly disappeared, leaving Logan to deal with the aftermath. Logan's gaze went from Ty's retreating back to Quinn's flushed face.

“We didn't mean to exclude you.”

Quinn didn't say anything, and Logan frowned.

“We figured you'd be sore from this afternoon.” That was stretching it a little, but mostly true. They hadn't wanted to disturb her; they should have stayed in the living room. “Quinn?”

Her eyes had a glazed look about them, and now the curiosity was killing him.

“Quinn?”

He crawled closer to her and realized he only could account for one of her arms. The other was hidden below the sheet.

Shit.

"Quinn…?" He placed a hand over the sheet where hers was, and he felt her moving. "Need help?"

She barely nodded as she let out a breath between parted lips. With the sheet between them, he guided her fingers, circling her nub, stroking her lips. He could feel the damp heat even through the cotton. Her hips lifted a bit, and her hand movement became frantic.

She flung her head back against the headboard, and Logan leaned in, speaking softly into her ear, "C'mon, let go."

Her frantic pace slowed as her hand jerked beneath his. Quinn cried out, her chest heaving as she shuddered beneath their touch.

After a moment, her breathing slowed, and her eyes cleared.

He gave her a smile. "Feel better?"

She laughed shakily, and he gathered her into his arms, tucking the sheet around her. The bed smelled like sex, and they would be definitely changing the sheets.

She leaned her head into his shoulder, and he brushed his lips against her temple.

"Again, I'm sorry."

She twisted in his arms to look him in the eye. "For what?"

"Oh…let's see. Waking you up, not including you… I don't know. Pick something."

"Logan, I am the third wheel here. I know that. This has been fun, but…"

"But?" He prodded.

She shrugged. “But it's going to end.”

He decided not to reveal his and Ty's earlier discussion. He'd wait until tomorrow. They had time.

“Your relationship with Ty is special. Watching you two be intimate… Well, all I can say is, it was moving. I mean, I can see how much you guys love each other. I can actually *see* it. Taste it. *Feel* it, just being around you two.”

“But you can—” *Be a part of this.* Logan stopped himself.

Quinn wanted to hear the rest. “I can…?”

“You can enjoy this while you're here.”

“I will. I am. But I wish I had the emotional connection with someone special like you two have.”

Logan didn't say anything, and Quinn really didn't expect a response. She didn't want him to throw her a pity party. She was just feeling a bit emotional at the moment. It would pass.

She decided to change the subject to something she was dying to hear an explanation about. “You guys didn't use a condom.”

“No.” He nuzzled her hair, breathing deeply.

He wasn't going to get off so easily. “Why not?”

“We test regularly.”

“So if I were tested and on birth control, we wouldn't need to use condoms?”

“Are you on birth control?”

A question answered—or not answered—with a question.

She was, but she wasn't sure if she was ready to reveal that yet. Or if she'd ever reveal it. "No."

"Okay. That settles it."

"Would you ever want children?"

There was a long pause.

"I don't know. Ty and I never discussed it. You?"

"I don't know either. I'm not at that point in my life where I'm ready to make that decision."

"When would that point be?"

"When I'm with someone I love, and that someone loves me back and just doesn't say the empty words."

Logan didn't say anything, but he nodded.

Whether he was agreeing with her decision or agreeing with the idea someone could be capable of saying the three little words, "I love you," and not meaning it, she'd never know.

Ty came into the room, naked but fresh out of the shower. It gave an excuse for Logan to peel away from her and go clean up.

She helped Ty change the sheets and straighten out the bedcovers. She watched, in appreciation, his muscular body move. He truly was like a moving piece of art, a sculpture made of flesh.

Logan returned shortly, his hair pulled back in a ponytail, she assumed to keep it dry while he had washed up. He pulled the hair band out and threw it on the nightstand before shaking his head, his hair swinging freely around his face. She most definitely preferred his hair loose.

He grabbed her waist and tumbled her to the bed. He laughed when she squealed in surprise. A moment later Ty followed, curling up next to her. The boys sandwiched her tightly between them, bringing to mind the saying, "As snug as a bug in a rug."

The bug fell asleep, feeling secure within the embrace of their arms.

Chapter Nine

Quinn didn't want to believe Sunday was here already. She delayed opening her eyes, because she wasn't ready to leave.

But she had to. She needed to get back to reality. Back to her life. Her job. Her responsibilities. Her parents.

Blah.

She would have missed this whole weekend if she hadn't gone to that wedding wearing that god-awful dress. She'd have to thank Gina for getting married.

She'd have to thank Lana and Paula for daring her to pick up Logan.

And she'd have to thank Peter for pissing her off enough to make her get drunk, which in turn made her brave enough to actually try to pick up Logan.

Even though the original attempt had failed.

Quinn smiled and stretched lazily, her limbs coming in contact with smooth skin. The body heat that emanated from both of the boys warmed her to her bones.

An arm came from behind her, wrapping around just below her breasts, to pull her close into a hard but wiry chest. *Logan.*

His face buried his face into her hair, and he inhaled deeply. “Morning.”

She reached out and made contact with Ty, who was still snoring softly. Quinn opened her eyes and saw he was flat on his back, the sheet not covering his morning wood, or any other part of his magnificent body, except from his knees down.

She reached out a finger and traced along the edge of the thick black-flame tattoo running up his sides. She followed it all the way around to the bottom of the large tat, which ended below his hips. His hard cock twitched in response, and she let out a little snort and looked up. He was now wide awake and watching her intently.

“Are you going to finish what you've started?” Ty's voice was raspy from nonuse and deeper than normal, sending a shiver down to her toes. The shiver hit a few sensitive spots along the way. And a few which were a little sore.

“Sure.” She pulled out of Logan's arms and climbed onto Ty, straddling his waist while placing her palms on his chest to keep her balance while she got settled. She ran her palms down his rib cage and over his hip bones.

“When did you get this one?”

His muscles moved under her palms in response, reminding her of Magnum twitching in his sleep.

“My senior year in college.”

She marveled at just how dark his skin tone was and how a black tattoo was even visible against it. But it was, and it turned her on. She had never been attracted to men with tattoos—they'd always seemed too dangerous. Nor men with long hair—too wild. But she had been wrong. At least with these two.

Two. Well, that was another thing she had never thought she'd be interested in.

And here she was, straddling a big, black, tattooed—not to mention, naked—man and being watched by another. She glanced over at Logan. He was lying on his side, his head propped up by his elbow, and was doing just that—staring at them.

He studied them intently, his cock not quite hard, lying against his naked thigh. He was stretched out like a scrumptious breakfast buffet.

Quinn was suddenly aware of the way her pussy pressed against Ty's lower belly; he could probably feel how wet she was already.

She shifted a little, just enough to spread the folds so he could feel more of her against his skin, the heat, the slickness. Her clit just touched his skin. His hands came up to grasp her hips.

"Was there any meaning to it?" She shifted once again, tilting her hips until her clit pushed against him harder, making it swell and harden.

He grimaced and gave her a tight smile. "Not really. I just thought it was cool."

She bit back a smile as she twisted around to look at his ankle, purposely pushing harder against him, teasing. "And that one?"

Ty shrugged powerfully beneath her, and she had to bite back a gasp. The movement against her sensitive flesh made her want to grind against him.

The son of a bitch was getting her back.

One tease deserved another.

"I got it when I was doing a bit too much celebrating after the NFL draft."

She turned back and scanned the rest of him. She leaned forward to put a finger on his right bicep, going out of her way to brush against his nipple.

"Drunk, huh? And what's with the matching white tigers?"

She slid back until Ty's cock lodged between the crevice of her ass cheeks. There was no way she wanted to take him that way. She was still too sore from the first time; plus, Ty was much bigger than Logan. And Logan had been plenty enough.

She could feel the warm stickiness from his cock on her back. She leaned forward and barely brushed her puckered nipples against his abs. Just enough so they could both feel it. He clenched his abdominal muscles, and her nipples pebbled harder.

He still hadn't answered her.

"The matching tigers?" She prodded.

Her pussy was riding his pubic bone, and it wouldn't take much for her to get off this way. But she wanted more—even if she *was* a bit sore.

She wanted a parting gift. Something for her to remember them by. This was her last day, and she wanted both of them at least once more.

Ty released a ragged breath before answering. "Lo, you want to answer that one?"

From the corner of her eye, she saw Logan finally move. He came behind her and lifted her hair, peppering kisses on the back of her neck and along her shoulders.

"Hmm. The white tiger." He pressed his lips to the top of her spine and then started a trail down the crease in her back. His lips were warm and soft against her skin.

Ty released her hips and cupped her breasts, pushing them together. Kneading. Squeezing. Quinn arched her back, encouraging him to do more.

Logan's lips were at the small of her back when he said, "Our first date was at the Franklin Park Zoo, and they had just acquired a white tiger named Luther."

When he didn't continue for a few moments, Quinn glanced over her shoulder. Logan was licking the glistening precum off the crown of Ty's cock. He swirled his tongue along the swollen head before looking up and catching her watching him.

"We were standing in front of Luther's exhibit when we first kissed—"

"And we wanted to remember that turning point forever," Ty finished for him, his jaw tight as Logan continued to lick down Ty's hard length, his hot breath beating against Quinn's skin.

Ty jerked underneath her and tilted his head back into his pillow. Quinn reached up to cup his hands, which still clutched her breasts, and she guided his fingers to her nipples, where she squeezed, showing him what she wanted.

He gave her a crooked smile, as if he was amused but was in the middle of too much pleasure to laugh. Quinn leaned down, careful not to dislodge his fingers, which were working her nipples just right, and captured his lips. Their tongues fenced and fought, and she moaned into his mouth as he tweaked her nipples even harder, causing her to thrust once against his pelvis bone.

Only once. Once more and she would come. She wanted to wait.

Logan planted a hand on the center of her back and pushed her all the way down until she was lying on Ty's torso, his muscles hard against her breasts, hard where she was soft.

A moment later fingers entered her, probing, testing her wetness, rubbing along her cunt, dipping. Spreading her wide, exposing her, holding her open as Logan pressed his cock into her with agonizing slowness. Little by little, giving her only a taste before pulling out. Each time he took her, he went a little deeper, giving her a little more before leaving her empty and wanting.

Finally he was fully seated in her. He ground small circles deep within her, not moving in or out at all, just rotating his hips enough to make her break her kiss with Ty, bury her face in his neck, and curse against his skin.

She wanted Logan to thrust, to fuck her hard; these small movements were driving her crazy.

Something pushed against her clit, something hot, smooth, and slick. Not a finger, no. The thick head of Ty's cock rubbed against her sensitive button. Pushing and circling the same way Logan did with his hips.

Quinn slammed her palms into Ty's chest and arched her back, shoving hard against the both of them as she fell over the edge, her pussy clenching down on Logan, her lips entrapping Ty. Her core pulsed as she threw back her head and screamed, "Oh God. Oh my God!"

Before she could even catch her breath, Logan was gone. Roughly pulling off his condom and grabbing another.

Her breathing under control, Quinn sucked Ty's lower lip into her mouth and nibbled. It was full and luscious and tasted just like Ty.

Yes, she was getting to know his taste. His scent. The texture of his skin, the way the tone of his skin changed. Darker around his joints, slightly lighter around the curves of his muscles. Dark nipples…

And a deep purplish cock that Logan was guiding toward her still-wet, still-ready pussy. He had taken the time to roll the fresh condom on his lover, and with one hand on Quinn's hip and one on Ty's cock, he brought them together like a puzzle. Fitting one piece into the other. Only these pieces didn't fit quite so perfectly. One was too big to fit the other. But it worked just the same.

Ah.

Ty watched her intently. Quinn didn't break his gaze as he lifted his hips and slid in and out of her, filling her until she couldn't be filled any more. Stretching her until there was no more room.

What should have been painful wasn't. It was—

Right.

Quinn pushed herself back into a sitting position, taking as much as she could of her dark lover. Wishing she could take more. Take all of him. Her pale hands against the darkness of his skin were a startling contrast, catching her attention for a moment until she heard Logan's voice.

"Are you curious about mine too?"

His?

Of course.

She let out a breathless "yes."

Logan moved behind her, pushing Ty's knees back, spreading the other man's legs, causing Quinn to almost lose her balance.

Ty grabbed her arms and held tight, keeping her still while he took Logan's lead: pulling his legs back, exposing both of them to Logan. Giving the other man complete access to do whatever he wanted. To her. To him.

To them.

Logan's chest pressed against Quinn's back as he reached around her to cup her breasts, to pick up where Ty had left off. Pinching and twisting her nipples until she squirmed and cried out.

"The tribal band was my first tattoo. My wife wanted me to get it."

Wife.

Quinn wanted to question, but she couldn't. Her mind was spinning, with Ty's cock buried deep within her, his balls pushing against her anus, Logan's fingers teasing and playing along her nipples, the curve of her breasts.

"The coral snake..."

Logan's teeth grazed along the sensitive skin of her neck, along her jugular. He nipped the length of her jaw.

"I did to piss her off. She was afraid of snakes and had told me no..."

Logan pushed his chest harder against her, and she felt Ty jerk beneath her as Logan entered him in one thrust.

Ty's fingers dug into Quinn's wrists, and Logan let out a hissing breath against her ear.

"The nipple ring..."

Logan grunted as he thrust hard again. Ty threw his head back, a long, low groan escaping him. His chest heaved, his cock lifting, trying to go deeper into Quinn.

She cried out and ground against him.

"Well, the nipple ring..." Logan grunted again, his lower belly slapping against the small of Quinn's back. "That was what broke the camel's back."

Camel?

Quinn was losing the point of this one-sided conversation. She didn't want to think so hard. She only wanted to feel.

With one hand still on her breast, Logan wrapped the other around her waist and began a rhythm for the both of them: Quinn riding Ty's cock and Logan taking Ty's ass. Logan moved his hips, bringing Quinn along for the ride.

Ty closed his eyes, his lips parted, and let her wrists go before he bruised or broke them.

"Holy fuck, Lo—"

Logan continued his assault on Ty's ass, plunging deep and hard, never pausing, causing Ty to buck against him, to buck against Quinn.

She fell forward, capturing his nipple in her mouth, sucking hard, raking her teeth across the small, stiff tip.

"Jesus, I'm going… Ah fuck!"

He thrust upward and tensed, his cock jerking within her. She tensed also as she felt the ripples within her begin, holding Ty like a fist, milking him of his hot seed.

She collapsed on Ty's chest bonelessly until Logan smacked her ass lightly. He gripped her, pushing his fingers deep into the flesh of her hips, and he pumped. Even though he pumped into Ty's hole, it was almost as if he were fucking her from behind. She watched him over her shoulder with unfettered interest. His long hair partially covered his face, but she could see him tightening, his jaw, his neck, his chest muscles. His buttocks clenched and unclenched with each draw of his hips until he just stopped.

He squeezed his eyes shut and grimaced, and Quinn could imagine Logan's hot cum filling Ty's canal. One lover filling another.

Then it was over. Silence. Stillness.

They were still connected. Pieced together. No one wanting to move…

No one wanting to be the first to break their closeness.

Chapter Ten

Quinn shut the door of her town house with her foot, her arms full of groceries.

Silence greeted her. The house was quiet and empty.

Lonely.

She moved toward the back of her two-story townhome to the small kitchen, where she sat the brown paper bags stuffed full of necessities on the tiny kitchen island.

The kitchen at the farm was at least three times the size of hers. She didn't even have room for a table. Since she'd been home, she hadn't felt like cooking anyway.

She felt empty deep down in the pit of her stomach. Like something was missing.

Ignoring the groceries, she moved to the sliding-glass door, which led out to a small deck. A deck the size of a postage stamp that looked out to the back side of someone else's town house. No fields of grass here. No wide-open spaces.

No Logan. No Ty.

She already missed the boys. And it was only Monday.

She had left the farm Sunday night after they cooked up an unbelievable dinner. She had watched in amazement as they moved around the kitchen, snapping towels at each other, joking around, occasionally brushing against each other and pretending it was accidental.

After dinner, they had sat around the table, and the conversation had gotten serious.

Logan had asked her to stay. At least for a while.

She told him no. She had a job. A family. But really, it wasn't a good excuse.

The truth was that she worried what people would say. What people would think. Her coworkers, her friends? Her family? Argh.

She had to weigh her options. Was enjoying two men worth the price of possible censure? Before her weekend out on the farm, she would have said no. Now…

She couldn't say.

She had to remind herself she was a practical person. She was a financial analyst, for God's sake. Sleeping with two men wasn't practical. Especially when it was at the same time.

Logan finally let her leave with a parting suggestion: "*Think about it.*"

She had been thinking about it. Nonstop. At work. And definitely at home, when she was at her loneliest.

One weekend. Two men. And she felt…she felt something had changed inside of her. Something that would never go back to normal.

Normal.

Crap. What *was* normal? A relationship with Peter? Hardly.

Her cell phone vibrated across the kitchen counter, making her jump. It was probably Lana. Or Paula.

She picked it up and looked at the caller ID. *Logan.* Damn, how had he known she was thinking of him? Of Ty?

She flipped it open.

Before she could even say hello, he started talking. "Quinn. I miss you."

Quinn moved out of the kitchen and into the adjoining living room. She sank into the leather recliner she loved, and tucked her feet under her legs.

"You miss me. Does Ty?"

"Ty's right here. He misses you too."

"It was fun…"

"Was that all?"

Was it? No.

But before that reception two weekends ago, she had sworn off men. She had needed another man in her life like a hole in the head. And now? Now she was going to get involved with two?

She was crazy.

Okay. Maybe she *needed* men. For certain functions. But she didn't need a relationship.

"It was a stupid dare…"

"You're fooling yourself. It had nothing to do with the dare. You didn't have to come back last weekend, but you did."

Quinn couldn't disagree with what he was saying. She gripped the phone tighter.

"Do you regret it?"

"You know I don't."

"So come back." She could hear Ty in the background but couldn't make out his words. "Come back for the weekend."

"I don't know…"

"What's one more weekend?"

"I have plans." It was true, but stretching it.

"For the whole weekend?"

Quinn silently cursed. She should have known Logan wasn't going to back down, take a simple answer, and leave it at that.

"I promised my parents I'd meet them for dinner."

He was a dominant. He was going to press until he got the answers he wanted. "When?"

"Sunday."

He was in control. "So meet them. Leave Sunday morning after breakfast."

She couldn't argue with that.

He knew what he wanted, when he wanted it, and how to get it. And that knowledge made her toes curl and her blood rush through her veins.

His voice got low, forceful. "We dare you."

In the end, she agreed. She accepted their dare.

* * *

The anticipation of waiting four more days was killing her.

She was restless at work on Tuesday, and Paula and Lana showed up unexpectedly at her office on Wednesday. They plopped themselves in the chairs that sat across from her desk and dumped greasy bags of food on her formerly clean desktop.

"Fried chicken from Charlie's Chicken Shack," Lana crowed, propping her feet on Quinn's desk.

"Your favorite."

Quinn didn't agree. It was Paula's favorite, not hers. But it did smell good.

Paula started digging through the bags, dragging out cheap plastic utensils and a wad of napkins, scattering food and crumbs and plasticware all over her desk.

Quinn grimaced and squirmed in her chair. Not only didn't she like someone messing up her personal space, but her ass was still sore from last weekend's extracurricular activities.

She half listened to the girls chatter away about stuff that wasn't really important, but they were her friends, and she loved them. So she tried to pay attention.

"Where were you Saturday? I called your cell. *And* left a message. Which you didn't return, by the way."

Quinn waved a hand carelessly. She glanced at Lana quickly, then away to papers on her desk, shuffling them around. "I, uh…"

Crap. She had never been good at making excuses on the fly.

"I forgot to charge my phone."

Lame. So lame. But Lana didn't question it, because Paula was on to the next topic.

"What are your plans *this* weekend?"

Quinn's computer dinged, and she pulled up her in-box.

Distracted, she answered, "Parents."

An e-mail from Ty.

She had already said yes. Did they really think she needed more convincing?

Paula crumpled up one of the brown bags and tossed it into Quinn's wastebasket. Quinn gritted her teeth. Just what she wanted: her office to smell like fried chicken for the rest of the day.

"You're going to your parents' house for the weekend?"

The subject of the e-mail was *IMPORTANT* and had a red exclamation point next to it. Crap, maybe something was wrong with Logan or Ty.

"Uh...yep."

Lana cut into her thoughts. "Unreachable last weekend, gone this one. I think she has a secret lover."

Both of the girls looked at each other and laughed. Quinn's eyebrows pinned together. They didn't think she could have a lover? She was tempted to tell them but knew better. She didn't want that can of worms opened. That would mean spending the rest of the night dodging questions. They would want *all* the details. Details she wasn't willing to spill.

Lana snorted. “Quinn, you don't even *like* your parents. Why would you go out there for the weekend?”

“Hey, I like my parents!”

“Yeah, all you do is bitch about how controlling they are—”

“How snobby—” Paula chimed in.

Lana made a face. “How highbrow. Should we go on?”

They forgot judgmental.

“I'm trying to make amends.”

Lana and Paula looked at each other and laughed. Again.

Jeez, the girls weren't giving her a break today. But then, they knew her. Too well. Crap. E-mail. E-mail. She turned her attention back to her computer.

She double-clicked, and when she did, a photo popped up in the body of the message. Two naked males stood in an embrace kissing, hands caressing each other's erections. The photo cut off just above their mouths, so she couldn't see their faces. But she recognized the muscular bodies, the beautiful colors of the coral snake wrapped around Logan's hips, his nipple ring, the deep dark coloring of Ty's skin and his recognizable tattoos. Under the photo it said, *Something to get you over hump day.*

Her breath caught as she studied the photo again. She wanted to be there. She wanted to jump into her computer screen and be instantly there, touching them. Exploring them. Being caressed and held by them.

“What's the matter, Quinn?”

She moved the cursor away from the Delete button and just minimized the screen instead. She wanted to look at the picture again later. When she was alone.

"Nothing. Just some Nigerian scam e-mail."

She crossed her legs under her desk and squeezed her thighs together.

That's it. She was calling the boys, taking a personal day on Friday, and heading out early.

Chapter Eleven

It was like déjà vu. Another Friday and another drive down the long, dusty stone lane to Logan and Ty's farm.

And Quinn was just as anxious this time as she had been the last.

Looking for a song that would calm her nerves, she switched back and forth from one radio station to another. She finally settled on a classic-rock station. When she lifted her eyes back to the lane, she let out a gasp and slammed her foot on the brake pedal. The Infiniti's ABS brakes brought the car to a grinding halt on the stones, a cloud of dust rising around it.

In the cloud sat a four-wheel all-terrain vehicle, parked diagonally in the lane. Blocking her path.

On the ATV sat a figure dressed all in black from head to toe: mask, long-sleeved shirt, gloves, cargo pants, and combat-style boots.

Thoughts spun in her head. Words like *highwayman, robber, hijacker. Sinister.* And a split second later she had another ridiculous thought: it was too hot out to be dressed like that.

Quinn gripped the steering wheel, unable to move. She just stared at the man, unable to look away. Her heart pounded in her chest as he lifted a hand and pointed at her. Her breath caught in her throat.

"What…the hell?"

Whoever it was, whatever game he was playing, whatever his intentions were…she needed to get out of there.

Pronto.

Her hand went to the shifter, ready to shove it into reverse, when a dark figure was at her door, ripping it open and pulling her out, while the first one came through the passenger side.

She should have locked her fucking doors!

The second person slammed her vehicle into park and unhooked her seat belt as the first dragged her out of the driver's seat. He grabbed her wrists and pinned them together behind her back.

Quinn screamed and kicked out with her heels, aiming for shins and higher. She was quickly blindfolded and gagged, her hands bound behind her with a soft rope. She was thrown onto her stomach and, from what she could tell, onto the backseat of her own car.

The attackers never said a word as they bound her ankles to stop her from kicking.

She gasped for breath, the gag making her panic. She forced herself to breathe out of her nose. Slow, steady. Until she heard the car door slam and felt the vehicle move forward. She held her breath, trying to see if she could tell if they continued down the lane or turned around. But between being frightened and blindfolded, her sense of direction was skewed.

She had no idea where they were taking her. She had no idea who they were.

She was fucked.

Quinn attempted to rub the blindfold off with her shoulder. She failed. She was able to push it up a little, but not enough to be able to see anything other than a splinter of light.

The car bounced underneath her, and even through the blood rushing in her ears, she heard the stones pinging off the bottom of her car. And suddenly her body was thrown forward and came to rest against the back of the bench seat. She let out a muffled "oof" around the awful-tasting cloth in her mouth.

She heard the whine of the ATV as it approached the stopped vehicle, and within seconds both back doors of her car were opened and hands were grabbing at her, pulling and tugging.

Above the sound of feet scrambling on stones, she heard an angel.

Magnum.

The dog circled them, barking excitedly. His deep shepherd bark was unmistakable. She was saved.

She heard a deep grunt to her right as the kidnapper grabbed her elbow.

She heard a squeal, Magnum crying out in pain.

"Shit! Magnum! Get out of the way!"

Logan. It was Logan's voice to her right.

"Get that dog out from underfoot."

She wanted to ask what was happening. What was going on? But the cotton in her mouth had sucked all the saliva from her mouth. Even if they removed it, she wasn't sure she would be able speak.

She heard a sharp whistle somewhere in front of her and the dog scrambling up the stairs. She could picture exactly where she was now.

Her pulse slowed a fraction, and her breathing calmed a bit.

What was their intention? Was this a game?

Shit. It *was* a game; they were role-playing.

At least she hoped so.

Because if they weren't, she was going back to idea number one: she was fucked.

Ty held open the front door for Logan, who had Quinn thrown over his shoulder as he struggled up the front steps, clearly trying not to lose his balance. Ty shook his head. He was stronger; he should have been the one to carry her into the house.

He was glad to remove the hot ski masks he and Logan had worn for the mock kidnapping.

He was the one who had thought of this. He hoped he didn't regret it.

He hoped she didn't get too mad.

At first he thought the idea would be fun, until he saw how scared Quinn was when they hijacked her car. And those nasty heels she had on. Jesus, she could have maimed them.

Logan moved past him, and Ty locked the door behind them. That was the last thing they needed: to have someone show up and just walk in unannounced. The cops would be up to their ears thinking they were kidnapping Quinn against her will.

Ty caught up to Logan and took Quinn from him. Logan was already showing fatigue, and Ty didn't want to risk them falling when they headed down the basement steps.

He was glad Quinn had stopped struggling, and hoped she realized this was all in fun. He slung her over his shoulder. She smelled so good. One of his arms gripped her thighs, holding her in place, leaving his other hand to support her ass. And her ass was so soft…

He brought his attention back to the basement steps. Another thing he needed to avoid was missing a step and having the two of them tumble down them. Logan had gone on ahead and was setting up the contraption Ty had built just in preparation for this.

Logan waited for him with an anxious, if not horny, look in his eyes.

Ty had to chuckle. Logan had gone along with his idea with great anticipation.

He felt Quinn relax even further when he laughed. He was now sure she knew it was them and not some crazy fiends.

He stepped up to the homemade St. Andrew's cross. He had worked all week on it. Logan had wanted to try it out and use it in their play during the week, but Ty had refused. He wanted Quinn on it first.

He had attached the X-shaped wooden frame onto the basement wall, making sure it was secure, making sure no one would get hurt. He had made it secure enough that it would be a permanent fixture in the basement and could be used for future play. Whether Quinn was a part of that or not.

Instead of shackles and cuffs, he had set it up with soft rope loops that would be used to restrain the wrists and ankles and even her waist, if needed. The soft rope he'd purchased was made of silk, soft enough not to cause chafing of her delicate skin. He didn't want to cause any pain or discomfort—just wanting and desire.

He leaned Quinn against the St. Andrew's cross, and she collapsed against it, her knees flexing slightly. Logan dropped to her ankles, released the temporary restraints, and placed her feet into the looped ropes, while Ty unbound her wrists from behind her back and placed them into the loops at the top of the cross.

Within minutes she was spread-eagle on the upright restraint system. Her wrists and ankles were bound and spread wide, giving them complete access to her. Now they just needed to get rid of her clothes. The high heels—something she would wear to her job—slipped easily off her feet. Logan took his time removing them, caressing her arches, slipping fingers between her toes until she curled them.

Logan slid his palms up her calves, taking his time, while Ty grabbed a sharp knife. He had no other way to undress her while she was restrained. He would have to cut off her clothes. As he slowly cut them off—first her skirt, then her blouse, leaving her in only panties and a bra—he promised himself he would replace them.

Her lingerie set looked fancy and expensive—well thought out. He hesitated before cutting them off.

Quinn was still blindfolded and gagged. He leaned in close to her ear as Logan stood and snagged the knife from his hand.

"We're going to replace everything we ruin."

With that, Logan slipped the knife between her breasts, freeing them as he cut through the elastic holding the cups together. He cut both of the shoulder straps and tossed the now-useless bra across the room. Ty watched goose bumps break out over Quinn's skin as Logan returned to his knees and caressed the tight skin of her stomach and hips before slicing the black lacy fabric of her panties also.

Quinn's nipples were tight and tempting. Ty ran his tongue over one and then the other. Her back arched, and a moan escaped from around the cloth gag. She tasted sweet and wicked, and he loved her flavor. He was amazed at the contrast between the paleness of her skin and the dark pink color of her nipples. It reminded him of strawberry frosting.

Logan took his time after cutting off her panties; still crouched between Quinn's legs, he kissed along her thighs. He plunged his fingers into her pussy, and Quinn's hips began to rotate in the same rhythm as Logan's wrist.

Quinn gasped into the gag as fingers buried deep into her. She was wet and enjoying every second of the boys' attention. Now she knew this was definitely kinky play.

She had never been one for being tied up. She had never wanted it for herself and never wanted to do it to anyone else.

There was something to be said about being blindfolded, gagged, and restrained to some contraption. She had no idea what it was. She still couldn't see.

Hell, there could be an audience watching what the boys were doing to her and she wouldn't know. That thought alone sent hot lightning through her core.

But her hearing was a bit sharper, and she couldn't hear anything but Ty's and Logan's breathing. And a few murmurs against her skin.

Logan—it had to be Logan—spread her pussy lips with his fingers, separating her, exposing her to his mouth as he pressed it against her clit, sucking and circling it with his tongue.

Quinn whimpered helplessly. She couldn't reach for his long hair, couldn't hold him where she wanted him. She was completely under their control. Again.

This was a hell of a start to the weekend.

They continued to surprise her and open her eyes to the unexpected.

Ty's hands kneaded her breasts, squeezing and pinching one nipple, while he sucked the other into his mouth. Her nipples were aching, hard peaks. She wanted him to pinch her harder, twist them harder, but she couldn't tell him that. She just had to wait for him to decide to do it on his own.

The frustration was like an aphrodisiac. It made her squirm.

She tried pulling against the soft restraints, yanking her limbs with a jerk.

"Shh. Don't hurt yourself." Ty's voice, so close to her ear, made her shiver.

She felt a warm, wet tongue against her lobe, down her neck. Then it stroked along her bottom lip. He kissed her against the gag, his tongue rubbing against the wet fabric.

Quinn's breath caught. She wanted to touch him with her tongue, touch him with her hands. She pulled against the ropes harder.

She didn't necessarily want to be released—at least from the restraints. She wanted release in a different way.

Logan's mouth still worked her clit, his teeth nipping against the sensitive nub, and his fingers played along her labia. He inserted one finger in her. One finger was only a tease! And then he...hummed. Oh God, he was humming against her clit. The vibrations drove her crazy, and she screamed into the cloth, which muffled it to a dull whimper.

She mentally cursed. They wanted to drive her batty. It had to be the plan. Ty bit down on her nipple as Logan continued his humming.

Fuck!

She came, her body convulsing against Logan's measly sole finger as he teased it in and out of her.

Before her last whimper, before her last wave of the orgasm, they were both gone. She felt suddenly alone; nothing but silence and emptiness remained. She sagged against the ropes.

Where did they go?

What were they doing?

She finally heard a scuffling sound and felt someone's body heat near her.

Then she felt it.

Silky heat. Hot oil dripping over her chest, running down her body, over her nipples, down her belly, pooling around her feet.

It was hot, but not burning hot. Warm enough to feel good, like sensual fingers running over her body.

More dripped over her. A sea of heat. Over her shoulders, down her arms, trickling onto her breasts, her nipples. Quinn sucked in her stomach as the rivulets of warm liquid snaked down her skin.

A finger, she didn't care whose, drew lines against her skin, through the slippery warmth. Fingers circled around the edge of her areolae, along her ribs, dipped into her navel, smoothed the oil over her thighs. Hands cupped her calves, tickled the backs of her knees, wrapped around her ankles.

More and more hands. Too many. It felt like more than four. Dripping more oil, massaging it into her skin, working her muscles. Pinching, pulling, pushing. Plucking. Teasing the hard nubs of her nipples, the hard nub of her clit. She wanted to grip her thighs together to capture those sinful fingers, but she couldn't move. She wanted to beg for more of those wickedly wild touches, but she couldn't speak. She wanted to watch what they were doing and who was doing it, but she couldn't see.

And that made it all the more sinful, wicked, and wild.

They found sensually sensitive parts of her, hidden secret spots they manipulated *just* right. Quinn worked the fabric between her teeth, biting down in pleasure and in painful need. She wanted release. Just one more…

Fingers continued their paths along the lines of her body, and suddenly she was blinded…

Not by the blindfold…but by the light hitting her eyes. An amber light. Someone had removed the blindfold. She blinked, trying to focus.

They were there. Her two men. Her lovers. Divested of their clothes, gloriously naked, both slick and shiny with oil. Their muscles gleamed and reflected the light as they moved away from her and went to each other.

She watched helplessly, still unable to move, still unable to ask—*beg*—for her freedom. Freedom to go to them instead of just watching them.

Like a voyeur.

Her pussy clenched with want and need as she watched them slide oiled palms, glistening fingers over each other, ignoring her. Making her suffer alone.

They embraced and kissed, making sure she had the perfect view. Quinn could see their tongues tangling; she could imagine the taste of them against her own tongue. She wanted to be free, to be a part of it. Their hands found each other, each caressing the other's cock. Both hard and thick, their veins prominent underneath the thin, sensitive skin covering their steely lengths.

Large hands stroked as they continued to kiss. From tip to root, fisting, palming each other's cocks. Quinn clenched her fingers into fists and screamed with frustration into the cloth gag. They ignored her muffled protests, and she wanted to ignore them…but she couldn't. She couldn't look away.

She didn't want to.

Logan broke the kiss and nuzzled Ty's neck. Quinn could feel the grazing of his teeth against Ty's skin as if it were her own skin. A shiver shot down her spine as Logan swept his lips over the gleaming, hard pecs of Ty's chest, down his rippled abs, over one hip, and then the other, until he was on his knees before his dark lover.

He took Ty into his mouth, his lips stretching around the girth of Ty's cock. Quinn closed her eyes. Her pussy was throbbing—actually throbbing—and she couldn't even relieve herself!

Ty's low groan and hiss of breath made her look at him. His fingers were wrapped around Logan's head, guiding him along his shaft. His head was slightly back, his eyes unfocused. His hips pushed forward with every stroke of Logan's mouth. Ty's cock glistened like the rest of his body. Quinn could taste the saltiness of his precum on her tongue. She could feel the pressure of her weight on her knees. She could feel her fingers digging into his rock-hard buttocks.

She screamed in frustration again and yanked on the ropes, hard enough this time she heard the wood of the contraption she was attached to creak.

So did they.

They both shot her a worried look, but after a moment they ignored her once again. As Logan rose to his feet, Ty leaned forward and snagged Logan's pierced nipple in his mouth. He sucked and flicked the gold ring with his tongue, unmistakably pulling it hard with his teeth.

"Fuck!" Logan cried out. "Hands on your knees," he ordered.

Ty immediately did was he was told, planting his hands on his knees, giving Logan full access to what he demanded. Logan spit on his palm before stroking his damp hand along his own cock.

Suddenly Logan pinned Quinn with a stare. Their eyes met and held. He stroked his cock again, this time slower, squeezing the bulbous head when he came to it.

"Watch," he commanded her.

With one hand on Ty's back and one on his hip, Logan plunged deep, thrusting quickly. Ty moaned and wrapped a hand around his own cock, stroking it with the same rhythm as Logan fucked him.

Quinn watched the muscles in Logan's ass flex with every push and pull. She watched Ty's ass flex as he received everything Logan gave him.

Ty grimaced; his body was practically bent in half, one hand still on his knees, keeping his balance while the other stroked himself so fast, it was nothing but a blur to Quinn.

She felt a tickle of dampness run down her thighs. She ached. She watched Logan's hard cock thrusting in and out of Ty's ass, as Logan gripped his cheeks hard, making indents with his fingers, holding Ty's hips still as he pumped even faster.

He was going to come soon. He was on the edge. Quinn just knew it. She could see his body tense, his lips part, his eyelids lower.

Logan planted himself deep within Ty one last time and made small, deep jerks against him as he cried out.

Quinn could feel the warm liquid spilling into Ty's canal. Logan, once again, claiming Ty as his own. Logan curled himself over Ty's back and reached around to lay a hand over Ty's as the larger man continued to thrust into his own fist.

Logan sank his teeth into Ty's back, and Ty groaned as he came in streaming spurts.

Both men were taking quick, heaving breaths, and Quinn could imagine their hearts were still pounding.

Hers was.

Quinn's body hummed. She wanted someone, anyone. And she wanted him, them, now.

Both of her boys had just spent themselves on each other. Here she was: still hanging on the wooden X, all oiled up, and gagged.

It just wasn't fair.

She couldn't wait to get even.

Chapter Twelve

They showered her, fed her, and made her come at least twice more Friday night. It definitely made up for the earlier frustration Quinn had gone through. She made it quite clear to them that she didn't mind them tying her up, though they'd better make sure she was good and satisfied before they went off and took care of each other.

But role-playing kidnappers was now out of the question. It had scared the shit out of her, until she recognized it for what it really was. Other role-playing, depending on what it was, might be acceptable. They would take it on a case-by-case basis.

But she felt good, really good, as they settled for bed that night. Deep in her heart she felt at home sandwiched between the two of them in the large bed. She fell asleep with a long, satisfied sigh.

It felt like minutes, but it must have been hours—definitely hours, since the morning light crept through the curtains—when Quinn awoke with a start. Her body jerked, and her heel made contact with Logan's shin.

"Shit!" he yelped, pinning her legs between his. Grabbing her hips, he snuggled his groin into her rump, his morning hard-on wedged between her ass cheeks. She giggled and, not wanting to leave Ty out, pulled the other man into her arms, feeling his very ready cock brushing against her belly.

She turned a bit to give him better access and…

Screamed.

Paige Reed stood at the foot of the bed, looking at the three of them. Quinn's heart kicked into overdrive, thumping rapidly. She tugged the sheet higher up to her neck and stared at the petite brunette, who was standing with hands on her hips and a huge grin.

Shit. Shit, shit, shit.

Logan rolled onto his back and folded his arms behind his head, giving his sister a welcoming smile. Quinn noticed how he bent his knees to make sure there wasn't any obvious tenting of the sheet.

Ty apparently didn't care who knew what was lurking under the covers. And Paige's appearance sure hadn't dampened his desire. Sheesh.

Paige had noticed too, causing her smile to widen.

"Morning, boys. Just wanted to drop in and see how things were going."

She couldn't call first?

"From my perspective, it looks like things are going pretty well." Paige pinned Quinn with a stare. "How are you, Quinn?"

For a moment, Quinn had hoped she had turned into a superhero and had become invisible. Apparently not. "Oh… Uh, fine." *Until you showed up.*

"Yes…I see." And then she had the nerve to wink at Ty. "Well." She sank down onto the foot of the bed, folding her hands into her lap. "I actually came to make you guys some breakfast."

She had settled on the bed like it was a normal occurrence to see her brother in bed with not only another man but a woman too.

"If you are up for eating?" she asked carefully.

Ty chuckled and gave her one of his blinding smiles. "We never pass up one of your meals, Paige."

Paige snagged his foot, which was buried under the covers, and wiggled it playfully. "I know."

Stop touching my… Quinn gasped. *Man.* Crap.

All eyes turned to her, and she felt the blood drain from her face. Her man. She was already getting possessive of Ty and Logan. That was not a good sign.

"I'm sorry." She looked pointedly at Quinn. "I didn't mean to intrude."

Ty reached out to Paige, his voice low and raspy. "You could join us." And he had the nerve to waggle his brows up and down.

Quinn wanted to smack him.

But oh, yuck! Quinn quickly looked at Logan. He was just lying beside her with a dumb smile on his face, taking this intrusion all in stride. Acting like Ty's suggestion wasn't weird… *Oh.* Ty had been joking. This had to be a long-standing joke between them.

She felt like such a dope for being jealous.

A male voice from outside the room yelled out, "Honey?"

Ty smirked. "So you did bring breakfast, I see."

Paige smacked him lightly on the foot. "Don't even try it. He's mine. You pull him over to the dark side, and I'll never get him back."

"The dark side as in men? Or the dark side as in a black man. You know the saying—"

Paige held out her hand, stopping his words. "I know. I know." She turned her head and yelled, "Con, honey, don't bother coming in here—*Never mind*."

Connor Morgan—because who else could it be?—pushed the bedroom door open wider and took in the sight of his woman sitting on a bed with her brother and another couple quite well, Quinn thought.

Paige shrugged, leaned over, and said in a loud, dramatic whisper, "I think I'm finally figuring out I need to tell him the opposite of what I really want him to do, and *then* he'll actually do what I wanted in the first place." She gave Connor a big, syrupy smile.

"Like I didn't hear that." The tall, blond man with the Aussie accent moved over to Paige and placed a hand over her shoulder, squeezing fondly. "You know I try to do everything to please you."

"And what about last night?"

"Hey, I'm not that flexible. Sorry."

Ty's interest perked up. "I can help you train to be more flexible."

Paige yelled out a sharp "no!"

Ty laughed. "She thinks I'm going to pull you over to the dark side."

"Well, if I were going over, you wouldn't be a bad choice." Connor laughed and sat behind Paige, pulling her into his arms. "Sorry, Logan. No offense."

Logan gave a half shrug. "None taken."

The bed was getting slightly crowded. Quinn wondered who was going to join them next.

"But," Connor continued. "I think I'll stick with this little one." Paige leaned back against his chest and looked up at him lovingly. Almost with puppy-dog eyes.

For God's sake, did she look at Ty or Logan with that expression? Quinn clenched her fists tightly around the sheet.

Connor's vibrant blue eyes caught her. He released Paige long enough to extend his hand. Quinn carefully released one hand from her death grip on the sheet and shook his. His grasp was firm as he pumped her hand up and down.

"Hi, I'm Connor Morgan."

Logan finally sat up, the sheet pooling around his lap. "Sorry, I should have done introductions."

Paige did a delicate snort. "Yeah, like this is a formal setting. Puh-leeze. Connor, that's Quinn—"

"Shorty! Let me do it, damn it."

Paige held up her hands in surrender. "Okay, okay."

"Connor, this is Quinn Preston. She's our—"

"Friend," Quinn quickly interrupted, not having any idea what description, what label, Logan might put on her. This whole situation was embarrassing enough.

"She speaks!" Paige squealed and then laughed.

Quinn pressed her lips together. She had only met Paige a few times before, and each time she had liked her, but today she was getting on Quinn's nerves. It could have been because Quinn was naked under the sheets along with two other men while Paige and Connor sat there having idle conversation.

That would be reason enough in her book.

Maybe Paige saw the discomfort on Quinn's face, or maybe it was the sudden flush of heat crawling up Quinn's neck, but she quickly cleared her throat and got down to business. "Well, the reason we stopped by was—"

"We wanted you two, er, three, to be the first to know—"

"We're engaged!" Paige squealed loudly and shoved her left hand under their noses, flashing the huge diamond on her ring finger.

There were moments of hand shaking and good-natured shoulder bumps between the guys, and Logan and Ty took turns hugging Paige.

Maybe she was supposed to hug Paige too. But instead Quinn just mumbled out a "congratulations." Without warning, Connor pulled her up into a smothering hug while Quinn struggled to keep the sheet over her naked breasts.

Quinn let out a muffled "oof."

"If you want to cop a feel, come over here and give *me* a hug," Logan said to Connor.

"Oh no, brother. He's mine. Hands off."

"You're no fun, Shorty."

"Okay, here's some fun… I want you to give me away."

Paige's tumble of words had Logan leaning back against the headboard and just staring at her. Seconds ticked by, and Quinn wondered if he had even heard his sister.

In fact, she started getting worried.

So did Ty. "Lo?"

Paige went on as if Logan wasn't weren't acting strangely. "And, Ty, we want you to be one of the groomsmen. If that's okay with you?"

Ty gave her a small smile, still watching Logan with a concerned eye. "Yeah, I'd love that. Lo?" He reached behind Quinn to put a hand on Logan's upper arm; he gave him a slight nudge.

Finally Logan seemed to snap out of his…whatever it was. And Quinn realized she had been holding her breath. She let it out and unclenched her fingers from her firm grip on the sheet.

She leaned over to Logan and asked softly, "Are you okay?"

Logan held her gaze for a moment, his unreadable but intense look causing the hairs on the back of her neck to rise. Then he broke the eye contact and looked at Paige.

"I'd be honored to give you away, Shorty." His voice had cracked a bit.

Brother and sister stared at each other as if they were sharing a secret. Everyone in the room froze for a second, before Connor squeezed Paige's shoulders, breaking the spell.

"Paige wanted that more than anything," Connor said.

"Are you getting married in a church?" Logan asked Paige.

She just laughed in answer, causing Logan to groan in response. "Shorty, you know how I feel about churches."

Ty nudged him one more time before settling his arm around Quinn's bare shoulders. "We'll just get out your aluminum-foil hat to protect you from God's fury when you're at the church."

"No!" Paige's eyes became as big a platters. "Aluminum foil is forbidden as part of the wardrobe."

"Yeah, T. You think it's funny, but—"

"But what? Don't you think the man upstairs has bigger things to worry about than your past?"

Jeez. What had Logan done?

Ty's fingertips traced circles over Quinn's shoulder, drawing a shiver from her. Her nipples hardened like two big goose bumps underneath the sheet, which instantly drew Connor's gaze.

That didn't go unnoticed from Logan.

"Okay, let's let the women have some girl talk as we men go into the kitchen and do some real men's work, like starting breakfast."

The three guys laughed in agreement, and Ty and Logan started to peel the sheet away to get up when Paige yelled for them to hold it. They did. She exclaimed she didn't want to see her brother's naked nether area, so she dug around in the dresser drawers and pulled out two pairs of boxer-briefs. She tossed one pair to Logan, who began to pull them on immediately, and went to toss the other pair to Ty, when she hesitated.

"Forget it. You don't need these. I want to see what you've got."

With a grumble of fake exasperation, Connor snagged the pair of underwear from Paige's fingers and threw them at Ty. "Oh no. You are not showing her shit. If she sees what you have, I will never be able to live up to that. It's better she doesn't know there's anything bigger than what she's already getting."

"Oh, sweetie, I already know…but I love you anyway."

With some good-natured ribbing, all three men departed, leaving Quinn and Paige alone.

"You'll come too, Quinn?"

Her soft question caught Quinn off guard. "Come?"

"To our wedding."

She wants me to say yes, when it could be a year away?

"Oh. I don't know. We'll see." *We'll see where we all are at that time.*

"The guys will need a date."

Now she was just trying to get on Quinn's good side. A date.

Quinn shook her head. "They have each other."

Paige pursed her lips and hesitated a second before saying cautiously, "They do, but…now you're here."

Quinn narrowed her eyes. Just what did Paige think was going on? Besides what was obvious, of course.

"I think you are mistaken in—"

"Listen," Paige interrupted. "I'm sorry for barging in on you guys. I had no idea. In fact, I never would have expected to find a woman in Logan's bed again."

"Why? I thought they—"

"Did this with other women?" Paige frowned. "I don't know. I don't think so." Her delicate eyebrows pinned together. "At least, I've never caught other women here. I mean, I'm not here all the time, but I do stop in quite often. I help with the books for the business."

Paige shifted and pulled herself on the bed farther. Closer to Quinn. Quinn wasn't sure if she liked that. The other woman was getting a bit too comfortable on the bed for her liking. But Paige curled her legs underneath her. It didn't look like she planned on leaving the bedroom anytime soon. And Quinn wasn't either, since she was naked under the sheet. She slid farther beneath said sheet.

Well, she might as well take advantage of this bonding—or whatever it was—and get some good info out of Logan's sister.

"Why do you think that is? Why me? Why now?"

Paige put up a hand to stop Quinn's questions and just shook her head. "I don't know the answers. You would have to talk to them. Logan, maybe. Don't know." She tilted her head and studied Quinn for a moment. "Look, I love my brother, and Ty coming into his life was the best thing that ever happened to him. I don't want anything ruining that.

I'm not saying you would, but Logan's happy now. He has a good relationship, a successful business, and"—she waved a hand around the room—"look at this place."

She was acting like this was something permanent. It wasn't. Quinn wanted to clarify that, but when she opened her mouth, Paige stopped her again.

"Listen. His wife screwed him up for a while. She made him feel dirty and abnormal. He's not. He just wants to love someone who loves him back."

That last sounded very familiar to Quinn. She had said something similar to Logan when he had asked her about kids.

"Logan's wife…" Quinn prodded after Paige hadn't said anything after a few moments.

Paige just about spit on the floor. "That self-righteous bitch."

Quinn winced. "Ouch."

"Oh. She deserves the title, believe me. Logan…Logan had a relationship with an older man when he was a teenager."

"Okay." That news did not surprise Quinn. Paige wanted to explain but acted a bit reluctant. She was curious as to why. "And?"

"When my mother found out—Did Logan tell you she raised us by herself? He did? Okay, well… When Mom found out, she sent Logan to our uncle's place in Kentucky for the summer. She thought he was just experimenting, that he was hanging around with the wrong crowd. She believed he just needed a male figure in his life. Believe me, Logan was always all male, so it was all just bunk. But Mom thought he would grow out of it." Paige took a deep breath.

"He says he's not gay. He's bi."

Paige waved a hand. "Semantics. Samantha and Logan met in college. I think he married her to get back into my mom's good graces. Not sure. But when my mom spilled the beans about the summer he turned seventeen—whoa. Logan was suddenly a pariah. No matter that Logan was completely faithful to her. Samantha didn't care. All her little Catholic ass cared about was that he had sullied himself with another man. Totally unacceptable. She left so quick, the front door was still swinging when the annulment papers were signed."

"He was devastated."

"Yes. To put it mildly. He was condemned by her and her religious views. That's why the reaction to the church thing."

"Does he want you to be telling me all of this? Is he going to mind?"

Paige shrugged. "I don't know. I'm sure he knows we're talking about something in here, and it's not crocheting." Paige laughed at her own funny. She sobered quickly. "You seem to be accepting of the situation, with Logan and Ty."

"Well, honestly, it caught me off guard at first. But I'm an adult. I could have left."

"But you didn't want to."

No. She didn't want to. She didn't want to admit it out loud to Paige. Paige who was friends with Lana.

Shit.

If Paige says anything to Lana... If Lana finds out where I spent the last couple of weekends, what I've been doing...who I've been doing it with...

Quinn released her bottom lip when she tasted blood. Damn. She hadn't even realized she'd been gnawing at it.

If Lana finds out, everyone will know. As much as she loved her friend, Quinn knew Lana had loose lips. It was one of her endearing but exasperating faults.

Quinn sat up quickly, the sheet slipping down, dangerously close to showing some nipple. "Paige, please, you can't tell anybody," she begged as she pulled the edge of the cover up higher, trying to keep at least *some* semblance of modesty.

Though she wondered why she bothered.

Paige was giving her a surprised but disappointed look. "Why? Are you embarrassed to be with my brother?"

"No. No! It's not like that."

"No? Then what is it like?"

"It's the complexity of the issue, I guess."

"Complexity? Hmm. You mean screwing two men at once?"

Quinn felt the heat of her blush. Her cheeks were burning. She couldn't meet Paige's eyes, even though the other woman was only stating facts; what she had said was true.

But that didn't mean it wasn't uncomfortable to admit.

"Quinn, you're lucky."

Quinn looked up in surprise. "What do you mean?"

"You're lucky to have two guys like these, wanting you. I'm jealous."

"Why would you be jealous? You have Connor."

"You're right. I do, and I love him. A lot." Paige's lips twitched. "But sometimes I wonder what it would be like to have the attention of two men…"

"Does Connor have any big, beefy friends?"

"Oh yeah. He certainly does!"

They both laughed, feeling absolutely wicked.

But Quinn sobered quickly. "So…can you keep this to yourself?"

Paige looked down at the floor for a moment before meeting Quinn's eyes. The perky little brunette was gone, replaced with someone fiercely serious.

"I don't have a problem with keeping a secret. I understand this isn't the norm and might not be received well in certain—oh hell—most circles. I wouldn't do anything to hurt you, nor to jeopardize my brother's happiness. If he's happy with this arrangement, then so am I."

Quinn reached out tentatively and touched Paige's arm. "Thank you."

Maybe there might be a friendship in the future between her and Logan's sister. Just maybe.

Chapter Thirteen

As Quinn sat in the stuffy dining room at the Mandolin Bay Country Club Sunday night, she already regretted having to leave the farm early. She wished she was sitting at the large butcher-block table instead of here. She hated her parents' favorite hangout—the place to see and be seen by the wealthy. It was gaudy and ostentatious. Too much so for Quinn's taste.

Even the waiters were snobs, she thought, as their waiter, Robert—no, that wasn't Robert like the normal American way of saying it. *Ro-bear*, as it was pronounced, insisted on draping her stiff, ultrawhite cloth napkin in her lap like it was too heavy for Quinn to do it herself.

As soon as he sauntered away, Quinn threw the napkin back on the table.

"Quinn, stop being so difficult," her mother tsk-tsked.

"You know I don't like being fussed over." Well, at least not by snobby waiters dressed like penguins. She had reluctantly left two men an hour ago who she didn't mind fussing over her. In fact, she enjoyed it. Couldn't get enough of it.

Quinn sighed.

Her father sat silently across from her, nursing his Tanqueray and tonic, while her mother started on a diatribe of useless gossip and information that Quinn couldn't care less about. Her father was obviously blocking out her mother's rambling, clearly noticeable by his glassy-eyed, blank stare and the fact that his glass never touched the table. His elbow was getting quite a workout.

As her mother had nothing important to talk about, and her father had absolutely nothing at all to discuss—not that he was allowed a chance—Quinn wondered why they had even wanted to get together for dinner.

She got her answer when the one person she didn't want to see just *happened* to run into them during their main course. Quinn almost choked on her squab—she had ordered the most expensive entrée on the menu to make it worth her while—when Peter did a drive-by of their table. Only he didn't just strike and run. Unfortunately.

Quinn hadn't seen her father move so fast in a long time. He was up and out of his chair, pumping Peter's hand enthusiastically, while her mother fussed with her primped hair and cooed as Peter kissed her knuckles with exaggeration. In exchange, he received air kisses on both cheeks.

Quinn fought back her vomit. She looked down at her squab and suddenly saw it with new eyes. She saw it for the pigeon it really was. She covered her plate with her napkin and sucked down a mouthful of cabernet.

Peter pulled out the empty chair next to her and plopped down, giving her a big grin. If he tried to kiss her hello, he was going to get a dead pigeon shoved up his nose. She didn't care what kind of scene that would make.

"Imagine my surprise, running into you here."

Yes, she could just imagine. Her parents had settled back into their chairs, and her father was waving Ro-bear over, his glassy-eyed stare long gone.

Quinn watched in disgust as Ro-bear brought over another place setting and poured Peter a glass of wine. Her cabernet. She curled her fingers against the urge to selfishly yank the bottle out of the waiter's pale fingers and scream: *mine, mine, mine!* If she had to sit with Peter for the rest of the ruined meal, she would need the remainder of the bottle. At least.

"So…"

So, you are an asshole.

"…you look great." He leaned over toward her a fraction. "Positively glowing."

Maybe because she had just gotten laid just a few hours ago by two men? Maybe that was it. It was a postcoital glow. She was so tempted to let that fact fly. But she gritted her teeth, pinned on a fake smile, and glanced over at her father.

She didn't want him to drop dead on her account. Now Peter, on the other hand…

Peter squirmed in his seat a bit when Quinn's only answer was the evil eye. He quickly cleared his throat and turned his charm on her mother.

"So, I'm looking forward to the House to Home Charity Monte Carlo Night next weekend."

House to Home Charity? Monte Carlo Night? Was that another reason her parents wanted to have dinner with her? Her mother knew it would be harder for Quinn to turn her down in person than if she had just called. Excuses were so much easier to give over the phone.

Trapped again.

Quinn looked over at her mother expectantly. At least she had the grace to look a little uncomfortable. Her mother's fingers fussed with the string of pearls around her neck.

“Yes, our Society Ladies' Charity Club has worked very hard on this. We want it to be a great success.”

Okay, this was such a setup. She couldn't believe she had stepped right into it.

“Mother, why haven't I heard anything about this before now?”

“Oh. I thought I told you.”

Uh-huh.

“No. You didn't.”

“Well, I talked to Frank, and the company is making a large donation,” her mother said.

Frank. Quinn mentally groaned. Now other was dragging her boss into this. Frank was one of the senior partners in the insurance company she worked for.

“He can't make it, so he suggested you present the check next weekend.”

Oh no. Now she couldn't refuse to come. Couldn't make excuses. She would look like a big schmuck if she refused to go. Not to mention that refusing to represent the company at her mother's charity event might be detrimental to her career.

Especially a worthwhile charity, one that rebuilt homes for victims of natural disasters.

Even so, Quinn didn't like being backed into a corner.

"And you're going to bring in a great price at the date auction." Peter gave her a knowing look.

The corner was getting much, much smaller.

"That was my idea, dear." Her father finally spoke. Since when had her father had his own ideas? Her mother might as well surgically implant her thoughts right into his brain.

Her gaze flashed to her father before returning to study Peter's sickening grin. Quinn pressed a finger to her ear and wiggled it. Maybe she had imagined what he had just said. "I'm sorry? I thought you said *date auction*."

Her mother leaned over the table and patted her hand automatically. There wasn't a drop of sympathy coming from her; she just didn't want Quinn to make a scene. As if Quinn would do that.

Ha.

"You heard Peter right. We have had quite a selection of volunteers. A few local newscasters and local athletes, like Ben Johnson. Do you know who Ben Johnson is?"

Of course she did. He was a popular player for the local NHL farm team. She, apparently, just didn't know anything about the NFL. The NHL she had covered. Right.

"But, Mother, I didn't agree to this."

Her mother swooshed a well-manicured, heavily bejeweled hand in the air. "Quinn, you can't turn us down.

The evening's program has been already printed up. And anyway, it would be selfish if you turned it down. We need all the money we can get."

Quinn took a deep breath and counted to ten. When she finished, she glanced at Peter's smug expression and decided to count to twenty.

They were all in cahoots. All of them.

"Are you in this auction too?" she asked Peter, though she already knew the answer.

"No, I'll be one of the bidders. Should be an exciting night."

It certainly would be. There was no way she was going to have Peter win a date with her. He'd had his chance with her. And blew it. It was too late for him.

She would have to figure something out. Some way to escape the evening with her sanity. But without Peter.

"If you need me to go shopping with you, honey, I can. It's going to be black-tie."

"No, Mother, I'll do my own shopping. What else is going on at this Monte Carlo Night, besides you pimping me out?"

"Oh, dear, don't be so crass," her father said before finishing off the last of his gin and tonic. He caught Ro-bear's attention and pointed to his glass. Ro-bear scurried away to retrieve a fresh drink like the good little waiter he was.

Her father had the right idea. Alcohol. Quinn drained the last of her glass and then snagged Peter's. He hadn't touched his with his cheating lips. It would be a shame to let it go to waste.

"There's the dinner and cocktail hour, the gaming tables, like blackjack and poker. After that, we'll have the live bachelor and bachelorette auction. We might have a couple of celebrities stopping by to sign autographs and take pictures."

"And the cost?"

"Oh, honey, we covered your plate."

Her plate.

"It's going to be a cash bar, with all the proceeds going to the fund, and of course, all of the auction monies will be too."

"Cost per plate?"

Her mother hesitated for a split second. "Oh, it's reasonable."

"Mother—"

Her father, looking around desperately for Ro-bear, interrupted. "It's a thousand dollars a plate, sweetie. Very reasonable."

Quinn put her, or actually Peter's, wineglass down before she spit all over her father. "You paid for a plate for me?"

"I told you it's covered."

"But, Dad—"

He pinned her with a very fatherlike stare. "Enough. It's covered."

She suddenly felt thirteen again.

Things hadn't changed. Her father was her mother's puppet. Even if he disagreed with something she said or did or wanted, he felt it was easier to appease her. Easier for him. Not for Quinn. Never for Quinn. He had never stood up for her.

Peter curled a hand around Quinn's shoulder. "Your parents are generous, and they want you to be there."

Quinn glared at his hand and bit back a growl. She must have sneered, though, because Peter quickly removed his endangered digits as if he had touched a flame.

Not only were her parents throwing her in Peter's path tonight, but they were forcing her to attend a function she did not want to attend *just* so that they could throw her in his path again—even when they *knew* what he had done to her. They should have just thrown her under a bus. It would have been quicker and more effective.

She looked down at her cold squab, the juice gelling on the plate. She pushed it away in disgust.

What she had eaten already felt like a lead balloon in her stomach. She couldn't believe just a few hours ago she had been happy and actually feeling carefree. In the arms of her two lovers. And now?

Quinn pushed her chair back and popped to her feet.

Her father and Peter jumped up, like the true gentlemen they were supposed to be.

"I've got to go."

"Are you okay, honey?"

Her mother had the nerve to ask her that? When she had just effectively trapped Quinn into something she didn't want to do?

"Just peachy."

Quinn strode quickly away from the table, knocking into Ro-bear on her way out. He fought to not spill her father's fresh Tanqueray and tonic. As Quinn gave him an evil grin, she thought she couldn't escape this nightmare soon enough.

* * *

"They're pimping me out." A tear plopped heavily into her glass of wine.

Logan *shhed* her over the phone, trying his best to soothe her. It wasn't working.

"What are you talking about?"

"They are whoring me out."

What part of pimping and whoring wasn't clear?

Logan's chuckle grated on her nerves. "C'mon, Quinn. Really. What's going on?"

He wasn't taking her seriously. If he needed her to spell it out…"They are selling me to the highest bidder."

"What do you mean? Like an arranged marriage?"

"No." Her lips quivered, and she sniffled loudly. She never cried. So why now? "They are auctioning me off, and Peter is going to win me."

"Who the hell is Peter?"

Ah. Now he was taking her a little more seriously. Mention one man to make another more interested. "My ex."

There was a pregnant pause on the other end of the phone.

"Okay. Still a little confused. Have you been drinking?"

"Do you blame me? They are purposely doing shit to get Peter and me back together."

"And you don't want that."

"Of course not! I'm—"*Happy being with you two.* "I don't want him."

She didn't even want to think about him, let alone go out on a pimped-out, bought-with-cold-cash date with him. Charity or not.

"What do you want?"

"Not to be auctioned off. Not to go to this charity event. I hate black-tie affairs."

She heard him sigh. "I'm not real fond of them myself."

She needed to stop feeling sorry for herself and get to the reason why she had called him in the first place. "I need Ty's and your help."

"Sure. What do you need?"

"I need a date for this *thing*."

"*Thing*. A date." Another pause, as if he was turning the idea over in his head. "Okay, but who do you want to go?"

Who?

"Quinn, which one of us do you want to go?"

Which one? As if she'd be able to choose. She didn't even think of them individually. They were a bonded pair. A couple. "Both. I want you both to come with me. I want you both to be my dates."

Another pause. A long one this time. "I don't know, Quinn. That might not be such a good idea."

"I don't care."

"You might think differently in the morning, after whatever you're drinking is out of your system."

"Wine."

"What?"

Quinn picked up the bottle and turned it to read the label. "Wine. A really nice, tasty merlot."

She splashed a little more in her glass and pushed the bottle aside. She got up from the kitchen stool and paced around the room, the cordless phone to her ear.

Would he—they—turn her down? Would he refuse to go or let Ty go because of a possible controversy? Because it might cause problems with her parents? No, not might, she had a good idea it definitely would. But she didn't want them to feel as if they were being used. Pawns in her revenge against her parents. Against Peter.

But if anyone was going to be at her side that night, she wanted Logan and Ty. Not one or the other. Both.

"Are you sure about this?"

"I've never been so sure in my life."

"Things might never be the same again."

"I'm hoping so."

"I want you to think hard about this."

"I don't have time to think about this. The Monte Carlo Night is Saturday."

"Wait. This Saturday?"

"Mmm hmm."

"Shit. I'd have to get a tux."

"I don't care what you wear. Come naked, for all I care." Naked, in a tux—he would look hot either way. The coral snake tattoo wrapping around his hip was gorgeous. Everyone should see that. All right, maybe her mother wouldn't be so impressed.

Logan laughed. "Yeah, you think you have problems now? Think about the problems you'd have if Ty and I showed up naked."

Quinn wiped the moisture from her cheek and smiled. "Nobody would be able to stop looking at Ty's package."

"Hey! I'm no slouch."

"No, you're not. I wish you were here right now, showing me what you've got."

"I wish I were too."

"I miss you guys," she said.

"We miss you too, baby, but you only left here a few hours ago."

"It seems like forever."

"Maybe it's because it's close to midnight."

"Crap. Is it?" The clock hanging above the sink said he was right. She groaned. "I have to go to the office in the morning."

"Then you'd better go to bed."

Yes, bed would be good. But not alone. Not by choice. "With you."

"Okay." His voice changed, getting a little gruffer, a little more demanding. "Go to your room."

"Why?"

"Don't question me. Just do it. Go to your room."

She had already kicked off her shoes earlier when she had gone through the front door, so she now padded up the carpeted steps to the second floor in just her stocking feet.

When she got to the top of the stairway, she balanced her half-full wineglass in one hand and held the cordless phone to her ear in the other.

"You still there?" she asked him breathlessly.

"Are you in your bedroom?"

A few more steps and she was. She moved through the room and set her glass down on the nightstand.

"Yes."

"What are you wearing?"

A streak of hot lightning shot through her, and her toes curled against the Berber carpeting.

"I have on a V-neck dress and stockings."

"Okay, we'll start with those."

Quinn's heart beat rapidly. She wished the boys were there, where she could touch them. Feel them.

"Does your dress have a zipper?" Logan's voice made her nipples pebble hard, and they began to ache. She needed his touch. Badly.

"Yes," she whispered.

"Unzip it. Slowly."

She grabbed the zipper at the back of her neck.

"Make sure you do it slowly, and I want to hear the zipper opening."

Quinn transferred the phone into her other hand, while she did as she was told. She reached behind her to work the zipper down, making sure the receiver was close enough to pick up the grating of the metallic teeth as they parted. The zipper stopped at the small of her back.

She put the phone back up to her ear.

"What color is your dress?"

"Red."

"Push that red dress down over your shoulders. Now over your arms. Let it drop to the floor."

She did just that, feeling the soft fabric caressing her skin as it slipped off her shoulders. The dress gathered for a moment at her elbows before landing at her feet with a soft swish.

"Now. Describe what you are wearing."

"I—" Her voice caught. She had to look down at herself, because her brain was spinning, and at the moment, she could have been naked and not remembered. "A black bra, lacy on the top, black satin bikini panties, and nude stockings that come up almost to the tops of my thighs."

"Get on the bed."

"Logan—"

"Do it."

Those two words, even through the phone, were powerful. That simple command made her body quiver. Made her ache. Made her wet with wanting.

She loved it when he took command.

"Are you on the bed yet?"

She scrambled onto the bed, sitting back against the decorative pillows she had piled near the carved oak headboard.

His voice now sounded different.

“Did you put me on speakerphone?”

“Yes,” Logan said. “Ty is here. I want you to put us on speakerphone too.”

She heard Ty's voice, though at a distance. “Did you do what he told you yet? Are you on the bed?”

“I'm on the bed.” She hit the Speaker button on the receiver and laid it next to her hip.

Logan's commanding voice came clearly through the cordless phone. “Unhook your bra. I want to feel your breasts.”

Quinn reached behind her and unfastened the little eye hooks. The bra fell forward, and she pulled her arms out of the straps and threw the bra to the end of the bed. Her nipples were at hard points, begging for a greedy mouth. Or two.

“Quinn, I want to feel your breasts,” Logan repeated.

She had never had phone sex before and wasn't sure what he wanted her to do. She ran her hands down around the heavy curves of her breasts and lifted them up, squeezing them together.

“Quinn?”

“Yesss?” The word hissed out of her.

“Are your nipples hard?”

“Very.”

"Do they need pinched?"

"Yes." Oh yes. By very unforgiving male fingers.

"Do it."

She did as she was told. Gladly.

Her eyes drifted shut as she pushed her breasts together again and brushed the pads of her thumbs over the tips of her nipples. She imagined them to be Logan's thumbs. Ty's thumbs.

She arched her back and moaned. She plucked at them with her forefingers and thumbs and then clamped down, twisting them until she cried out.

Quinn kept her eyes closed as she imagined the boys with her. Doing to her what she was doing to herself. "They're very hard. I love it when you twist them like that. I love it when you pluck at them and suck them deep into your mouth. Twist them and nip them until the pain is so incredibly pleasurable. I need you to squeeze them with your big, rough hands until I want you to fuck me."

She wasn't paying attention to what she was saying; she was babbling. Her mouth was open, and words were coming out.

"Ah. *Jesus*," came from the speaker on her phone.

She released one breast to run her right palm down her stomach and into her panties.

"I'm so wet for you now. I'm dripping. I need you guys to be deep inside me, plunging in and out until I cry out. Until you cry out."

She pressed a finger between her slick folds and teased her swollen clit. "My clit is so hard; it feels so good when you circle it with your fingers and your tongue."

Her finger found a rhythm of pressing the hard button and circling. She added a second finger and circled harder. Her left hand continued to play with her breasts, plucking and pulling one nipple and then the other.

She pushed her hips into her hand, her fingers abandoning her clit and shoving deep within her pussy. "*Oh*... Ah, fuck." She pushed her palm against her mound, keeping pressure against her clit with the heel of her hand as she moved her fingers in the opposite rhythm of her hips. Her head fell back against the headboard, and she caught her bottom lip in her teeth.

"Omigod. *Shit*."

"Feels good, doesn't it, baby?"

"So good."

"Are we deep enough inside you? Are we hard enough for you?"

"Always hard enough... Always... No. I want you deeper." She rolled her head back and forth against the headboard as she tried to sink her fingers deeper. It wasn't deep enough. Not nearly deep enough.

"Are you going to pull us in deeper?"

Logan's voice rushed over her like a wave. She could feel his breath against her neck, his teeth grazing against her earlobe.

She opened her eyes suddenly and jerked her hands away from herself. She rolled over quickly to the nightstand, knocking the cordless handset over. She yanked the nightstand drawer open and blindly grabbed for her girl's best friend. A strange mix between a giggle and a sigh bubbled out of her when her fingers bumped against what she was looking for. Her seven-inch, multispeed, flexible, jelly vibrator.

Logan's voice was muffled against the bedspread. "Quinn? Quinn? Are you all right?"

She held the pink battery-operated piece of heaven to her chest and shuffled back to the middle of the bed. She uprighted the phone.

"Now I am."

"What happened?"

Quinn twisted the dial on the bottom of the vibrator to full speed, and it came to life, humming against her skin.

"Oh," was all Logan said, and she swore she heard Ty in the background laughing.

He could laugh all he wanted. She was past the point of caring.

She was at the point of desperation. Of need.

She rolled the humming vibrator across her one tight nipple as she fingered the other. It only took her seconds to get back into her sex play. Her eyes drifted shut once more as she pictured the boys in the bed with her, with Logan taking charge, of course.

"How does it feel?"

Quinn rolled the sex toy back and forth over her nipple, the pulsations shooting from the hard tip down to her toes, which curled in pleasure.

"You...you have no...idea."

"Put it against your clit."

She slid the head of the realistic-looking vibrator between her breasts and over her sternum, past her belly button. She pressed it to her clit through the silky fabric of her panties. Her hips shot up as the vibrations rocked her to the core.

She must have made a sound, or many sounds, but she never heard them; she could only hear the blood rushing in her ears.

It took her a second before she realized Logan was speaking to her. Giving her the next command.

"Peel your panties down. I want you to expose yourself to me."

That would mean putting down her toy. But it felt so good...

She stroked it over her folds, feeling the heat already emanating from her pussy. She slid it along the damp fabric one more time before putting it aside with regret.

She hooked her thumbs into the waistband of her black panties and wiggled them over her hips.

"They are over my hips, down my thighs, brushing against my stockings, now over my knees, ankles. Okay, they're off."

"Run your hands over your ankles and go up slowly."

She encircled her ankles with her hands and lightly brushed her fingers over her stocking-encased calves, around the back of her knees, and up over her thighs. She rounded the tops of her thigh-high stockings until the backs of her hands met near the apex of her thighs.

"Spread your legs and bend your knees."

Again, she did as she was told. She had no reason not to.

"Tell me how wet you are."

Quinn strummed fingers over her folds, feeling the moisture around her tightly trimmed pubic area. Her labia were swollen, slick, in desperate need of attention.

"Very wet. I'm so slick, you won't need lube."

"I'd bet you'd taste really sweet right now."

The high-pitched buzz of the vibrator brought her attention back to it. Her pussy contracted at the thought of what it would do to her. How it would make her come, so easily. How it had been her only form of release many times in the past.

It had been a better companion than her former lover.

She had two good—no, great—lovers now. Not one but two. She might be able to retire her toy forever. That was, if they kept her in their lives. Forever.

Or at least for a while.

But the toy would have to do for now. They weren't here. They were a half hour away, probably entangled with each other, touching each other, while she lay in her bed alone.

"Quinn."

She picked up the vibrator and ran her fingers over it, wishing it were real. She looked at the head, wishing it were glistening with precum.

"Quinn."

"I'm here."

"Touch yourself."

The vibrator shook within her hand, and she slid the toy over her slick pussy lips, spreading her juices, getting herself—once again—back into the game. With two fingers, she spread herself and worked the length of the toy back and forth from the tip to the root, but not penetrating. Just teasing herself, telling herself how good it felt. And it did.

Conceivably it could take her seconds to orgasm with her toy. She knew how to please herself quickly, but that wasn't what this was about. It was about making a connection with the boys—her boys—even when they were not close by.

She put the vibrating tip against her clit, just lightly, and her pussy clenched, wanting a hard length within it, wanting to be filled. She didn't move the toy, just held it still, and before she knew it, she was crying out as her clit twitched and pulsed. The intense spasms were over quickly, and she heard heavy breathing on the phone.

She closed her eyes and stretched out on the bed, trying to picture what they were doing with each other. Probably running hands over their hard bodies, stroking themselves, kissing.

Quinn let out a long, shuddering sigh.

"Did you come?" Logan's voice sounded strained.

It wasn't over yet. That small explosion of pleasure was just the beginning.

She still had the urge. The deep itch that needed scratched. That little orgasm was nice, but she'd had better.

"I want more," she told him.

Her clit was now a bit on the sensitive side, so she bypassed it this time, again sliding the vibrating toy over her slick, swollen folds. She pinned her thighs together, trapping the vibrator between her legs. The sensations of the toy echoed through her thighs, hips, and lower belly.

"I want to come harder."

She forced herself to spread her thighs as she slipped the end of the vibrator inside her. Just head-deep. The latex cock hummed away, and she pushed it deeper, her hips rising to meet it. She spread her lips to accommodate the girth of the fake cock.

"I want your big cock in me. I want it in me so far, your balls are smacking against my ass."

She thought she heard Logan drop the phone.

"How deep do you want us?"

"To the hilt."

"Are your thighs spread?"

"Yes."

"Okay, I want you to slide that thing in you as deep as possible."

Quinn twisted the vibrator, working it in deeper, burying it as far as it would go.

The vibrations radiated throughout her core, driving her mad. She didn't know what to do first, whether to jam it in deep over and over or to just let it ride. Let it sit as the pleasure slowly built until the climax crept up on her. Those were usually her most intense orgasms. The ones that came from nowhere. So unexpected.

She decided to keep it buried and tilted it toward the front of her body just to make sure it hit that special spot. When she found it, Quinn kept the toy there. Let the vibrations work their magic.

"Oh God!" Her hips lifted off the bed, and suddenly the pulsing began. It began deep within her and radiated out. Her thighs tensed and quivered, and she finally bucked against the bed as little mews escaped her.

Her eyes were pinned tightly closed, and her breathing rasped from between her lips as she floated down from the orgasm high she had. Her body felt boneless, her chest rising and falling with each gasp of breath she took. She drew the now-glistening vibrator from her pussy. She dropped the toy to the bedspread and ran a hand languidly up her stomach and over her chest until her fingers rested on her throat.

The phone was silent next to her. She called out, "Are you there?"

"We're here."

Quinn's eyes popped open at Ty's voice. It was close, but it wasn't coming from the phone. Logan snapped his cell phone shut and tucked it into his jeans' pocket. He gave her a heated smile.

They were there. In her house. Her two boys. Unbelievable.

They crowded the door to her bedroom, staring at her naked and spread-eagled on her bed. Just barely after she had finished pleasuring herself.

She had wished they were there.

They were.

How?

With a hand on Ty's wrist, Logan pulled him a few steps farther into the bedroom. He turned to the darker man and grabbed the hem of Ty's shirt, whisking it up and off his torso, exposing the rich cocoa brown of the taller man's skin, the solid black flames licking up his rib cage and his perfect black nipples.

Those nipples were at a hard point, and Logan did what Quinn wanted to do. He flicked one with his tongue before pulling it deep into his mouth.

Ty's chest surged, and he sank his fingers into Logan's ponytailed hair. Quinn rose up on her elbows to watch her men. *Her* men.

But Logan pulled back. He turned suddenly, his eyes piercing her.

"We were on our way back from dinner in the city when you called."

Ah. That couldn't have been more convenient for her. For all of them.

Ty pushed past Logan, unsnapping the top of his jeans as he approached the bed. "We skipped dessert." He dropped to his knees at the foot of the bed, his expression heated as he looked at Quinn. His gaze raked down her face, over her chest, and landed on her cunt. "I intend to change that." In a flash, he had wrapped his fingers around her hips and dragged her to the edge of the bed.

When her rear end was at the edge of the mattress, he parted her thighs. Dragging a finger in between her folds, he parted her swollen lips.

"You are so juicy. I'd bet you taste perfect." With that, he buried his face between her legs.

Ty's tongue against her heated skin made her gasp. His hands slid underneath her hips, lifting her until she was at a better angle, giving him full access to his "dessert."

His tongue felt rough against her already-sensitive nub. Her clit jerked against every stroke of his tongue, every pluck of his lips.

In her peripheral vision, she saw Logan stripping out of his clothes. She tried to turn her attention toward him. He was a sight to be seen. His body almost perfect. But Ty's actions between her thighs kept drawing her back.

He sucked her clitoris, spreading her labia with his thumbs to open her up wide. Two large fingers entered her and curved upward, stroking her special spot as his lips, his tongue, and his teeth teased her hard button, which again protruded from its hood.

A long breath hissed from between her lips. Ty's smooth head looked out of place between her thighs; his cocoa brown fingers dug into her pale skin, holding her in place.

The bed tilted as Logan climbed onto the mattress and positioned himself at her head. He nestled her between his thighs, his hard cock brushing against her cheek, his warm sac against her hair.

Quinn tilted her head back, wanting access to him, wanting to taste him. He had wedged her head tightly into the apex of his thighs, and she couldn't move.

Once again, he was in control.

She looked up as he knelt above her, the vibrant colors of his coral snake catching her eye. And upward, to the gleaming golden ring in his nipple. It protruded more than normal, as if someone had been tugging it, playing with it, teasing Logan.

She had a fleeting question on what had gone on between the two of them after she had left the farm earlier that day. She reminded herself she was the third wheel in the dynamics of their relationship. She was the extra. Though every time she was with them, she never felt as if that were true.

Logan dropped forward, his chest hairs tickling her face as he scooped her breasts into his palms and squeezed them together.

Finally she had something close to her mouth. She snagged his pierced nipple as soon it was within range and poked her tongue through the ring to tug not so gently.

Logan pushed his chest against her mouth, his body tensing.

"Oh, you are fucking wicked." He grasped both of her nipples between his fingers and yanked.

Quinn quickly let him go and cried out. She didn't cry out for him to stop, though; she wanted him to continue.

He leaned over again, his nipple tantalizingly close once more. She sucked it into her mouth and worked it with her tongue, flipping the nipple ring back and forth.

She reached up and grabbed his other nipple and mirrored what he was doing to her. His mouth fell greedily upon her breast, and he nipped at her while Ty continued to devour her as if she were a buffet.

Ty's fingers teased her sweet spot until she tilted her hips, shoving her throbbing pussy harder against his mouth. He pressed his forearm over her hips, pinning her down to the mattress. Logan quickly flipped around, straddling her chest, careful to keep his weight on his knees. His slick head bumped against her lips.

Quinn took Logan's cock deep as he wrapped his hands around the back of her head, lifting. Logan thrust in and out between her lips, his fingers winding into her hair and pulling tight.

The tight skin over Logan's cock tasted sweet but salty. It was silk over steel against her tongue and between her lips as she created suction from the root to the tip. Logan kept eye contact with her, which made it all the more erotic.

Quinn moaned around his hard length when Ty grasped her clit between his lips and sucked hard. His fingers continued an assault on her wet pussy, increasing the intensity and speed. She quickly pulled away from Logan's cock as her orgasm exploded from her core; she didn't want to accidently maim him.

She sucked in a shaky breath and released a long wail, throwing her head back and feeling the pull of her hair that was still wrapped around Logan's fingers. He refused to release her, and as soon as she stopped convulsing and caught her breath, he pushed his cock back between her lips.

Her coming had made him even harder, and the precum was leaking faster than she could lap it up.

The bed shifted again as Ty moved up behind Logan, framing his muscular thighs around Quinn's waist. The contrast of the dark chocolate hue of Ty's arms enveloping the golden skin of Logan was jolting. It made her pulse hammer through her, all the way to her core. She wanted to pin her thighs together to relieve the ache.

Ty's large hands caressed Logan's nipples as he buried his lips against Logan's shoulder. Logan leaned his head back on Ty's shoulder, giving his lover access to lick along his collarbone and up his neck. Ty pinned Logan's chin with his fingers and turned him enough so he could capture Logan's mouth and take it like he owned it.

Quinn worked her tongue around Logan's engorged head as she grabbed the root of his cock and worked it between her fingers. She felt Ty shifting his hips above her and knew he was thrusting his hard cock along Logan's crease.

Ty continued to plunder Logan's mouth with his lips and tongue, tightening his arm around Logan's chest, pulling the smaller man back against him. His other palm smoothed over Logan's abs and downward, until he collided with Quinn's hand, which was stroking along Logan's slick cock. Ty's hand covered hers, moving along Logan's length as her mouth worked Logan's head.

Watching them kiss so intimately, so intensely, made Quinn's nipples harden painfully. The thought of Logan tasting her on Ty's lips excited her even more. Though she had just had her release, better than the one earlier with the vibrator, she felt greedy and wanted more.

Her boys always made her want more.

She released her hold on Logan's cock and ran her hands up Ty's arms, over Logan's biceps, around his waist, his hips, down over his thighs. She brushed her palms along Ty's smooth thighs to his hips until she couldn't reach any farther.

Quinn took Logan deeper into her mouth as Ty squeezed Logan's root and sac, causing Logan to break the kiss when he cried out. His chest heaved, and his cock twitched. He quickly freed her hair, letting his cock slip from between her lips. Leaning down, he took her mouth, his tongue exploring hers. He cupped her cheeks and kissed her harder and deeper, letting her discover what it was like when the two men had shared their kiss.

Ty sat back on his heels and pulled Logan by his waist, up and away from Quinn. She scrambled from underneath the two of them toward the headboard and watched as Logan, who was still on his knees, settled back against Ty's lap. Logan tensed as he sank onto Ty's cock. As Logan relaxed a bit, his eyelids became heavy, his gaze unseeing.

Quinn was surprised it happened that way. Logan was the top between the two men; Logan was the dominant. That he hadn't stopped Ty from taking him made her wonder if there had been a shift in the relationship that she didn't know about.

But Logan's next command threw that thought right out the window. "Lube. Condom." Spoken from between gritted teeth, Logan now looked irritated, as if he realized Ty had gotten the upper hand when Logan was in a weak moment.

Quinn didn't dare laugh, though she desperately wanted to. The expression on Logan's face was priceless.

Quinn dug in the still-open bed-stand drawer and tossed a bottle of lube to Logan. It thumped him in the chest and landed between his knees. Ty snagged it quickly, popping open the top. It disappeared behind Logan's back, and a second later Ty threw it on the bed next to them. There was a wide grin on his face as he pulled Logan back against him harder.

"You know you are going to pay for this," Logan told him, trying to sound angry, but the look on his face was all pleasure.

"I sure hope so," Ty answered against Logan's neck, his teeth nipping along the other man's skin.

Condom in hand, Quinn sat against the headboard, watching the two of them move against each other. Ty's hands splayed over Logan's chest as his hips thrust against Logan's buttocks. The smacking of skin against skin made Quinn's breath catch. Logan let out a little sound with each surge, while Ty kept whispering Logan's name into his neck.

Logan suddenly pinned her with a stare and extended his hand to her. She moved closer, facing him.

"Sheath me."

Her heart thumped wildly as she tore the foil package open, grabbed his still-hard cock, and rolled the condom over the crown and down its length. Her pussy clenched as his cock bobbed with every movement Ty made.

Ty paused for a moment and let out a long breath. Quinn took advantage of the timing and climbed on Logan's lap, adjusting her balance until she was basically squatting over him. Logan grabbed her hips and guided himself to her opening. She was ready for him. No lube necessary.

Ty thrust hard against Logan, causing Logan's cock to bump against Quinn's clit. She groaned and lowered herself on him until he was fully seated, deep inside her, impaling her.

She didn't think it would work, but it did, with Ty sitting on his heels, Logan leaning back on Ty's lap, and Quinn riding Logan. She kept her weight in her heels, and she posted as if riding a horse, while Ty picked up his rhythm once again.

Since Logan was relinquishing his dominant status, at least for the moment, Quinn decided to take advantage of it. She wrapped his ponytail around her hand and pulled his head back, exposing more of his neck to Ty and to her. She grazed her teeth along the curve of his neck, then met Ty over Logan's shoulder. She brushed her lips against his before tracing her tongue along the edge of his lips.

Ty had such a beautiful mouth, and he knew how to use it skillfully too. Just remembering his lips on her clit made her grind against Logan. She ground once more and came. But it still wasn't enough.

She released Logan's hair and slipped off him, grabbing the tube of lube. She squirted some on his cock and turned away from him, shifting backward until his cock nestled between her ass cheeks. She looked over her shoulder at him.

"Help me."

His lips twitched. Most likely in amusement, but he became dead serious as he held his cock still, the head pressed against her tight ring.

"Slow," he told her.

No doubt about it, she was going to take it slow. As she pushed back against him, she felt the rim of her anus open and stretch to accept him. Quinn stilled, getting used to the sensation and the feeling of fullness. She swallowed hard but pressed onward until she had him fully.

"You okay?" he whispered against her ear. He sounded out of breath.

She couldn't answer him; she just nodded slightly.

Ty hadn't moved while Quinn was getting settled, but now she was, and he began his pace once again.

Logan reached around her to slip two fingers into her swollen pussy and put his thumb against her clit. Ty's cadence jostled her enough, any discomfort she felt quickly melted into pleasure.

"Oh my God. That feels so good."

"Yes," Logan answered tightly. His chest was pressed against her back, and she could feel how quickly he was breathing.

She couldn't imagine what it was like to be him right now, one cock in his ass and his own in another's. It had to feel like heaven.

Logan gasped. "Ty. *Stop.*"

Ty did, and Logan began tilting his hips; each thrust into Quinn worked Ty's cock in and out of him as well. Ty teased her nipples as Logan played with her pussy. Just when she thought she couldn't take any more, that she was going to explode into a thousand little pieces, Ty's fingers clamped down on her nipples, and he groaned, fucking Logan's ass at a quick pace until he stiffened. His climax set Logan off. Logan pulled Quinn tighter against him, his thumb making frantic circles around her clit as he began to make long strokes, driving deep into her anal canal.

Quinn cried out as each thrust became harder than the one before.

"Come, baby," he said before he tensed deep within her. His teeth sank into her shoulder, sending a jolt down into her pussy, where it exploded, and she came for a fifth time that evening.

By the time she came down from the clouds and her vision cleared, Ty had extracted himself from the tangle of arms and legs. He disappeared down the hall, and a few moments later, she heard the shower running.

"He's got the right idea, but I'm feeling too lazy to move." Logan groaned as she rolled over and settled against him.

"Me too." Quinn sighed, her cheek resting against Logan's damp chest. His chest hairs tickled her nose, and she wiggled it to keep from sneezing.

Logan shifted, tucking Quinn securely underneath his arm, pinning her snugly against him.

"How did you know where I lived?"

"I had Ty call Paige on his cell phone while I talked to you."

Paige? Paige didn't know where she lived.

"But—"

"But one of your friends, who is friends with Paige, provided the address."

Crap. Lana.

"But—"

"Paige didn't tell her why she needed the address. Don't worry." He rose to his elbows, looking down at her. "And anyway, isn't everyone going to know next weekend?"

Logan searched Quinn's face. He knew next weekend was going to be difficult for her. It was not every day someone let their friends and family know they were sleeping with two men at one. Especially in public. It was kind of a bizarre coming-out.

"Yes," she said cautiously. "However, Lana has a problem with keeping her mouth shut. I want to be in control of when and where and to whom I tell that we are together."

He didn't say anything for a long second.

"Define *together*."

"Having sex."

He shook his head.

He did not want Quinn only as a sex toy. Something—someone—for him and Ty to play with occasionally.

And he didn't want her thinking of herself that way either.

"I would hope you think of us as more than just sex partners."

Her expression closed; she became unreadable, and that concerned him.

"You do know that, right?" He prodded her. She tried to roll away, but he held on to her tighter.

"I know I enjoy both of your company. I know I love having sex with you guys. I know the two of you love each other…a lot." She sighed. "I'm not sure what is going on between the three of us. We haven't known each other long enough. I don't want to assume anything."

Before he could answer her, Ty came in only wearing one of her bath towels wrapped around his lean hips. His ebony skin was still damp from the shower, a few stray beads of water running down it.

Logan had a tough time pulling his gaze away from him. No matter how many times he had seen his lover naked or nearly naked, it never failed that he would feel the thrill of loving him run through him. That Ty was his and his alone.

Shit. That was no longer true, which brought him back to the problem at hand—Quinn's not feeling secure in where she fit within their relationship.

Ty was no longer just his. Logan now shared him with Quinn.

Their relationship dynamic was something they would have to discuss in greater depth. But he wanted to talk to Ty about it first.

Ty broke into his thoughts. "There is something else we need to discuss."

Ty was right.

She tried to roll away from him again, and this time he let her go. She sat up on the edge of the bed, clearly not even remotely self-conscious of her nudity. It was one thing he loved about her.

She asked, “What's that?”

Ty sat next to her, the mattress sinking under his solid body weight. He laid a hand on her bare thigh and squeezed. “The fact you left your front door unlocked.”

“Oh.”

“Yeah. Oh. You're lucky it was us coming in and not some psycho. You never heard us in the house. We completely caught you off guard.”

They certainly had. They had caught her in a very compromising position, one in which she had been the throes of an orgasm. As much as Logan had enjoyed watching Quinn get herself off, he had to consider her safety.

“Ty's right.” Logan said. “What if Peter had shown up and caught you in that position? Would you have invited him into your bed? Or if you weren't interested, would he have taken no for an answer?”

“I doubt Peter would have acted upon seeing me all spread-eagle and horny on the bed.”

Her comment caught Logan's attention. “Why not?”

Was she blushing?

“He never seemed that interested before.”

Logan hooked an arm around her shoulders and gave her a quick kiss on her forehead. “Then he's crazy, and it was his loss.” He moved off the bed. He felt sticky, and his skin tightened as the sweat dried. He needed a shower. "But you do deserve a spanking for being so careless."

Quinn's eyes glittered. "Really?"

"Uh-huh. But right now I'm going to go clean up." He looked at Ty, who had shifted closer to Quinn. "Did you leave me any hot water?"

"Do you need me to wash your back?" Ty asked him.

The offer was tempting. He wanted to say yes, but he just wanted to jump into the shower quickly to leave enough hot water for Quinn. It was her condo, after all.

"Another time. I'll just be a minute."

After they'd all taken showers, Quinn went downstairs to make them a midnight snack.

They fed each other grapes and pieces of cheese while cuddling in bed watching a late-night rerun of *M*A*S*H.*

Logan lay in the dark later, feeling complete; Ty and Quinn curled up with him in her queen-size bed, which seemed miniature in comparison to their king-size bed at the farm. He listened to the soothing sounds of their breathing and eventually succumbed to sleep himself.

Not a couple of hours later, the alarm jerked them all out of sleep. Logan turned to look at the alarm clock. Five o'clock. He groaned and turned over, pulling a pillow over his head. He didn't realize she had to get up at this ungodly hour.

After a few minutes, the alarm was quiet. He pulled the pillow off his face and noticed Quinn had slipped from the bed.

He shifted closer to Ty, who had fallen quickly back to sleep and was snoring softly. He brushed his hand over Ty's muscular, tight ass before spooning his body and nuzzling his face into Ty's neck.

* * *

Quinn padded barefoot back up the stairs. She had gone down to call her boss, even though it was way too early for anyone to be at work. She had left Frank a message informing him she was taking a personal day. When she got to her bedroom, she stopped to take in the scene.

Ty and Logan were snuggled tightly together. Ty had the sheet all pulled to one side, the fabric clutched in his fists, though none of that sheet covered his dark, chiseled form. He lay facing the wall with Logan's leg tucked between his heavily muscled legs. Logan was pressed against Ty's wide back. She was unable to see Logan's face; his hair was loose and hid his features.

When Logan had showered last night, Ty had gotten really serious while the other man was out of the room. He had gathered her hands within his and given her a crooked smile.

"*Quinn.*" He had squeezed her fingers lightly. "*I've been meaning to talk to you alone, and now may be the perfect time.*"

Her mind had begun to spin, wondering what it was about. It couldn't have been about the simple fact of her leaving her door unlocked. Could it?

"*I'm not sure if you realized it, but I was having some doubts about Logan bringing you...*" He had stopped and grimaced.

It had been her turn to squeeze his fingers, encouraging him to continue. She had no idea where this conversation would be going.

"*I had concerns.*"

"*Concerns,*" she had repeated.

He had looked uncomfortable and seemed to have a hard time getting out what he was trying to say.

Ah. "*About me?*"

"*Yes. Sorry. I didn't really want to bring it up. Felt it wasn't necessary, but Logan said I should say something anyway, just in case you wondered...*"

Quinn had been amazed. She had never seen the man so unsure of himself. She'd caught herself wringing her own hands and flattened her fingers against her thighs to prevent the nervous action.

"*Just spit it out.*"

He had finally grinned, the tension obviously draining away. "*Sorry. I was concerned when Logan first brought you home that you'd come between Logan and me. I could see the attraction between you. I got a little jealous. I love Logan with all my heart.*" He had paused for a moment and cleared his throat before continuing. "*All my heart.*"

"*I know,*" Quinn had murmured.

"*And I was interested in bringing in a third person—a woman—but I also was worried that our relationship might not survive it if it wasn't the right person.*"

"*Okay.*"

"*Quinn, I just wanted to tell you that I really think you are the right person.*"

As she stepped through the bedroom doorway, Quinn smiled, remembering that conversation. Her heart almost burst even now from what Ty had said.

She approached the bed, and when she put a knee on the mattress, Logan brushed the hair out of his face to look at her. He gave her a sleepy smile and made some space between them, patting his hand on the bed. She climbed in between the two and wiggled to get settled. Her bed wasn't nearly big enough for the three of them. It was a tight fit, but she wasn't complaining.

She ended up snuggled against Ty's back with Logan behind her. She felt like she was between a slice of pumpernickel and a slice of whole-wheat bread. This was a sandwich she'd be happy to enjoy anytime.

Logan's warm breath stirred her hair around her ear, tickling her. He murmured something sounding like, "You're ours. No one will win you but us."

She closed her eyes against the tears burning them. She truly felt wanted.

* * *

Her earlier feeling of being wanted quickly waned.

"So now you are saying you won't go?" Panic rose to the top of Quinn's throat. She set her coffee mug down on the small kitchen table with a *thump.*

"I never said we would definitely go. You just assumed that."

"Like Logan said earlier, you really need to think hard about this. I think you're going about it the wrong way." Ty pushed his chair back from the table and crossed his arms over his broad chest.

Logan grabbed one of her fisted hands. "I agree. I think it's selfish. You want to use us to get back at your mother."

Quinn pulled her hand out of his grasp and stuffed both fists into her lap. "My parents. Peter."

Logan frowned. "Your mother. You've said that your father just follows her lead."

"Doesn't make it right," Quinn grumbled.

"Maybe not. But wanting us to go with you as dates—*both* of us—I don't know, Quinn. You could do permanent damage."

"To what?"

Logan groaned, his frustration clearly shown on his face. "To you. Your relationship with your parents, your friends. Your career."

"To us. Our business. Possibly my friendships with my former teammates," Ty added. "I'm not sure if I'm ready to make *our* relationship public." He waved a hand between Logan and himself. "Not to mention letting the world know about the three of us."

"You, yourself, didn't want to let your friends know. You didn't want to be the topic of gossip. But now you want to make us the center of attention at a charity event? To embarrass your parents?" Logan shook his head. "That's just fucked-up, Quinn."

She opened her mouth, then snapped it shut.

The pressure in her chest increased and became suffocating. Her heart squeezed. She should have known better. Men continually let her down. Peter, who had cheated on her. Her father, who jumped when her mother said jump. Now these two. They were no different.

She needed to strike out. For them to hurt as she was hurting. Quinn could only think of one thing to say. "Get out."

Ty straightened up in his seat. "Quinn—"

"Quinn, you can't be serious." Logan's eyebrows lowered, anger flashing in his eyes.

He was not used to being told what to do. Too bad for him. "Oh I'm serious. You guys need to get out." She pointed a shaky finger toward the front of the house. "Last night everything you said made me believe that you would go…"

Logan shook his head. "You are making a mistake," he warned.

Whether he meant by her throwing them out or by the way she was going to handle Peter and her parents, she didn't care at the moment. She was upset. Upset they wouldn't stand by her side and support her while she was at the benefit.

She had done everything they asked of her. And more. "I've trusted you. I've let you do whatever you wanted to do with me. I put myself in your hands. And now? You can't do this one little thing for me?" Her words were gritty and thick.

"Quinn, this isn't little. This could affect us big-time. We could possibly lose business..."

She closed her eyes to stop the stinging. She did not want them to see her cry.

"Get out!" She sat stiffly, breathing through her nose. Struggling to keep herself together.

She heard the sharp scrape of a chair and then Logan's low, tight voice. "Okay. We'll leave for now. But think hard on this, Quinn. You'll see that we're right. You're going about this the wrong way."

She had a niggling feeling they were right. That they were looking at it from a better point of view. But she hoped they were wrong.

She didn't move until she heard the last of their footsteps and the soft *click* of her front door.

The silence of the condo became deafening. The fridge powered on, and she started, opening her eyes.

Before that very moment, she had never felt so alone.

Chapter Fourteen

Quinn nervously smoothed a hand over her hip. She'd had to suffer through dealing with the highbrow saleswomen in four boutiques before finally settling on the dress she now wore. It was midcalf length, sleeveless, and white, decorated beautifully with sparkly sequins. And it fit very, very snugly, hugging all her curves and framing her cleavage perfectly. Her back was completely exposed, all the way down to just above her buttocks, where the silky fabric draped softly, barely hiding the top of her crease. A silver and rhinestone chain hung midway across her back. It bridged both sides of the dress, keeping it from separating and gaping enough to show her bare breasts.

Just enough fabric covered her breasts; she went without any form of bra or support. The neckline—if it could be called that—went so low, she was surprised her navel wasn't exposed. Her breasts bounced firmly with every step she took in her four-inch heels. Even though she was in her thirties now, her breasts hadn't gone south yet, and she was proud of that. Her shoes were also white, with matching satin ribbon. They laced around her ankles and up her calves. The dress had a slit up the left side to midthigh, making her feel extraordinarily sexy.

She decided to forgo the panties also, since any panty line would be noticeable with the tight fit. Going commando had never been her style, but she felt daring tonight. If not a little reckless.

And very determined to make a point.

A huge square-cut sapphire solitaire, handed down to her from her late grandmother, hung heavily between her breasts on a platinum chain. Two more sapphires dripped from her ears. A twenty-thousand-dollar tennis bracelet sparkled on her right wrist—a present from her father when she graduated college summa cum laude.

She was dressed to kill.

And she didn't look anything like she had in that ugly bridesmaid dress the night she had met Logan. It had only been a few weeks ago, but it felt like months.

She wasn't going to dwell on the fact that she was just as alone tonight as she had been on that night. Even though a lot had happened since then, everything seemed to be back to where it was. No one was going to change that but herself. It was time to take control of her own life. To do what *she* wanted, not what everyone else wanted just because it was expected of her.

Maybe the boys thought that was selfish. Maybe it was.

She pushed the what-ifs and possible future regrets out of her mind. She couldn't worry about them right now…

She pasted on a sexy smile and put an extra oomph into the swing in her hips as she came around her Infiniti. She plucked the ticket out of the valet's fingers and shoved it into her clutch. The poor young valet continued to stand there and stare at her, his mouth gaping. Well, he wasn't staring at her. He was staring at her breasts. She was beginning to think he could see the pink of her nipples through the dress, when he finally snapped into motion, wiping a bit of spit from the corner of his mouth.

Quinn laughed as he scrambled around her car. This was the exact effect she was striving for.

The dress was worth the week's salary she had paid for it.

She snapped her clutch closed and walked through the double doors of the country club.

Her ears were immediately assaulted by the din of the banquet room, which was directly across from the country club's main entrance. Monte Carlo nights seemed to be loud and boisterous as participants got caught up with the games.

She paused at the double doors to the room where the charity event was being held, and surveyed the crowd. She relaxed a little when she didn't spot Peter. It gave her a little time to deal with her parents first. She was sure her mother wouldn't be pleased with what she was wearing.

And that had been another selling point for this particular dress.

She startled when a hand grasped her elbow firmly from behind. Quinn was dragged backward, farther away from the event, and she struggled to keep upright. She dug her heels in and turned to meet her mother's displeased expression.

"You look like a whore."

Quinn sharply pulled her sore elbow out of her mother's grasp. A bruise would not make a nice accessory. "An expensive one, I hope. I was going for the Julia Roberts in *Pretty Woman* type of look. Did I succeed?"

"Do you think this is funny?" her mother asked, her eyebrows pinned and lips tightly pressed together in displeasure.

"Look, Mother. You want to sell me off to the highest bidder. I might as well dress the part."

Her mother hissed at her. "This is a charity event. Not a sex-slave auction."

Quinn lifted a bare shoulder lazily in a half shrug, trying to appear much calmer than she was. She gave her best attempt to drum up the newfound confidence the boys had given her. At least until she noticed her father quickly striding toward them. His face didn't hold the displeasure her mother's did, but more of a shock and disappointment.

Quinn suddenly had the urge to run and hide. She loved her father and did not want to hurt him. But hell, she hadn't asked for any of this. She couldn't forget that. And she had come this far, did she really want to back out now?

As he approached, her father stripped off his tuxedo jacket and extended it to her. "Put this on."

Quinn shook her head and backed up a step, careful not to catch her narrow heel on the rug. "No."

"You can't go in there looking like that. You look like a...a..."

"Yes, I know. Mother's already said."

"You need to go home and change." Her father looked annoyed, ready to ground her for a week and take away her phone privileges.

She was an adult, damn it!

"No, Dad. I've spent a fortune on this dress, and I will wear it."

Her mother stepped a hairbreadth away from her and pointed a red-lacquered fingertip into her face. "We'll remove you from the list of auctionees."

As if *that* would punish Quinn.

"No, you won't. You will reap what you have sowed. This money is going toward a good charity. You can't let the charity suffer due to your uptight attitude."

"This is not about being uptight. This is about how it looks—" Her mother stopped abruptly.

"How it looks to your friends and peers," Quinn finished for her. *Anything to keep up appearances.*

"Do you think Peter is going to be happy when he sees you dressed like that?"

If he were normal, he'd be hard when he saw her. But then, Peter wasn't normal.

Did she say that out loud?

No. Phew. She needed to get away from them before she said something she shouldn't. As if she hadn't already.

Her father's disappointed and almost-hurt expression sent a sharp pain through her chest. Maybe she should leave and forget the whole thing… Maybe the boys were right.

She moved away from her parents as fast as her high heels would take her. She answered over her shoulder, "I don't care if Peter is happy." She'd make her decision whether to leave or to stay once she returned to the lobby.

"Well, you should!"

Her mother's comment brought Quinn up short. She spun to face her parents. "Why? When was Peter ever concerned if I was happy?"

If it had been funny, she would have laughed at her parents' stunned expressions. Her mother was actually speechless for a split second... Imagine that!

"That's what I thought," Quinn said before continuing her escape.

"Peter loves you," her mother yelled to Quinn's back as she strode away.

Quinn just shook her head in disgust. Peter was a cheating bastard, but her mother still thought he was perfect. Hell, she didn't have to wait until the lobby to make up her mind. After tonight, there would be no doubt in her mother's mind—in Peter's mind—that Quinn wanted nothing more to do with him. She deserved better.

When she got to the banquet room, she took a deep, bolstering breath and sauntered into the crowded room and right up to the bar.

* * *

It was déjà vu for Logan. When he had first spotted Quinn weeks ago at the reception, she had been tying one on at the bar. Tonight she was doing the same thing, only this time she wasn't wearing that ugly pink monstrosity. She was wearing some sleek number that made him as hard as hell.

And he was sure it made every other man in the room as hard as hell too. Well, except maybe her father, who he supposed was somewhere in the crowd.

While that bridesmaid's dress had done nothing to show off her attributes, this one did *everything* to show them off. It actually showed off too much.

But he wasn't complaining. No, sir. All he could think about was stripping the little covering she was wearing off later tonight. *If* she forgave them. He hoped them showing up tonight was enough. If not, he might be tempted to beg.

His lips twitched with amusement at that thought.

At least until he heard, "Mr. Reed! Mr. Reed!"

Every muscle tensed in his body as he heard footsteps rushing toward him.

He turned to face the squat little man who was the general manager of the Mandolin Bay Country Club.

He lifted one eyebrow. "Mr. Lawson?"

"Yes, yes. I saw your helper dropping you off at the front door. The head groundskeeper is not here right now, but he needs to speak to you regarding an issue with the sod."

"My *helper* was just parking the car. He should be in here momentarily."

"Then I'm glad I caught you. Again, the head groundskeeper has been meaning to meet with you. He is down at the maintenance shed."

Logan crossed his arms over his chest and looked down at the man. Was he kidding?

"Do I look like I'm dressed to work on the greens?"

The man's mouth opened and closed like a gasping fish as he finally noticed Logan's attire. Which just happened to be a tuxedo, not coveralls.

After a moment, Lawson sputtered, "Why, no."

"I'm here for the House to Home Charity."

Lawson had the gall to step in front of Logan, blocking his way. He put out a chubby hand, as if that could stop Logan from entering. "Sir, it's by invitation only."

"I've been invited," Logan growled. His patience was wearing thin.

"By whom?"

"Quinn Preston."

"But Ms. Preston…" Lawson stopped.

"Yes? Ms. Preston?"

His gaze shot back and forth as if he was trying to avoid making eye contact with Logan. "Uh. Ms. Preston has a date."

"Yeah? Who?"

"I…I… Peter Harrington."

"Oh. Well, I brought my own date." Logan glanced behind him to see Ty approaching. His "date" looked very handsome in his tux. "Here he is now." Logan slipped an arm through Ty's and gave him a quick kiss.

Lawson turned a sickly shade of pale, and his eyes widened to large circles as he stumbled away from the two of them.

Jeez. You would have thought he and Ty were lepers the way the manager acted.

"Was that smart?" Ty asked as Logan led him into the event.

"Probably not."

Logan felt a twinge of regret at shocking the man. He didn't want his actions to jeopardize his contract with the club. He'd had it for years, and it brought in a nice chunk of change.

Well, if needed, he'd do damage control later.

Right now he had something more important to deal with.

A group of men gathered around Quinn. Three untouched drinks sat on the bar in front of her as she sipped the one already in her fingers.

"Alabama slammers?"

A quick outtake of breath escaped her gaping mouth before she quickly schooled her expression. Logan was impressed how rapidly she recovered from her shock at seeing the both of them there. But he could still see the question in her eyes.

Her lips turned up at the corners. "No. Tonight's a perfect night for Long Island iced teas. Not quite as potent as slammers, but they will do the trick."

He handed one of the extra drinks to Ty and picked one up for himself. He took a long swig. A little too sweet for his taste, but not bad.

"Hey," yelled one of the men crowding against Quinn. "The drink was bought for the lady."

Logan looked Quinn up and down and bit back a snort of laughter. *Lady.* Quinn hardly looked like a lady tonight. She looked like a vixen. A sex kitten who knew how to bring a man to his knees.

She had effectively brought both him and Ty to their knees. Their showing up tonight proved it. Not that either were complaining.

Her hair was pulled up, exposing the long line of her neck. A few stray tendrils framed her face delicately. The sapphires at her ears brought out a tinge of blue in her gray eyes. Those eyes that currently held a glint of evil.

She gave him a wicked smile and slipped her left leg out of the slit in her dress, showing off a very shapely thigh. "You like?"

"Very much." He glanced at Ty, whose gaze was glued to Quinn's leg.

She shifted her leg out of the slit a little more, and Logan saw she wore no panties. He stepped a little closer to her to block the view from the other men.

Not pleased at her display, he leaned in close, murmuring into her ear, "What are you doing?"

"I thought you guys weren't coming," she murmured back.

"I'll explain later," he grumbled. He didn't mind her dressing sexy, but she was wearing the dress for the wrong reasons.

One of the wrong reasons just happened to saunter up at that moment.

Quinn quickly pulled her leg back, once again hiding herself before turning to her ex. "Peter! How are you?"

Logan winced at Quinn's overly sweet, obviously exaggerated speech.

When Peter stepped up, the rest of the men melted away. It was as if Peter had come to claim his prize, and they were gracious enough to recognize it.

Bullshit. Logan wasn't leaving her alone with him.

Quinn put a newly manicured hand on Peter's upper arm and pulled him closer. "Peter, I want you to meet some friends of mine. Peter Harrington, this is Logan Reed and Tyson White."

The shit extended his hand, and Logan was polite enough to accept it. When Peter shook Ty's hand, a look of recognition crossed Peter's face. "Tyson White? As in Tyson 'T-Bone' White of the Boston Bulldogs?"

Don't tell me the little geek bastard knows football, Logan thought. He probably takes part in office football pools. And loses his ass.

"That's me," Ty answered, twirling the tiny straw in his drink. He was acting as if being recognized as a famous athlete was nothing.

Logan's cock twitched. Quinn in her outfit wasn't the only thing flipping his switch. His dark lover, whose ebony skin shone under the club's recessed lighting, made his gut do a little flip.

"Amazing. I didn't realize Quinn's mother had arranged for two Bulldog stars to be here tonight."

Both Logan and Ty opened their mouths simultaneously to question Peter, but Quinn held up a hand, stopping them both.

"Two?"

"Yes, Long Arm Landis is here."

"Long Arm?" Quinn asked, her delicate eyebrows pinching together.

Both she and Logan looked at Ty questioningly.

"Quarterback," he answered them and sipped his drink.

Logan shook his head. "I know who Long Arm is. Why would he be here?"

And why wasn't Ty concerned about his former teammate finding out Ty was in a relationship with a man? Not that Logan believed Ty wanted to keep it a secret. At least, if he did, he wouldn't have agreed to come here.

Logan figured tonight was a night for discoveries. When they had decided to come show Quinn their support, to prove to her how much they cared, they knew this was the risk.

But shit—

Like it or not, Ty most likely would end up being outed, and if Quinn had her way, so would she. But Ty's outing would be to a former teammate, something he'd managed to avoid all these years. They had both decided being with Quinn tonight was worth the risk to themselves. Even so, Ty still had a chance to back out from this possible debacle; Logan would respect any decision he made.

Seemingly unconcerned, Ty looked at Quinn expectantly. "I don't know. Why would he be here?"

Quinn gave a slight shrug and sipped her own drink.

"The Society Ladies' Charity Club did want to bring in some celebs to sell off some signed memorabilia. Maybe it's that, or he's part of the bachelor/bachelorette auction," the dweeb answered.

Unexpectedly, Quinn's ex turned his attention to her. Her dress seemed to suddenly draw Peter's attention more than the prospect of having two NFL stars in the room.

"Is that dress new?"

Quinn smiled into her drink. "You don't remember it?"

"I think I would remember a dress like that. Doesn't leave much to the imagination, does it?"

She tossed her head back, her breasts jiggling enough with the movement that they almost escaped the narrow strips of white fabric that barely contained them. "It's not meant to. It's supposed to show off my attributes."

Peter cupped the large sapphire nestled between her breasts. "Is this your grandmother's stone?"

Logan felt Ty tense beside him. He gave Ty a look that said Quinn could handle herself.

Though he wasn't sure he liked the way she was doing it. Especially when she trapped Peter's hand with hers and pressed his knuckles against the bare curves of her breasts. Her voice got low and smoky. "Familiar, is it?"

"Uh." Peter yanked his hand away as if he had been burned. "Yes, I thought it looked familiar."

Logan couldn't believe it. Her ex actually looked uncomfortable, embarrassed that his hand had brushed against Quinn's breasts.

Logan barked out laughter, making the blood rush to Peter's face.

Peter stepped back and stared at Logan for a moment before appearing to gather some confidence.

Logan'd had enough. He slid an arm around Quinn until his hand splayed on the warm skin of her lower back. He picked up the square vibrant blue stone and pretended to study it. “It's a beautiful gem.” He met her gaze as he laid it gently against the delicate skin between her breasts, his fingers lingering against her soft cleavage. “Just like the woman wearing it.”

Peter cleared his throat. Loudly.

“Would you like me to get you another drink, Quinn?”

Before Quinn could answer him, Logan said softly, “We can handle it from here, Pete.”

“It's Peter. Quinn?”

Quinn finally broke their locked gaze. But instead of looking at Peter, she looked at Ty, who gave her a bright white smile. A knowing smile, an unspoken promise of what was to come later. Quinn's hand fluttered to her throat.

“I'm fine. Thank you,” she answered Peter absently.

“Oh. Okay.” Peter tugged at the lapels of his jacket. “Well. I…I'm going to go mingle. I'll see you a little later, Quinn.” He nodded to both Logan and Ty. “Nice meeting you, gentlemen.”

Logan gave him an answering nod and a predatory smile. Ty shook Peter's hand, then gave him a slap on the back as he scurried away.

A band on a stage at one end of the large hall started to play, drowning out some of the noise from the gaming tables.

Ty noticed a dance floor in front of the stage, with only few couples dancing.

He offered his hand to Quinn. “Dance with me?”

She smiled warmly and accepted his offer, linking her fingers with his. She handed her Long Island iced tea to Logan as Ty led her toward the parquet-covered dance area.

Once there, Ty pulled her into his arms and pressed his hips to hers. He brushed his nose against her hair. “You smell good.”

Her low chuckle vibrated against his chest. “And you look very handsome tonight.”

“Just tonight?”

“Well, you look extremely handsome in your tux. But honestly, I prefer you naked.”

He smiled into her hair, careful not to wreck all the work she had put into styling it.

“Well, if we are being honest here, you *are* practically naked.”

“I'm covered where I need to be.”

He wasn't the best dancer, but he managed through the slow dance, shuffling his feet. He was careful not to pinch her pedicured toes.

“Ty, what's going on? Logan said he'd explain later, but—”

“We couldn't let you do this on your own.”

“But—”

“But we realized we were being as stubborn as you were by refusing to come.” He chuckled. “I guess we are just not as stubborn as you. We were willing to bend." He suddenly felt fiercely possessive of the woman he held in his arms. "We want you, Quinn. We care about you. We want you to realize it."

Her fingers clenched against his back. Hard enough that he could feel them through his tux coat.

He heard what suspiciously sounded like a sniffle. He leaned back slightly to look at her. She turned her face away.

"Hey now. You need to stay strong. Isn't this what this whole display is supposed to be about?"

"Yes," she whispered against his lapel. "I just don't want you guys to do what you don't want to do."

"If we didn't want to do it, we wouldn't be here."

"You don't know what this means to me," she said as her body melted against him, cementing the fact that he and Logan had made the right decision to come tonight. No matter what it cost them otherwise, Quinn needed to be a part of their lives. Maybe they didn't agree 100 percent with her decisions, but they were hers to make, and he and Logan would be there to help pick up the pieces if need be.

"Do you feel how much I want you right now?"

She pulled back a little in his arms and looked up at him seriously. "Oh, is that you? I thought you had a salami in your pocket."

Her eyes crinkled at the corners, and he pulled her close once more, his fingers skimming down the smooth skin along her spine. She shivered against him, rocking her hips with an exaggerated motion.

"*Careful*," he warned her. His balls tightened as his cock hardened even more.

He pulled her hips against him even tighter, making sure she felt every inch of him. A shoehorn would be needed to separate them.

Or not. He noticed the glances they were getting from couples on the dance floor and others who were gathered at the gaming tables nearest the dance floor. Some of the rich biddies were shooting nasty looks toward them; others were whispering to each other.

Ty sighed. He put a little space between him and Quinn.

"What's wrong?"

"Oh. The same old, same old."

An expression of concern crossed her face. "What does that mean?"

Ty shook his head in disgust. "Never mind."

"Oh no, you don't. Tell me what's wrong." Quinn looked around at the surrounding charity participants. "Ah. Never mind. I understand now."

"I guess your mother's friends are still stuck in the Dark Ages."

"They are not all my mother's friends, but yes. This country club has a strict membership policy, if you know what I mean."

He stopped in the middle of the dance floor and studied her face. Logan said that they had to be there for her, no matter what, and he had agreed, but… "Quinn, do you know what you are doing tonight?"

"Absolutely."

"No. Look. These people don't even like the fact a black man is dancing with a white woman. How are they going to react when they find out you are not only dancing with one but sleeping with him?" He put up a finger to stop her from interrupting. "*And* you are not only sleeping with a black man you are sleeping with his white *male* lover. I don't think they are going to be real open to that concept."

The band transitioned from one slow song into another.

Quinn grabbed his arms and wrapped them around her. She laid her head against his lapel. "I don't care."

Lord, she felt good in his arms. "Quinn, you had better be sure about this."

"You sound like Logan."

Ty bit back a laugh. As funny as it was being accused of sounding like Logan, what Quinn was doing tonight was serious business. "Well, maybe he's right. Do you really want to alienate your family because they want you to be with that analyst geek?"

She gave him a light punch in the arm. "Hey! I'm an analyst geek."

"Hardly."

He moved her slowly around the dance floor, his fingers pressed into her hips.

"If my parents can't accept my decisions—can't accept me the way I am—then, well, to hell with them."

"Quinn, they are your family."

"Then they need to accept my choices. They need to let me choose who to love."

Ty stopped again, catching her chin and tilting her head up. He squinted, looking deep into her eyes. She met his gaze defiantly, as if daring him to question her. He decided to let the comment go. The dance floor at a charity event—a crowded one at that—was no place to explore what her last comment meant.

"Why no earrings tonight?" she asked him.

"Because I leaned toward the more-conservative side tonight."

"So you decided to change yourself to fit in?"

She was purposely challenging him. Ty bit back a curse. Instead he said, "Does it look like I fit in here?"

"Do *I* look like I fit in here?"

Where was she going with this? "Yes."

"Well, that proves it: looks are deceiving."

He snorted. "You can't judge a book by its cover?"

"Looks are only skin deep."

"Beauty fades; stupidity lasts forever."

Quinn threw her head back and laughed loudly, drawing more attention to them. Not that they already hadn't drawn enough attention. But her laughter made a little of the tension in his body disappear.

As the song changed again, he decided he'd had enough of trying to fake that he could dance. His whole point of asking her to dance was for some alone time and to feel her against him. A little something to tide him over until later. He had achieved his goal; now he could return her safely, with all her toes still intact.

He cupped her elbow, leading her from the dance floor. And directly into Long Arm Landis.

"Holy shit, T. Never would have expected to see you here."

"How are you doing, Renny?"

Quinn looked from one man to the other. "Renny? I thought his name was Long Arm."

Ty kept a grasp on Quinn's arm, holding her close to his side. "Ren, this is Quinn Preston. Quinn, this is Lawrence 'Long Arm' Landis. Known around the locker room as Ren or Renny. The public and the media nicknamed him Long Arm."

Quinn eyed the other man's arms, which were encased in a very expensive tux. "His arms look like a normal length to me."

Both of the men laughed.

"Where did you find her?" Renny asked him.

"His nickname comes from how far he throws on the field," Ty explained to Quinn.

"Oh. Sorry." Her cheeks were unmistakably pink.

Renny eyed Quinn's dress. Or rather, the lack thereof. Ty suddenly felt a bit protective. He was close with all his former teammates; they were like brothers. But not close enough to share. Logan was off-limits. And now so was Quinn.

That realization smacked Ty right between the eyes. Logan was right. She belonged with them. Any remaining doubts he'd held on to vanished.

"My agent didn't mention you'd be here. Hey, T, you find it a bit odd we are the only brothers here tonight?"

"We were just discussing that fact."

"Are you here to sign autographs?"

"No. I'm here escorting Quinn."

Ty's declaration drew Renny's attention back to Quinn. He gave her a big smile and leaned toward her, whispering, "You like dark meat?"

"Are we talking about a Thanksgiving turkey?" Quinn countered.

Renny laughed, his gaze raking over her from the top of her head to the tips of her toes and back. "Wow. Looks and a sense of humor. Quite the package." Renny fingered the sapphire. "Nice piece of bling."

What was with that fucking sapphire? The next person who touched Quinn between her breasts was getting his fingers broken.

Ty stepped between him and Quinn, breaking the contact. "You can look, but you can't touch."

"What's up, T? Is she yours?"

She's mine. She's Logan's.

"She's ours."

Chapter Fifteen

She's ours.

Those two little words resonated through Quinn. They meant a lot to her. To be claimed outright like that felt good. Especially since she'd thought she was going to have to face this night by herself.

Ty's former teammate lifted his hands in front of him as if in surrender. “Hey, man, white looks good on you. No harm, no foul.”

The jury was still out on how Quinn felt about Ty's friend. He was a little overconfident, if not arrogant. But then, he was apparently a famous pro football player. And not a bad-looking one to boot.

Renny sure hadn't come dressed conservatively. He had a huge diamond solitaire in each ear. Quinn guessed they had to be two carats a piece. One of his long fingers sported a large square ring. She had been able to read the ring when he touched her sapphire. It said *World Champions*, and it was encrusted with diamonds and colored stones that looked like rubies, in the shape of a bulldog.

She wondered if Ty had one of those rings.

Even though Renny was dressed in a tux, he had a large gold cross hanging from his neck, and his dress shirt had the top two buttons undone. His cummerbund was Bulldog red. His hair was tightly braided into cornrows against his head. He had beautiful white teeth and large dark brown eyes.

And he was watching her checking him out.

Crap.

She didn't want to give him the wrong impression.

"So," Renny asked, "what's with the *she's ours*?"

Quinn saw Ty's gaze bounce from Logan, who was still at the bar, to her, and back to Renny. A mix of emotions crossed Ty's face, and suddenly Quinn realized he was struggling with admitting the truth about his relationships. Or at least one in particular.

His former teammate had no idea Ty was in a relationship with—in love with—another man.

A lump formed in the pit of her stomach. By throwing her relationship in her parents' faces, in Peter's face, she was outing both Logan and Ty. She knew that. The boys had warned her about that. And she hadn't listened. Hadn't seriously thought about the consequences.

She slid an arm inside his jacket to hug his waist. The heat from his body was overly warm against her bare skin as she gave him a little squeeze.

She was such a selfish shit.

She never should have come. She never should have dragged them into this. Yes, they ultimately had decided to come on their own. But only to please her.

The sting of tears bit at the corners of her eyes. She looked up into Ty's face and said, "I'm sorry."

He brushed the pad of his thumb over her cheek and gave her a tender smile.

“Don't be. We wanted to be here for you.”

“But I didn't want you guys to be a sacrifice for my benefit.”

“We're not, Quinn. Believe me, we're not.”

The last came from Logan, who had moved up to join them, looking concerned.

“Is everything okay?” Logan asked.

Ty nodded. “Fine.”

He introduced Logan to Renny. The two men shook hands.

“I think I remember you. You laid the sod at our stadium. What are you doing here?”

Logan answered honestly. “I'm with Quinn.”

A look of confusion crossed Renny's features. “I don't get it. I thought T was with her.”

Quinn laid a hand against Logan's chest. An unspoken warning that they did not have to do this. They did not have to go through with this tonight.

Logan went on anyway. “He is. We both are.”

It took a minute, but finally the confusion cleared from Renny's face. But not for long. “So you guys are escorts.”

Quinn opened her mouth to say something, to stop them. But Logan put a hand over hers and squeezed. Her breath caught, and she helplessly watched everything unfold before her.

Ty shook his head, looking directly into Renny's eyes. “No, we're lovers,” he said.

“Yeah, I get it. You and Quinn are doing the bump and grind. So how does he”—he nodded his head toward Logan—“fit in?”

Logan brushed a piece of imaginary lint off Ty's shoulder. “Like he said. We're lovers.”

Renny stepped back, his eyes widening. “Wait. Wait.” He did a complete circle in place, stomping his feet and smacking his palms on his thighs. Then he planted his hands planted on his hips and stared at Ty. He opened his mouth and a second later closed it, before opening it once more. “T… Really?”

“Yeah, really,” Ty answered softly.

“Damn, man. Wow.”

Quinn decided it was time to step in. “*Wow* just about describes our relationship perfectly.”

The overhead lights flashed a couple of times to get the attendees' attention. The lights lowered to a more-ambient glow. A man Quinn didn't know was at the microphone on the stage, a soft spotlight shining off his bald head.

“Ladies and gentlemen, tonight's turnout for the House to Home Charity Monte Carlo Night has been exceptional. Thank you to the Mandolin Bay Country Club for allowing us to hold it here, and special thanks to the Society Ladies' Charity Club for all their hard work. Now, if you'd all take your seats, we'd like to get the bachelor/bachelorette auction started.”

A low murmur came from the crowd as they moved away from the gambling tables along the outer walls toward the round banquet tables surrounding the dance floor.

The man continued. "When we are finished with that, dinner will be served, followed by the reopening of the gaming tables. At that time, our local celebrities will be signing autographs and posing for pictures. And we have a special treat for our sports fanatics. Long Arm Landis is with us tonight."

A spotlight came from nowhere to shine on Renny. He pasted on a smile, covering up the fact he was still in shock, and gave a slight wave. Polite clapping came from around the large room.

As soon as the spotlight cut off from Renny, they all moved to the nearest empty table and sank into chairs. Ty and Logan flanked Quinn, while Renny settled to Ty's right.

Quinn adjusted her dress to make sure she wasn't giving the event goers a free show as the announcer continued with his speech.

"Just a reminder, the House to Home Charity needs your generous donations to continue to benefit the needy. This charity was put in place to help rebuild homes for the victims of natural disasters. Disasters which include hurricanes, like Hurricane Katrina, earthquakes, tornadoes, and mud slides. Just about any type of natural disaster. So without further ado, we will begin the auction…"

One by one, local celebrities, like newscasters, sports figures from local farm teams, and high-profile businesspeople, were called to the stage to be "sold" to the highest bidder. The winner received a date of their choice with the auctionee. It could consist of dinner or a movie, or just a meeting at a coffee shop.

When Logan suddenly nudged Quinn in the ribs, she realized she had stopped paying attention to what was happening on the stage.

Logan whispered against her ear, "You're up."

Quinn looked up at the announcer, who was doing double duty as the auctioneer. He was holding an arm out toward her, beckoning her to the stage.

"Ms. Preston is the daughter of Margaret Preston, the president of the Society Ladies' Charity Club. Her father is Charles Preston, retired senior partner of Morgan, Morgan and Chandler Accountants, one of the top ten accounting firms in the world."

Quinn felt self-conscious as she carefully made her way up to the stage. Okay, they had proved her blood was blue. Now did they want to check her teeth too?

"Ms. Preston is a senior financial analyst for the insurance firm of Anderson, Jameson and Coleman, LLC."

When she approached the microphone, she leaned into it and asked, "Would you like my weight, height, and age too?"

Chuckles came from the crowd, which she could not see because of the damn spotlight blinding her. From nowhere, someone shoved a large cardboard check into her hands, almost making her lose her balance.

"In addition to graciously agreeing to be one of our auctionees, Ms. Preston is presenting a donation check for one hundred thousand dollars from her firm."

Jesus, she'd had no idea how much Frank and the senior partners had donated. Her mother must have put the screws to him. She'd have to apologize to her boss on Monday.

In honor of the donation, the crowd did a courtesy clap, setting Quinn's teeth on edge. The man took the check from Quinn and leaned it against one of the amplifiers. "Now on to what all the gentlemen have been waiting for. How much will the bidding start for this beautiful lady?"

Dead silence met him, and panic started to creep up on her.

Then a lone voice yelled out, "Five hundred dollars!"

Five hundred? What the hell? The men had been bringing in thousands. And what was worse was that she didn't even recognize the voice.

The auctioneer said, "Okay, the bidding has started at five hundred dollars."

Quinn's father shouted, "One thousand."

"One thousand to Mr. Preston."

"Two thousand." As expected, Peter joined in on the bidding.

Her mother had conveniently volunteered her so Peter could win her. And of course, Peter did as Quinn expected... He didn't have the balls to go against Quinn's mother.

Well, he wouldn't win her, and if he did, she was going to make sure he spent a fortune.

"Twenty-five hundred."

Was that Renny? Shit.

Peter quickly countered with three thousand dollars.

Renny immediately upped the stakes to five thousand.

Renny was effectively putting a wrench into Quinn's plans. She had never expected him to bid on her.

With one more bidder than expected—hell, with her father, it was two—things were quickly getting out of hand. More out of control than she wanted. Before the evening she had expected the bidding to go no higher than a few hundred dollars. Then after the earlier auctionees had been won, she figured a couple of thousand at the most. But nothing like this.

Her father's voice rang out again. "Ten thousand."

Before she could stop herself, Quinn shouted, "Dad!"

Why would her father want to outbid Peter? Didn't he want her with Peter just like her mother did? Didn't they both think they knew what was best for her?

Peter, sounding a bit panicked, bid ten thousand five hundred.

The crowd became restless; she heard murmurs but could not make out what people were saying. She lifted a hand to shield her eyes from the glare, desperately trying to see out into the sea of tables.

She met Logan's eyes from a distance. He slowly got to his feet, not breaking their gaze.

"Twenty thousand."

Quinn sucked in a breath, and the blood rushed from her face. She had wanted the boys to win her. But not at this high of a price.

Never at this high of a price. Their business was still developing. They needed that money.

Peter jumped to his feet, his chair falling backward, clattering onto the floor. He was two tables away from her boys. "Twenty-two thousand."

Quinn pressed a hand to her chest. "*Jesus, stop*," she whispered, but no one heard her.

Renny, still sitting, brought the bidding up to twenty-five thousand. He barked out a laugh as if he was just as surprised as the crowd was at what he had just done.

The murmuring got louder throughout the crowd. All eyes were on the standing men, who were now challenging each other just with their body language.

Peter's gaze darted to Renny. "Twenty-six thousand."

The auctioneer had quit repeating the bids. He stood as helplessly on the stage as did Quinn. The microphone flopped by its cord from between his fingers.

Ty's chair scraped backward as he rose to stand next to Logan. He placed a hand on Logan's shoulder and shot Quinn a grin.

She wanted to scream *no*. She couldn't. She wanted to tell Logan, tell Ty, to let Renny and Peter just fight it out between them. Her mouth refused to work.

"Thirty thousand."

Though he hadn't yelled, everyone heard it. A collective gasp ascended from the crowd.

Peter openly gaped at the two of them. He looked up at Quinn, shook his head, then sat down abruptly.

As if the auctioneer suddenly awoke from a coma, he cleared his throat and lifted the microphone. "The bidding is at thirty thousand dollars, ladies and gentlemen! Are there any other bids for this lovely lady?"

Quinn wanted to sock the dude in the gut. Ty and Logan were winning, and the last thing she needed was to have someone else jump in on the bidding. To bring the bids up even higher.

Thirty thousand dollars. Quinn's chest ached. She became aware of her nails digging half-moons into her palms. She tried to relax but failed.

It was too much money. She couldn't let them do it. They needed the money for their irrigation system.

She looked over at Peter, who folded his arms over his chest. She willed him to outbid the boys. She cursed silently; she didn't want Peter to win. But damn, she was torn.

She'd just pay them back. That was all. She'd make sure she paid them back every penny. No matter how long it took her. Even if it meant selling off her diamond tennis bracelet her father had given her. She didn't need it. She'd even pawn off every other useless piece of jewelry she had. Except her grandmother's necklace. She couldn't bear to part with that.

The auctioneer yelled out the thirty-thousand-dollar amount several times and asked the crowd if there were any more bids. Not one person stood up or yelled out.

"Sold! The date with the young lady, for thirty thousand dollars, to the gentleman at that table." He pointed the microphone toward Ty.

The eerie silence was deafening. When there should have been clapping and cheering, there was none.

Those freaking rich snobs should be glad the charity was receiving such a great amount of money on her behalf. But instead of as a good thing, they were seeing it as a scandal. Quinn sighed in disgust.

Ty moved up toward the stage. She guessed to claim his win. Nothing like auctioning off live flesh for a good cause, she thought bitterly. When Ty approached, he held out his hand. Quinn took it and let him guide her to the steps and help her down to the dance floor. The spotlight followed her, as if the auction wasn't over.

As Quinn stepped down off the last step and reached solid ground, Ty swept her up in his arms and made a show of giving her a kiss. His broad, soft lips captured hers, and he cupped her hips against him. He took the quick brush of their lips and deepened it until his head tilted, and his tongue searched her mouth, sweeping against her tongue until she felt the pull of desire from deep within her.

For a few seconds she forgot they had an audience. Until a low murmur started. And the longer Ty and she kissed, the louder the event goers got until she heard a roar in her ears. Whether the roar was actually from the crowd or from inside her head, she didn't care. She broke away and looked around. All eyes were on them, and she was sure they had shocked everyone who knew her family. Not only was she showing unrestrained passion in public, but she had been locking lips with a black man. A cardinal sin for these country-club members.

She threw her head back and laughed loudly enough for everyone to hear.

She looked around until she found Logan. She grabbed Ty's hand tightly and dragged him to where Logan was, still standing at their table. Without releasing Ty's hand, she snagged the back of Logan's head with her free hand and yanked him down until she brushed her mouth against his. She wanted to give him as good of a kiss as she given Ty, but Logan kept his lips closed, making her keep it chaste.

When she let Logan go, he shook his head slowly at her but gave her a wicked grin. She returned it and snagged his hand too, so she had both of her men in tow as she approached her mother.

Her mother, appearing almost as pale as the tablecloth, sat stiffly at her table, surrounded by her snobby friends. She looked extremely disappointed that her plan had backfired. She couldn't be happy with the fact her club had made a nice chunk of change for the sponsored charity. No, that would make too much sense. She'd rather dwell on the fact Peter hadn't won Quinn. That Peter wasn't getting a second chance with her daughter.

Quinn stopped at the table and tilted her head at her. “Mother.” As the guys flanked her, Quinn tucked her arms in theirs. “I would like you to meet…” *My lovers.*

She hesitated. As much as she wanted to throw that fact in her mother's face, she couldn't. Not in front of everyone. Not tonight. No matter what, the woman was still her mother, and she still loved her. Faults and all. Her mother would figure it out soon enough anyway. “I'd like you to meet my good friends Ty White and Logan Reed.”

Her mother's mouth opened, but no sound came out. One of the other ladies at the table knocked over her water glass, crying out when water sloshed into her lap.

Logan nodded his head at her. “Mrs. Preston, we'll make sure you get the check for the charity as soon as possible.”

As her mother still sat there wordlessly, Quinn tugged on the boys' arms and led them toward the exit.

The night air was a bit cooler than expected, and Quinn gave a little shiver. Ty shed his jacket and slipped it over her bare shoulders. He curled his arm around her, holding the oversize jacket in place.

“Better?” he asked.

She gave him a warm smile. “It's all better.”

Logan stepped in front of them, giving them both a serious look. He tugged the lapels of Ty's jacket snuggly around Quinn.

“We—”

“Quinn!” Her mother trotted after them out of the double doors.

Not again. She could not take another berating from her mother again. Though she should have expected this one too.

Especially after the display the three of them had given to all her mother's peers.

Quinn quickly dug into her clutch and shoved her valet ticket at the wide-eyed young man. He gave the men a fleeting glance and then took off to the parking lot.

“Quinn, damn it!”

Quinn turned in surprise to meet her mother's angry gaze. Her mother never cursed. At least, Quinn couldn't remember her mother cursing. Ever.

"Quinn. I can't find your father. I think he has died of embarrassment." She looked at the three of them, her hands planted on her hips, anger twisting her face. "What is the meaning of all of this?"

Did her mother really want to know? They were no longer in front of a crowd. There was no time like the present for Quinn to get her point across. "Mother, these are my lovers."

"I don't understand."

Logan grabbed her upper arm through Ty's jacket, but Quinn ignored his unspoken warning and yanked her arm from his grasp. "What don't you understand? They're both my *lovers.*"

Her mother clasped a hand to her chest and stumbled back.

Logan rushed to assist her, but she stepped away from him, holding him off with a hand. "No, don't touch me." Her gaze pinned Quinn, who was still being held tightly by Ty. In fact, it was more like Ty was holding her back now. As if he was afraid of what Quinn would do to her mother if he let go.

"Quinn, this might not be the time," Logan warned.

"Are...are you saying you have sex with these men at the same time?"

"I didn't say that, but you can assume it."

"So they have sex with each other? They're gay?"

Logan backed stiffly away. “She's on her own.”

“Mother, that's one thing you don't get. You shouldn't label people like that.”

“Get real, Quinn. People are labeled all the time. That's life. If you think you can go through life and not be labeled and judged, you need to face reality.”

Quinn jerked forward, trying to pull away from Ty. He tightened his arm around her, holding her in place. “So how would you label me?”

“You tell me,” her mother countered.

Quinn heard the unspoken words between them.

Slut. Whore.

She could see it in her mother's face.

“Why, Quinn? Why would you bring these gays with you to my charity event?”

These gays.

“Why not? Why shouldn't I? Maybe they are a big part of my life. Maybe they are important to me. Maybe—”

Quinn's voice cracked, and she took a shaky breath as she fought back the sting of tears.

“Mother, these *gays*, as you so eloquently put it, are the best thing that has ever happened to me. They love each other. They cherish me. They don't judge me. Not like my family does. Maybe they mean more to me than you'd ever know.”

“More than your father and I?”

Quinn kept her mouth shut. She didn't want to slam all doors shut tonight. She really didn't. But it was going that direction, and she had known it might when she decided to invite Ty and Logan.

"I see. Well, I guess if you keep this up, don't expect for me or your father to be there for you when you need us. The charities would be more than happy to get your inheritance."

"Money isn't everything."

"No. It isn't. But how about some sense of pride? Decency?"

The valet pulled Quinn's Infiniti around the curved driveway to the entrance.

Quinn felt all the fight leave her body. She was drained. She needed to crawl into a corner, lick her wounds, and reevaluate.

She hadn't wanted to alienate her parents. She had only wanted to teach them a lesson about trying to control her life.

Quinn straightened her spine. "I have plenty of pride and decency. That's why I am not running back to Peter."

The valet finally found the nerve to exit the car. He stood by the open driver's door, his Adam's apple bobbing nervously. Logan finally took pity on him and moved around the car, shoving a tip into his hand. Ty tossed his keys to the young man and told him to retrieve his vehicle, giving him a description of his SUV. With a look of relief, the kid couldn't get out of there fast enough.

Logan went around to the passenger side of her car and opened the door. "Let's go, Quinn. Ty, take the SUV back to the farm."

Ty just nodded his head and steered Quinn over to Logan.

"C'mon. I'll drive you home." Logan helped her into the passenger seat, Ty's jacket still wrapped around her. The fabric held Ty's mix of woodsy, musky scent, comforting her somewhat.

Logan shut the door and moved around to the driver's side. The black SUV pulled up behind them, and Ty climbed in.

Quinn looked out of the window at her mother. She stood there, alone, watching her daughter, her only child, leave with two men she did not approve of, did not accept, and probably never would.

Quinn felt a pull of great sadness in her heart. If she thought she had disappointed her parents before by not accepting their choice in a mate, she couldn't imagine the disappointment her mother felt with her now.

Logan placed a comforting hand on her knee as he pulled away from the curb.

"It's a shame we are missing out on that dinner. Especially since it was a thousand bucks a plate."

Quinn pulled her eyes off her mother and turned to face Logan's profile.

There was no reason they should walk away from this evening with empty stomachs.

"Hold on."

He slammed on the brakes. "What?"

"Pull around to the back."

With her direction, he steered the car around to the back kitchen.

"I'll be right back."

Chapter Sixteen

Logan had spread out a picnic blanket in front of the fireplace. A mix of light contemporary hits and oldies drifted through the speakers strategically placed around the open great room. Because it was too warm, instead of lighting a fire, Ty had placed candles around the hearth and surrounding tables. Their light gave the room a soft romantic ambience.

The empty doggie bags Quinn had retrieved from the country club's kitchen littered the middle of the blanket.

The boys stretched out on the floor, digesting their meal of honey-orange duck breasts, wild-mushroom raviolis, and green bean amandine. Ty lay on his back, his arms folded under his head. He had stripped down to just his black suit pants and white tux shirt, the shirt unbuttoned, exposing a tight undershirt hugging his muscular chest.

Logan reclined on his side, his head propped in his hand, his eyes occasionally drifting shut. He had released his hair from his ponytail, and it draped softly around his face. His lips had a slight, satisfied curve to the corners. He was bare chested and barefoot, a pair of worn jeans pulled over his hips but not fastened.

The boys looked like the ultimate examples of relaxation, while Quinn gnawed on her bottom lip with anxiety.

She felt in limbo. Even two glasses of the champagne she had hijacked from one of the waitstaff hadn't seemed to take the edge from her nerves.

"That was sure some expensive takeout." Ty's voice was low and sounded groggy.

Quinn released a drawn-out breath before murmuring, "This whole evening ended up costing too much."

In more ways than one.

Logan brushed a palm over the short whiskers on his chin. "I don't want to tell you I told you so, but…" His voice drifted off.

"You told me so," Quinn finished for him. "I know. I know. Deep down inside, I knew what my mother's reaction would be, but I was hoping… I don't know what I was hoping for."

Actually she did. She had hoped her parents would finally see her as an adult, see she could make her own decisions, and most importantly, they would realize her happiness should be more important than having the *perfect* son-in-law.

Well, that had been a colossal failure. Times two.

Just like her relationship with Peter had been.

But no matter what her parents thought, her happiness was important. And if it meant being with Logan, being with Ty, then that's what needed to happen.

Ty sat up, reached for Quinn, and pulled her in between his legs. He cradled her against him, her back nestled against his chest. He stroked a hand through her hair, plucking the bobby pins out one by one. Tress by tress, he released her hair, until it fell around her shoulders. It felt good to have those nasty contraptions out of her hair and away from her scalp.

Ty tucked a strand of hair behind her ear. "Your parents will get over tonight. You'll see. Before you know it, they'll be calling and bugging you again."

Quinn inhaled deeply through her nose. "I don't think so. I made a scene in front of everyone who matters to them."

"Parents have a tendency to forgive and forget," Logan added. He frowned. "I can't believe I just said that. My mother never forgave me—or forgot." He released a long groan. "Sorry, I didn't mean to make it worse."

"I feel bad for my father. I know he loves me and only wants the best for me." She absently stroked her hands slowly up and down along the strong tendons in Ty's arms. A rhythm that soothed her.

"Then he should know that Peter wasn't what, or who, was best for you."

"But the way I went about making that point clear to him and to my mother was not best for you two." She tilted her head back, nestling it in the hollow between Ty's muscular pec and his collarbone. It was a perfect fit. She sighed. "I promise, I'll repay you every cent of that money, no matter what I have to do to get it. I know you need it for your business. And if you lose business, I'll go out and drum up some more. I don't want you two suffering for something I did."

"We did," Ty corrected her, curling a finger around a tress of her hair.

"What?"

He gave her hair a gentle tug. "Something that *we* did. We made the decision to go and be there with you. We all made a conscious choice tonight."

"But I proved tonight that I'm as bad as my mother. I used you to get what I wanted. I'm selfish."

"Then so are we. We want you. We didn't want to lose you. We want to be there for you, no matter what. Whenever you need us and for whatever reason."

"But—"

Quinn could feel Ty shaking his head above her; his chin brushed against her hair. "No buts. No regrets. What's done is done."

Ty picked up the closest champagne flute and took a sip. He handed the glass, which looked overly delicate in his large hands, to Quinn. Instead of taking the glass from him, she wrapped her fingers around his and lifted it to her lips. The bubbly alcohol tickled her nose when she sipped it.

She let Ty put the flute back on the hearth, and she leaned her head back into his chest as his strong arms came around her, making her feel secure. Wanted.

She had removed her heels earlier, but she still wore his tux jacket over her dress. She moved forward just long enough to remove the jacket and toss it on a nearby stuffed chair. She sank back into his arms.

She could stay like this forever.

This made her happy.

Seeing Quinn in her sexy little dress, enveloped in Ty's arms, made Logan catch his breath. He couldn't believe he could feel this way about a woman. Not again. At least not since Ty.

He never would have thought there would be a woman who would fit so nicely into his life. And it wasn't only his life. It was their life. Ty's and his.

He had been thinking about asking her to move in with them ever since she'd kicked them out of her condo. The sense of loss he had felt when he walked out that door that night had made his head spin. It was one of the reasons he decided to risk all by going to the benefit. He needed to show her they loved her. That all three of them were in it together. Or at least, that was what he had hoped.

He had discussed the new living arrangements with Ty, who at first seemed hesitant. But when Ty considered her not being in their lives at all, he'd quickly reconsidered.

Ty just needed some assurance Quinn wouldn't change their—Ty's and his—relationship. Logan couldn't promise that, but he did tell him inviting Quinn into their lives permanently might enhance it.

Now, after all that happened tonight, Quinn needed some assurance. Or even some reassurance.

She had just turned her life upside down and inside out. Logan remembered how that felt. When he came out. When his wife had discovered the truth about Logan's bisexuality.

He knew every day would not be perfect. A relationship was hard—it was real work—just with two people. And with three?

But as long as all three were willing to try…

"It amazes me…" Quinn said, breaking into his thoughts.

Logan rolled up to a sitting position. "What?" He shifted over until he was lounging next to Ty and leaned back against the larger man's powerful arm. Ty lifted his arm, an unspoken invitation for Logan to cuddle closer. Logan did just that.

"How you two can freely say you love each other."

Feeling content with Ty's arm hugging him, he reached out to brush back a wild lock of Quinn's honey-colored hair. "Why? Why is it amazing?"

"I've never—" Her voice cracked. She looked down into her lap and played with the hem of her dress. "I've never told anyone besides my parents that I loved them."

"No one? Not even Peter?" Her little confession surprised Logan. From what he understood, Peter and Quinn had been together for quite a while. Years, he thought.

"No. That's what amazes me so much, I guess. That you two can be so open with your feelings. There are no games between you."

Logan sighed. "A relationship shouldn't be made up of games. It should be made up of trust and honesty."

Ty brushed his fingers lazily down Logan's bare arm. "And telling someone you love them isn't necessary."

"But it's nice."

"Yes. It's nice," Logan agreed. "However, if you truly love someone, they'll know it with or without the words."

Ty's deep voice vibrated against Logan's back. "It's the respect you show them, the actions you take. It's all the little things that count more than words."

"Words are nice. But words can be empty," Quinn said.

Ty let out a long, low whistle. "Tell me if these words sound empty." His voice got low and husky. "Lo, I love you."

Logan turned his head and gave his lover a small smile. "I love you too."

Quinn protested, "But—"

Logan shushed her, putting a finger up to her lips. He rose to his knees, turning to face Ty. He gripped Ty's jaw and leaned in, his lips meeting the other man's. Ty's mouth parted, giving Logan access to his tongue. He tasted like champagne and the strawberries Quinn had added to their champagne flutes. He tasted wonderful.

Ty sucked Logan's lower lip and nipped gently, causing Logan to harden, his cock brushing against the rough zipper. Since Logan had never bothered to pull on a pair of boxer-briefs when he'd changed out of his monkey suit, his cock peeked from the top of his unfastened jeans. Ty's thumb found him and brushed against his sensitive head, capturing the drop of pearly precum on his finger.

"Ah fuck." Logan groaned, grinding his mouth harder against Ty's.

Ty wrapped his warm fingers around Logan's neck to keep him there, but Logan pulled away, leaning back to see Quinn's reaction.

As he expected, Quinn's breathing had become quick and shallow; her nipples were hard nubs under the pure white fabric of her dress.

"Undress Ty," he ordered her.

Quinn didn't hesitate. Like Logan, she rose to her knees and turned to face the darker man, while staying nestled between his thighs. She swept Ty's open dress shirt over his broad shoulders and threw it on top of the discarded tux jacket. She grabbed the bottom of his undershirt with both hands and slowly pulled it upward as if she were unwrapping a gift. Ty's dark skin gleamed over his lean, hard muscles, the black flames of his tattoo hardly visible against his skin tone in the low light.

The backs of Quinn's fingers brushed over Ty's nipples as she lifted the shirt higher. Ty ducked his head as she tugged the tee upward and off him completely. She tossed it onto the growing pile of clothes.

Quinn leaned close and captured one dark nipple into her mouth as she reached for the clasp on his tux pants. She struggled a bit to release the zipper, as Ty's cock was hard and ready, pushing tightly against the fabric. But after a couple of attempts, she had the zipper down, and Logan could see the impressive bulge in Ty's black boxer-briefs.

Logan would not feel that large cock in him tonight, but he would be taking advantage of Ty's tight hole. He planned on claiming his man tonight. And possibly his woman.

Quinn dipped her hand into his briefs, pushing them down, releasing Ty's cock. Her hand looked tiny in comparison, so pale against Ty's polished ebony shaft. She stroked up and down along his smooth length as she teased his nipple with her lips and tongue.

Logan's balls tightened painfully in the crotch of his jeans. He stood, his eyes never leaving what Quinn was doing to Ty, and he stripped the denim down his legs and over his feet. He tossed the jeans, not caring where they landed, before he dropped back to his knees, clutching the root of his cock tightly. He squeezed himself with the same rhythm as Quinn squeezed Ty. The head of Ty's cock was now shiny and slick with his fluids, something Logan wanted to taste. He imagined Ty's hard, smooth cock in his mouth, and Logan stroked himself faster.

Before he lost it completely, Logan jumped to his feet and said, “I expect you both to be naked when I get back.” And with that, he went to the bedroom to gather condoms and lube. The thought of what the two of them were doing out in the living room without him made him want to rush. He forced himself to take his time, though, even take extra time. The anticipation made him painfully harder.

Logan slowed his breathing as he moved back down the hallway, and when he saw Ty and Quinn, he was pleased. They were just as he had told them to be. They were naked, their skin glowing in the light of the candles. Ty's tight, round ass was in the air, tempting him as Ty knelt between Quinn's legs, his head buried between her thighs.

Logan paused to watch as Quinn's head was thrown back, her eyes closed, her lips parted. Ty had one of her nipples captured between his fingers as he twisted and pulled. Logan couldn't see his other hand; it had disappeared between Quinn's legs and was apparently working its magic, as Quinn was releasing small whimpers and arching her back in unmistakable ecstasy.

Logan palmed Ty's rounded ass cheeks as he moved behind him. Ty never lifted his head from Quinn's pussy but instead lifted his ass higher in a silent invitation. Logan quickly prepped himself, lubing his extremely hard cock, careful not to stroke himself too much, not wanting to lose it before he was deep in Ty's ass.

He positioned himself perfectly. He was lined up just where he needed to be to enter Ty, but still able to watch Ty pleasuring Quinn, to watch Quinn's uninhibited reactions.

With one hand around the base of his cock, he pressed the head against Ty's puckered hole, watching Ty relax his muscles in preparation. Logan pushed against him slowly, until his head just broke past the tight ring of muscle. Logan wanted to plunge deep, ram Ty hard with long strokes, but he held back. He gripped Ty's hips within his fingers and fought to keep control of himself. He closed his eyes from the sight in front of him; he sucked air into his nose and released it out of his mouth, trying to calm his rapid heartbeat, trying to fight the urge to thrust uncontrollably.

He pushed his shaft another inch into Ty, whose canal was like a warm cocoon over his throbbing cock. He took another inch, and then another, until he was seated fully. When Ty clenched his ass muscles, Logan cursed, his concentration almost breaking.

He looked down at Quinn's face, which twisted in pleasure under Ty's ministrations. Small sounds continued to escape her, and she had managed to dislodge Ty's fingers from her nipple; she was now playing with her breasts, her long nails flicking and scraping against the hard tips.

He lost it. Unable to hold back any longer, he surged against Ty's buttocks. He thrust quickly, deeply, and hard, holding Ty's hips in place. Ty cried out against Quinn's pussy, making her cry out in turn. Logan threw his head back and pounded hard. The heat surrounding his cock was scorching, and he wanted to put out the fire with his cum. Every time he fucked Ty, he felt as if he was claiming him all over again as his. Ty was his.

Ty was his.

He gave into the overwhelming desire to possess his lover fully. He pushed deep and made small thrusting movements, grinding his sac into Ty's ass. Logan leaned over and sank his teeth into the other man's smooth back, hard enough to emphasize the pleasure, but not enough to break the skin.

Ty groaned once more against Quinn, his long fingers digging into her thighs, spreading her wider. Quinn's eyes sprang open, and she lifted up, wrapping her hands around Ty's head, holding him tight against her as she cried out, her thighs shaking.

Logan felt the rush of heat from his balls as his orgasm overtook him. His seed spurted violently from him.

Logan wanted to collapse but didn't want to crush Ty. As his spasms faded, he waited a moment before carefully releasing Ty. He grabbed a nearby napkin to clean himself and Ty off.

He tossed the napkin aside and settled against the hearth, his back to the stone, his legs spread. He patted the blanket between his thighs.

"Quinn, c'mere."

She crawled over to him, and he settled her between his legs, her back against his chest. Ty sat on his haunches, watching them in anticipation, his cock still rock hard. Logan extended a hand to him, and Ty didn't hesitate. He moved closer.

Logan grabbed a condom and ripped open the foil packet.

"T," was all he had to say. Ty knelt between Logan's and Quinn's legs. Logan reached around Quinn to place the condom over Ty's leaking cock, rolling it down over his length. Logan took his time caressing Ty's shaft, feeling how soft and heavy his dark sac was. Reluctantly he let Ty go. Logan smoothed his palms along Quinn's inner thighs. He lifted her legs up and over his own, spreading her wide.

Ty shifted closer, his long cock bobbing straight out. Just waiting.

Logan ran his fingers along the edge of Quinn's folds, amazed at just how wet, how hot, she felt. He slipped two fingers into her, and she cried out.

"Are you ready?" he murmured against her ear.

"Oh God, yes. I am so ready."

"You are so wet. Do you want his big cock in you?"

"Yes. Oh yes. I want him to fuck me." Quinn reached out and splayed her hands on Ty's chest. "I need you to fuck me now, Ty. Now."

Ty lowered himself over her, over Logan, all his weight on his arms.

"I want you to wait until I tell you," Logan told him.

"Lo—"

"You will wait until I tell you."

"I need him now, Logan."

"You will wait."

Ty tilted his hips until his cock bumped against Quinn's entrance. Her fingers dug into his chest.

"Wait," Logan warned.

Ty closed his eyes, and Logan could see the internal struggle on his face. His brain was telling him to obey his lover; his body was saying otherwise.

Logan ran his hands up Quinn's sides, over her breasts, and up her neck. He turned her flushed face and took possession of her mouth. She kissed him back fiercely, biting his lip not so gently, capturing his tongue between her teeth. For a moment, he thought she was so worked up, she would actually bite his tongue off, but she let him go, and he pulled back just enough so their breath still mingled.

"Now."

Ty shifted as Logan kissed Quinn again. As Ty slid into her, she cried out into Logan's mouth. Quinn was shoved against him with each thrust Ty took. Ty's head hung, and his arms shook as he pumped into her, his buttocks flexing with each deep stroke.

Logan cupped Quinn's breasts, his thumbs circling over her nipples. He buried his face against her neck, his tongue stroking down her skin. He pressed his lips along her collarbone and squeezed the hard peaks of her nipples between his fingers.

"Ty, move up."

He did, changing the angle of his hips until he looked directly at Logan. Without releasing Quinn's breasts, Logan kissed Ty over her shoulder. Ty slowed his rhythm somewhat, taking longer, deeper strokes. Quinn wrapped her legs around his waist, hooking her ankles behind his broad back.

She pressed her face against them, making Logan pull back from the kiss.

"I want to kiss you too."

Their heads together, Quinn took turns kissing Logan and Ty.

"God, can it get any better than this?" she asked in a low whisper, her forehead pressed against both of them.

"Yes. You could love us," Logan answered her.

Ty stilled, his breathing ragged, and he waited. He waited for her answer like Logan did.

"I…I am loving you. Right now."

"No. I meant you could *love* us."

"I…I do."

"Then say it. We want to hear it."

She wiggled like she wanted to escape, but she was trapped securely between them. Her wiggling made Ty thrust once, twice, before becoming still once more. Still waiting for Quinn's admission.

"All right, damn it. I do. I love you. I love you both."

It wasn't a tender declaration of love; it was angry. She appeared angry that Logan had made her admit to her feelings.

She was pissed off, and she wanted to come. She bucked furiously against Ty, who could no longer hold back. Logan leaned back, pulling her against his chest, twisting her nipples. She rocked hard against him as Ty pounded into her.

"Fuck me harder," she taunted him.

"Do you want it hard, baby?" Logan rasped, catching her earlobe between his teeth.

"*Yes.*"

"Ah fuck, she's so tight," Ty ground out.

Logan pressed his cheek against hers. "Are you going to come?"

"I don't want this to end." Her breath caught, and Logan swore he heard her voice quiver, causing his chest to tighten.

There was more meaning to her words than she realized.

Or maybe she meant just what she said.

"It's not going to end. I promise. Let go."

Quinn slammed her head back into Logan's chest, making him grunt in pain. She dug her nails into his thighs, and her whole body quivered and arched like a bow.

"I'm coming," she cried out, her breathing harsh and rapid.

"That's it, baby. Feels so good. Doesn't it?"

He was talking to both of them. Both of his lovers. Both of his loves.

A warmth spread from the depth of his gut as Ty tensed in his arms and groaned loudly, his expression distorting with his release.

A few long seconds later, Ty relaxed his tight muscles and moved from between their legs to collapse on the blanket. He disposed of the condom in one of the empty food bags and then tucked an arm under his head.

Logan and Quinn moved to his side. Quinn stretched out next to Ty and laid her head on his chest. Logan spooned her from behind, his arm draped over her hip to lace his fingers with hers.

A sense of peace washed over him.

For the longest time, no one said a word. They lay together, the soothing rhythm of their breathing the only sound in the room.

"We have a proposition for you," Logan finally said, breaking the silence.

"Hmmm?" Quinn's sleepy response made Logan smile.

He leaned over and met Ty's gaze. Ty gave him a small nod.

"Quinn, this is serious."

"Okay. What's this proposition? Or is it just another new *position*?"

"We want you to come make your home with us."

"What? Wait. I confessed my love to you, making me vulnerable, but I didn't hear any declarations of undying love from either of you two."

"Do you have any doubt we love you?"

"Well, I've heard you tell each other. Why not me?"

"Okay..." Logan gave her a soft kiss, murmuring against her lips, "Quinn, I love you."

Quinn turned to look at Ty. He smiled at her, brushing his lips over her forehead. "I love you too, Quinn. I never thought I could love anyone else other than Logan. I was wrong."

"Okay, but even so. Don't you think it's too soon?"

"No. Not at all. This feels right. And it's more than that."

"More?"

"We don't want you just to live here. I...we"—Logan corrected himself—"want you to manage our business."

"But I'm good at my job. It pays pretty well."

"You can have a share of the farm. If you'd like, you can do consultations on the side for some extra cash. We'll set an office up for you. Our business is growing; we'd like you to be a part of that."

"We'd like you to be a part of our lives," Ty added.

"This is serious..." she whispered.

"Quinn, stay with us forever," Logan said. He fought back the panic that she might say no. A thought popped into his head. "I dare you."

"I double dare you," Ty said.

Quinn's answering laughter filled the room.

Both men joined in.

THE END

Jeanne St. James

Jeanne St. James loves to write about an Alpha Male (or two) who knows what he wants, when he wants it, and how to get it. Nothing turns her on more than a man in uniform, whether it's a police officer, a Federal agent, or even a pro football player.

She started writing when she was about 13 years old and found it great therapy. During her high school years she read loads of books, most of them historical romances and contemporary category romances. She fell in love with the genre and has been writing ever since.

Jeanne now concentrates on erotic romance. Why? Because it's a blast. There's nothing like a hot, spicy romance to get your juices flowing. But she still likes the HEA (happily ever after) ending. She believes a romance can involve more than just a man and a woman, so she writes *ménage a trois*, and, occasionally, stories including two men. Love and sex can be sizzling in any combination!

Her first published erotica piece was a fantasy short story in the July 2006 issue of *Playgirl*, which was titled "The Hot Ride."

Find Jeanne at http://www.jeannestjames.com